"Are you saying you didn't really want me?"

The question threw him. "I want you all right."

"You're not drunk this morning?"

"Dead sober." He'd *never* be drunk again.

"Then . . ." She shifted, looked up at him. "Okay."

His knees almost gave out. Was Grace trying to kill him? He tightened his hold on her upper arms and tugged her the smallest bit closer. "Okay? What the hell does *okay* mean?"

"Yesterday you were so drunk, I knew I couldn't take advantage of you."

"You couldn't . . ." She left him speechless.

"I especially wanted to touch you. Leaving you in your boxers wasn't easy. But I promise, I behaved."

She behaved? "Grace, are you saying we really didn't do anything? As in *nothing*? As in not even kissing?"

"You don't remember?"

"Not much."

"Oh." That one word held a wealth of disappointment. "You, uh, well you did kiss me a couple of times. It was . . . really nice."

The timid way she confessed that made Noah want to kiss her again. He *had* to kiss her.

The Novels of Lori Foster

Murphy's Law
Jude's Law
Jamie
Just a Hint—Clint
When Bruce Met Cyn
The Secret Life of Bryan
Say No to Joe?
Unexpected
Never Too Much
Too Much Temptation
Truth or Dare

Anthologies Featuring Lori Foster

I'm Your Santa
A Very Merry Christmas
Bad Boys of Summer
When Good Things Happen to Bad Boys
The Night Before Christmas
Star Quality
Perfect for the Beach
Bad Boys in Black Tie
Bad Boys to Go
Jingle Bell Rock
Bad Boys on Board
I Brake for Bad Boys
I Love Bad Boys
All Through the Night

Published by Kensington Books

Too Much Temptation

LORI
FOSTER

ZEBRA BOOKS
KENSINGTON PUBLISHING CORP.
www.kensingtonbooks.com

ZEBRA BOOKS are published by

Kensington Publishing Corp.
850 Third Avenue
New York, NY 10022

ISBN-13: 978-1-4201-0431-8
ISBN-10: 1-4201-0431-4

First Brava Books Trade Paperback Printing: March 200?
First Kensington Mass Market Paperback Printing
February 2003
First Zebra Mass Market Paperback Printing: Decembe
2007

10   9   8

Printed in the United States of America

Chapter One

Noah Harper stood frozen in the carpeted hallway of his fiancée's house while his skin pricked with some vague, unsettling emotion. It wasn't really anger or grief. It sure as hell wasn't jealousy.

If Noah hadn't known better, he might have sworn it was . . . relief. He shook his head at the thought. No, he'd wanted to marry Kara. He'd accepted it as his fate and even viewed it as part of a grand plan for the future. Not really *his* grand plan, but then, he didn't think in grand terms. His grandmother did.

Noah liked Kara, respected her and her parents, and his grandmother adored her. Almost from the time he'd met Kara, everyone had assumed they'd eventually marry. In one month, they would have.

But now . . .

Without a conscious decision, Noah moved toward the obvious sounds of soft moans, low encouragement, and rustling sheets. He wasn't in any particular hurry, because he already knew what he'd find.

He was wrong. *Very, very wrong.*

Oh, Kara was in bed all right, doing exactly wha[t] he'd suspected she was doing: having very passion[-] ate sex, when all he ever got from her was per[-] functory attendance. It was her partner who was s[o] unexpected.

Not that it really mattered.

Noah's eyes narrowed as Kara gave a particu[-] larly ardent moan and bowed her slender body i[n] a violent climax. He watched, unmoved.

Faced with such a bizarre circumstance, Noa[h] pondered what to do, and settled on propping on[e] shoulder on the door frame, crossing his arms[,] and waiting. Surely he'd be noticed soon enough[,] and at the moment, his territorial nature rejecte[d] the idea of offering them privacy. After all, Kar[a] was his fiancée—or rather, she had been.

That had all changed now.

Her skin dewy from exertion, her eyes daze[d] and soft in a way Noah had never experienced, Kar[a] leaned back and sighed. "Oh God, that was incred[-] ible."

"Mmm," came the husky, satisfied reply. "I ca[n] give you more."

Looking scandalized and anxious, Kara purred[,] "Yes?" and came up on one elbow to smile at he[r] lover.

That's when she noticed Noah.

Kara's beautiful face paled and her kiss-swolle[n] lips opened in a shocked, horrified *oh*. Her lover[,] with his dark eyes glittering and bold, lounge[d] back in antagonistic silence.

Amazingly enough, Kara snatched up the shee[t] to conceal her body . . . from Noah.

Noah shook his head in disgust—most of it self[-] directed. He'd been a royal fool. He'd treated he[r] gently, with deference, with patience. And she'd cheated on him.

"Don't faint, Kara. I'm not going to cause a scene." Noah didn't even bother to glance at the other man—there was no challenge there.

Instead, Noah lent all his attention to the woman he'd expected to be his wife. "Under the circumstances, I'm sure you'll agree the wedding is off."

Kara gasped in panic. Having said his piece, Noah turned on his heel to stalk away. He was aware of the race of his pulse, the pounding of determination that surged in his blood. It wouldn't be pleasant, ending elaborate plans already in progress. The upper society of Gillespe, Kentucky, was about to be rocked by a bit of a surprise.

Kara's parents, Hillary and Jorge, had gone all out on preparations for the celebration. They'd rented an enormous hall and purchased a wedding gown that had cost more than many houses. Guests were invited from around the country, and all of Gillespe was aware of the impending nuptials.

His grandmother . . . God, Noah didn't even want to think about Agatha's reaction. She fancied herself a leader of the community, and she was tight with Hillary and Jorge, treating them like relatives as well as her dearest friends. In many ways, she already thought of Kara as her own.

Noah bounded down the spiraling carpeted stairs two at a time, anxious to get away from the house so his mind could quit churning and settle on a course of action. He'd learned at an early age, while being shuffled from one foster home to another, to make cool, calculated decisions and then to analyze the repercussions so that nothing could ever again take him by surprise.

This time, he had few choices, so his decisions were easy. He wouldn't marry Kara now, but at the same time, he hated to disappoint his grandmother.

He'd just started to pull the front door open when a small hand grabbed his upper arm. "Noah!"

Damn. He'd really hoped to avoid this confrontation. He sighed and turned.

Kara stared up at him with wet eyes and a trembling mouth. Her fair skin blanched whiter than usual, with none of the rosy glow he'd grown used to. She wore only a hastily tied robe that emphasized the swells and hollows of her body—a body he'd once thought very sexy. Her short golden brown hair was becomingly tousled and as Noah watched, she released him and ran a shaking hand over her forehead, pushing her wispy bangs aside.

Her shoulders slumped and she looked down at her bare feet. "I'm sorry."

A cynical smile curled Noah's mouth. He could just imagine how sorry Kara felt right now. How could he ever have considered making her his wife? "Sorry you were caught?"

She clasped her hands together. "There's more than just our wedding at stake, Noah, you know that. My parents . . ." She shuddered. "Oh God, I can't imagine how they'll react. Everyone has been planning for us to marry for so long."

Noah snorted. "Your folks accepted me, Kara, mostly out of respect for my grandmother. I doubt they'll be brokenhearted not to have me in the family. There're plenty of other guys they'd rather you marry and we both know it."

"They love Agatha." Kara looked at him, her expression fierce. "*I* love Agatha."

At least that much was true, Noah decided.

"Yeah, my grandmother loves you, too." *Much more than she'll ever care about me.* "You're the daughter she never had, the granddaughter she wants, the female relative to fill all the slots. She dotes on you, and I doubt that'll change."

Kara swallowed hard. "This will kill her."

The laugh took him by surprise. "Kill Agatha? She'll outlive us all."

"Noah, please, don't do this."

"This?"

Big tears ran down her cheeks and she quivered all over, truly beside herself, pleading. Why the hell did women always resort to tears to get their way?

"Please don't ruin me. Don't ruin my family. I can't bear the thought of everyone—"

Realization dawned, and with it, a heavy dose of disgust. Didn't Kara know him at all?

Noah looked at her sad, panicked eyes and accepted that no, she didn't. She'd have married him, but she didn't really know him.

Just as she'd never really wanted him.

He said, "Hey," very softly, and watched her try to gather herself. Any second now he'd have a hysterical woman on his hands.

Looking at it from her perspective, now knowing what she expected of him, Noah could understand why.

Feeling a surge of compassion, Noah took her delicate hands in his. "Listen to me, Kara. The wedding is off; there's no changing that. But why we ended it is no one's business but our own, all right?"

Her mouth opened and she gulped air. She wiped her eyes on her shoulder, sniffed loudly. "You mean that? You really mean that?"

Hell, he was used to worse hardships than censure. Kara had led a pampered life protected from ugliness, never forced to face the harsh realities life often dealt.

Noah had learned to survive almost as a toddler. He could shoulder the heat much more easily than she. "Yeah, why not?" Then he added, "I'll break the news to everyone if you want."

She pulled her hands free and searched in her pocket for a tissue. "I don't believe you." A shaky laugh trickled out. "You're too damn good, Noah Harper."

Now there was a joke. "No, I just don't relish being humiliated either."

Rather than make her laugh, she covered her face and sobbed. "I'm so, so sorry. I didn't mean for this to happen."

"We were obviously never meant to marry, babe, you know that." It was Noah's turn to glance up the stairs, but her lover wisely stayed out of his sight. Noah shook his head, still bemused by her choice. "Your secret is safe with me."

She threw herself into his arms, leaving him to awkwardly deal with her gratitude. Noah wanted only to escape. Even at the best of times, he'd never totally felt at ease with Kara. She was too refined, too polished and proper—the opposite of him.

Noah set her aside and said, "Maybe you should think about a quick trip, until you have time to figure out what you want to say. I'll wait to tell Agatha until tomorrow, to give you time to get away."

She managed a pathetic smile. "Thank you, Noah. Really."

Kara had just saved him from making a horrible mistake. Though he felt like thanking her right back, Noah merely nodded and walked out. For more than the obvious reason waiting upstairs, tying himself to Kara would have been a disaster.

For one thing, he didn't love her. If he had, he wouldn't be so easy right now. He should have realized that sooner.

As he went down the walk, he felt the sun on his face, the chill of a late spring breeze, the freshness of the day—but he didn't feel hurt or heartsick. He felt no real sense of loss.

For another thing, sex with Kara had offered no more than base physical release. She'd never blown his mind, never burned him up. During their engagement, he'd been faithful, and he'd made do with the few quick, passionless screws he'd gotten from her.

But God, he missed the burning satisfaction of hot, sweaty, grinding sex. He missed the bite of a woman's nails, her teeth, when she felt too much pleasure to be gentle. He missed the clasp of sleek thighs wrapped around his waist and the softer, hungrier clasp of a woman's body on his cock. He missed the throaty, raw groans during a woman's climax.

He missed the wetness.

Kara had been a lady through and through, even while under him. Ha! He was a blind fool. A lucky blind fool, because now he was free.

It wouldn't be easy, but he'd deal with the families and the gossip sure to arise—and then he'd find himself a wild woman, a woman who matched him in every way. He'd ride her hard until he'd worked off every ounce of tension. Then *he'd* be the one to leave *her.*

Noah's last thought as he drove away from his ex-fiancée's house was that he could hardly wait.

* * *

Grace was so furious with herself, she felt like spitting. The near-torrential rainfall didn't slow her down as she splashed her way up the sidewalk to Noah's building, her every step punctuated by a passionate rage. Eight days. Eight hellish days she'd been away, probably when Noah had needed her most. She'd expected to come home to a list of things yet to be done for the wedding, because Agatha did love to give her lists.

Instead, she'd come home to the tail end of an uproar.

She swiped away a tear of fury that mingled with the rain dripping down her cheek. It was always that way. Hurt her, insult her, and she was fine. She'd summon up calm dignity and deal with it. But let her get really mad and look out—she cried like a baby.

Damn her car for breaking down, damn Agatha for being a hardheaded matriarch, and damn everyone for ever doubting him.

Poor Noah. Poor honorable, loyal Noah.

He *needed* her.

Spurred on by her convictions, Grace hurried on. She slipped as she jerked the foyer door open and bounded inside onto slick marble tile. She'd have landed on her well-padded behind if it weren't for Graham, the doorman, catching her arm and wrestling her upright.

"Here now!" Graham said with some surprise, maintaining his hold on her arm as Grace started to dart past.

It took him a moment to recognize her with her hair hanging in long, sodden ropes in her face and her clothes saturated through and through, making them baggier than usual. When he did recognize her, his old eyes widened.

"Ms. Jenkins! What in the world are you doing out in this storm?"

Grace forced herself to slow down. "Sorry, Graham. Is Noah in?"

"Yes, ma'am. He's with his brother."

Thank God. Grace would rather have had her visit with Noah in private, without Ben as an audience, but at least Noah was home. Besides, she should have known Ben would be close at hand. He very much respected his brother, and always offered unconditional support.

Grace was relieved that Noah hadn't been all alone during the ordeal.

"My stupid car broke down a few blocks from here," she told Graham. "I'll call triple A from Noah's."

"Should I announce you?"

Noah had a standing rule that his family was always welcome. Grace was in no way a blood relative, but as his grandmother's personal secretary, Noah granted her the same importance. She'd known Noah for three years. She'd loved him just about that long.

Not that she would ever tell anyone, especially not Noah.

"No, I'll go on up. But thanks."

The doorman shook his head as she turned away, probably thinking she had less sense than a turkey to go running through the stormy weather. But she simply hadn't possessed the patience to wait in her car for a cab. A little rain wouldn't melt her, and since hearing what Agatha had done yesterday, how she'd treated Noah because of the breakup, Grace had been filled with a driving urgency to reach him, to let him know that at least one person still . . . what? Still believed in him, still trusted in his innate honor?

The elevator moved so slowly, Grace couldn't stop tapping her foot, which jiggled drips of rainwater from her body onto the elevator floor. She now stood in a puddle.

The second the doors opened, she leaped out, then had to leap back in when she realized it was the wrong floor. The woman getting on the elevator gave her a funny look but said nothing, even when she had to step around the soggy carpeting.

Grace chewed her thumbnail. It was a disgusting habit—as Agatha had often told her—but she couldn't seem to help herself.

This time she checked the floor before getting off. Every step she took caused her feet to squish inside her pumps and left damp tracks across the carpeting. When she reached Noah's door, she drew a deep breath to fortify herself, pushed her long, wet hair behind her ears, and rapped sharply.

Nothing.

She knocked again, and even pushed the doorbell a few times, but still there was no answer. Refusing to give up, Grace tried the door and found it unlocked. She crept inside, calling out, "Noah?" but no one answered. And then she heard voices coming from the balcony.

Grace hurried through the apartment, noticing empty beer bottles everywhere, as well as pizza boxes and chip bags thrown about. A mostly empty, dried-up container of sour-cream-and-chive dip was half tucked into the sofa cushions.

The cleaning lady would have a fit.

Grace wondered if Noah had thrown a party, if he had actually celebrated the breakup. It seemed unlikely. For many years now everyone had expected him and Kara to marry and then be blissfully happy in their picture-perfect lives. The breakup had naturally thrown everyone for a loop, Grace especially.

She finally located him.

Noah sat on the covered balcony with his brother, and together they made such an impressive sight they stole Grace's breath. Oh boy, there were some outstanding genes running through those two. No wonder Agatha had put her pride aside and sought out her deceased son's illegitimate offspring. Noah was a man to make anyone proud.

The two brothers were talking, oblivious to Grace's presence, and she studied them. Their large, bare feet were propped on the edge of the railing, getting rained on. Both of them lounged back in chairs, Ben with his tilted on its back legs.

Noah had a long-necked bottle of beer dangling between his fingers, his other hand resting limply on his hard abdomen. He wore faded jeans, a gray sweatshirt with the sleeves cut off, and nothing else. His silky, coal-black hair was rumpled, his face shadowed with beard stubble. His entire body bespoke weariness.

He was the sexiest, most appealing man she'd ever known.

Even from where Grace stood, she could see the lush length of Noah's sooty lashes, sinfully long, too extravagant for a man. They lent a striking contrast to an otherwise hard-edged presence.

Grace sighed.

"To hell with all of 'em," Ben said. His words were slurred and thick and angry.

Grace tucked in her chin. Uh-oh. Ben sounded . . . drunk. Really drunk.

Like Noah, he seldom imbibed, so this must be a . . . commiseration-drinking binge? She didn't really know men well enough to know what their habits might be, but it seemed feasible.

She looked behind her, and this time counted the empty beer bottles littering the apartment. Oh Lord! They must have been at it since last night. Had Noah contacted Ben directly after leaving Agatha's? Had they been drinking ever since?

Wide-eyed, Grace turned back to the brothers.

Noah's voice, too, sounded slurred when he said, "It took them all by surprise, that's all."

"Yeah, so they jump to the conclusion that you're a heartbreaker. The asses."

"Heartbreaker?" Noah made a sound that wasn't quite a laugh, wasn't quite a curse. "Oh, they had better descriptions than that, believe me. You'd think I jilted her at the altar the way they went on."

Grace swallowed her choking pain and renewed annoyance. Agatha had told her all about the awful meeting, with Noah summoned to her house to face Kara, along with her mother and father and Agatha herself. He'd stood alone against them, bearing their insults and their blame without defending himself—the same way he'd faced the world most of his life.

They'd jointly called him to account, and when Noah had refused to explain why he'd ended the engagement, Agatha had threatened to disown him.

No. Grace curled her arms around the ache in her stomach, the pain in her heart. She would never let that happen. Noah was a part of the family now, and he'd damn well stay a part. She'd make Agatha relent. As her personal secretary, she carried some clout.

At least she hoped she did.

"Situations like this," Ben explained, waving his beer for emphasis, "are why I don't submit to her fucking blood tests."

Noah slanted his younger brother a look. "You know she has to be careful, Ben. In her heart, Agatha knows you're family, but she's stubborn and cautious."

"She should take my mother's word for it."

"Yeah. But it would damage her pride to do that."

"And to hell with anyone else's pride? Is that it?"

Noah shrugged. "Agatha has more pride than most."

"Ha! She's a—"

"Careful." Noah narrowed his eyes. "I'm madder than hell at her right now, too, but she's still my grandmother, *your* grandmother."

"Not that she'll admit it."

Noah ignored that to add, "Just as you're my brother."

"Half brother." Ben lifted the beer and guzzled down the remainder, then belched.

"Whole, half, who gives a rat's ass? You're my brother, and regardless of any damn blood test, we both know it."

Grace's heart expanded in her chest, her throat clogged with emotion. Yes, Ben was Noah's brother, and Agatha's grandson. It was there in the shiny black hair he shared with Noah, in the broad-shouldered physique, the olive skin tone.

At six feet, four inches, Noah was as impressively

tall as his father had been. Ben stood six feet even, but he carried himself the same, and their sexy, teasing smiles were identical.

Only the eyes were different. Noah had pale, striking blue eyes that could be either as cold as ice or hot enough to singe your soul. Ben's eyes were just the opposite, as black as a sinner's and equally as wicked. He looked at women and they blushed and stammered in reaction.

Agatha's son had fathered two sons by two different women, and he hadn't acknowledged either of them. Likely Agatha wouldn't have either if her son hadn't died, leaving her all alone with no other family. But fifteen years ago the private detective she'd hired had found Noah, and now Agatha loved him. Grace was sure of that much, even if Agatha never admitted it. Despite the current disharmony, Noah was her pride and joy.

Though Agatha had been fully appeased by locating one grandson to fill the void in her personal and business life, the detective had also found Ben before the search could be stopped.

From the first, when Ben had been an irreverent fourteen-year-old rascal, he and Agatha had rubbed each other the wrong way. But Grace knew that eventually Agatha would accept him. How could she not when Ben was so like Noah in the most important ways, proving he was her own flesh and blood?

Problem was, Agatha ruled with an iron fist and often placed her pride above everything else. Ben was his own boss, refusing to submit to the whims of an old woman. Secretly, Grace enjoyed Ben's rebellion. He infuriated Agatha, which kept her on her toes and sharp-witted.

"We need more beer," Noah announced, and

ropped his empty bottle with a clank onto the
alcony's stone floor.

More beer!

"You'll have to get it," Ben said without moving.
I can barely feel my legs."

"Wimp." Noah started to rise with a lusty groan.

"No." Grace stepped forward, drawing the at-
ention of both men. They slued around in their
hairs and stared at her in muddled surprise.

"Hey," Noah said. Then, with some confusion:
Where'd you come from?"

"The front door wasn't locked."

"It wasn't?"

Disapproving, Grace said, "I think you've both
ad quite enough to drink."

The two men shared a look, and Ben grinned.
Ah, Gracie, did someone try to drown you, sweet-
eart?"

"Ha, ha." She made a face at Ben. He was for-
ver teasing, and usually she liked it. "No, I got
aught in the rain." Self-conscious, she pushed her
air behind her ears again. Her sweater stuck to
er breasts and her back and her long skirt clung
o her plump thighs, her belly. "My stupid car
roke down," she explained, while trying to make
erself less noticeable.

Noah straightened, then came to his feet with
tiff-legged purpose. "Why the hell didn't you call
ne? I'd have picked you up."

He swayed, and Grace lifted a brow. "In your
ondition? I do believe that's not only dangerous
ut illegal."

He cupped her chin and leaned closer. "I'd
ave called a cab for you."

Just that simple touch on her chin and Grace's
eart was ready to pop. With a shuddering breath,

she lifted herself away from him and busied he
self by picking up empty bottles.

All around them, the storm raged, spraying int
the balcony every so often, lighting the earl
evening sky with a brilliant display of electrical er
ergy. The thunder rolled almost continually, ra
tling the windows and vibrating the floor, whic
explained why they hadn't heard her knock.

"It doesn't matter," Grace remarked when bot
men continued to watch her, putting her on edge
"I'm here now."

She started back into the apartment, aware c
them tottering along behind her. "Besides, I was i
a hurry."

Ben propped himself up against a wall. He, toc
had on jeans, now wet to the knees, and a pol
shirt that fit his broad chest perfectly. His face
throat, and brawny arms were tanned, testifying t
the amount of time he spent outdoors and nea
the pool.

"Yeah?" he asked. "How come?"

Distracted, Grace asked, "How come what?"

"How come you were in such an all-fire hurry?

The reason for her visit flooded back to Grac
and she gasped, almost dropping the bottles. Noal
relieved her of several and plopped them onto th
dinette table. "Grace? You okay?"

"Ohmigod," she said, and turned to Noah, grasp
ing his sweatshirt with both hands, holding on t
him while she stared up into his handsome face. "
almost forgot when I saw you both sitting ou
there, looking so cute in your drunken revelry.

Ben chuckled, muttering, "*Cute,*" under hi
breath, but Noah shook his head. "Quit pulling or
my clothes and tell me what you forgot."

"*Almost* forgot." Then Grace softened with emotion. "Oh, Noah. I am so, so sorry."

He and Ben shared another look, this one of concern and male speculation. "For what, exactly?"

"*For what?* For what's happened, that's what!" Her hands, curled in his shirt, thumped against his chest in emphasis. "For how Agatha jumped to the wrong conclusions and how everyone is acting and—"

Noah pressed two big, warm fingers against her lips, making her toes curl inside her waterlogged shoes and her belly curl in sensual delight. "What conclusion did Agatha jump to? And how in hell do you think everyone is treating me?"

His fingers were still over her mouth and Grace swallowed hard, then reached for his thick wrist and gently drew his hand down. Oh Lord, the man made her shake with . . . with all kinds of things.

"Agatha wrongly assumed you were to blame for the breakup. And from what she told me, Miss Callen's family was no better." Grace's temper ignited anew at her own reminder of how he'd been treated. "You'd think none of them knew you at all!"

Ben pushed away from the wall. His walk was only slightly steadier than the moment before. "You're saying you don't blame him?"

Grace whirled on him. "Ben Badwin! You should certainly know better!"

"Hey—" He held up both hands, on the verge of laughter. "I didn't say I blamed him."

"Well, I would hope not."

Noah crossed his arms and propped his hip against the dinette table. He still wavered a little, rocking back and forth. "So who do you blame?"

"Why . . . no one." Grace flapped a hand. "Oh,
heard all about Kara weeping and being deva
tated and all that. Agatha said you've humiliate
her in front of all of Gillespe by crying off after a
the arrangements had been made, and that Kara
emotionally crushed and may never recover. And
feel horrible for her, I really do."

Ben laughed again.

"But I know you both must have had your ow
reasons. At the very least, I know you wouldn'
have crushed her unless you had no other choice.

Grace squealed when Ben slipped his thic
arms around her from behind and lifted her o
her feet in a crushing hug. He treated her weigh
as negligible, and the thought occurred to Grac
that for a man of Ben's size, it might be.

And Noah was even bigger!

Ben's bear hug so surprised her, Grace's arm
and legs sort of stuck straight out, like a strangle
starfish trying to gain balance.

Rainwater squished out of her clothing, the
trickled down her body and onto Ben. He put
smacking kiss on the side of her neck, immobiliz
ing Grace with the impulsiveness of it. She coul
count on one hand the number of times a gor
geous man had kissed her neck.

Heck, she could count with one finger becaus
this time was a first.

Noah continued to study her, scrutinizing he
every reaction, which made Ben's behavior incon
sequential. She began to burn, and knew she had
to gain control of the situation.

She cast a wary glance at Ben, who, although h
released her, continued to grin like a rogue. Sh
looked back at Noah, and way up, to see his ex
pression. His muscled arms were crossed over hi

chest, his intense blue eyes narrowed, watchful. He looked bemused and something else, perhaps . . . tender.

"I'd have been here sooner," Grace told him in a croak, trying to collect herself. "But I was out of town."

"I remember," Noah murmured, still holding her fixed in his gaze. "Agatha had you doing some headhunting, didn't she?"

"Yes, for a new chef she'd heard about. He agreed to her terms and she, ah, hired him. He starts right away."

"Great."

Noah sounded more disgusted than enthused. It had been Noah's job for years now to do all the hiring. Agatha's interference often resulted in difficulties that Noah had to deal with.

Grace didn't want him sidetracked with worries about that now. "But that's not important."

"No? What *is* important?"

Grace chewed her lip, trying to decipher Noah's mood. He had the most stony, unreadable expression when he chose, and he'd just gone into full conceal mode. He appeared relaxed, unconcerned, no more than curious.

But oh, those silvery blue eyes of his, shadowed by his long thick lashes, continued to burn. And she felt the heat right down to the core of her being. She glanced at Ben, but he just winked, his own brown eyes alight with mischief.

"It's important," Grace said, "that you know everyone doesn't blame you."

"But everyone does."

"Not me."

Ben again laced his arms around her and propped his chin on her crown. "Why is that, sugar?"

Oh, please, Grace thought in a bit of a panic
Ben didn't really think she could talk with him
lined up behind her and Noah in front of her? She
felt surrounded by testosterone, hemmed in by
machismo. Impossible.

It was distracting enough that Ben had a body
like a steel statue and was sexy to boot. It was doubly bad that he touched her in ways she'd never
been touched before. It more than rattled her.

But while Ben could unsettle her with his dy-
namic presence, he'd never excited her emotions
the way Noah did, never made her alternately hot
and cold and so physically *aware*.

Yet, there Noah stood a mere foot in front of
her, bare feet braced apart, dark hair damp from
the humidity, eyes as hot as a blue flame. Grace's
heart pattered, and she wondered that Ben didn't
feel it.

Then Noah slanted his brother an amused look.
"You're going to make her faint, Ben."

"That right?" Ben peeked over her shoulder to
see Grace's face. She could feel his breath on her
cheek. "You feelin' faint, honey?"

"I, uh . . ."

"Knock it off, Ben." Noah watched her as if he
knew what she felt and even while he smiled at her
predicament, he wanted to protect her.

Grace drew a shuddering breath. "I'm, uh, not
used to guys touching me."

Noah's eyes glittered. "Huh. Now there's a con-
fession."

Before Grace could recover from the suggestion
in Noah's tone, Ben saved her by pretending to be
shocked. He said, very theatrically, "No! I won't believe it, Gracie."

Grace didn't mind Ben poking fun. Almost every other twenty-five-year-old woman she knew had left virginity far behind.

Without looking at Noah, she said, "Afraid so." Then, to try to relieve the tension, she added, "At least, not big, gorgeous, sexy guys like yourself."

"You hittin' on me?" Ben asked with a teasing grin. He could be such a charming scamp.

"No," Grace assured him, "because I'd have no idea what to do with you."

He laughed and shook his head, then touched her cheek before moving away. "She's all yours, Noah."

Noah smiled.

Seeing that smile, Grace gulped.

Apparently unaware of Grace's embarrassment, or at the least not caring, Ben added, "I suggest you get her out of those wet clothes before you continue your interrogation." He glanced back at Grace over his shoulder and bobbed his eyebrows. "I'd offer to help, you know, but I gotta get going. Hell, I'm so drunk, I hope I make it to my own bed."

Grace immediately turned and snagged the back waistband of Ben's jeans. She held on. "You can't drive in your condition!"

Ben was so unsteady on his feet he almost fell into Grace when she abruptly halted his forward momentum, causing him to stumble back two steps. He caught himself at the last second and laughed. "All I'm gonna do, Gracie, is pick up my shoes, shuffle to the elevator, and then ask Graham to call me a cab, assuming I make it to the lobby in an upright position. Noah here made me drink more than I'm used to."

"Made you?" asked Noah with one glossy black brow raised. "I seem to remember you're the one who showed up with the first case of beer."

First case of beer? Grace still held on to Ben. "I'll take you to Graham."

Ben looked down at her hands, latched tight to his waistband. "Turn me loose, woman. I can manage."

She gave Noah a questioning look.

"He'll be fine," Noah promised. "I'll call down and tell Graham to watch for him."

"Well, all right." Grace loosened her hold and Ben floundered forward. He fetched up against the couch, righted himself, then located his shoes. He didn't bother to put them on.

"You two kids behave now, okay?"

Noah, who was only slightly steadier than Ben, went to his brother to help him out, then used the intercom to call down to Graham.

While they were both occupied Grace picked up an empty beer case and began stowing bottles inside. She was only half done when Noah returned.

He still had that awesome fire burning in his eyes and it made her very nervous. And very, very aware of him as a man.

"You heard what Ben said," Noah told her while scrutinizing her every movement.

"Uh, no." Grace licked her dry lips. "What did he say?"

Noah started forward, faltering a little but with definite purpose. And damn if he didn't have a small, wicked smile tilting one side of his mouth. "You're all . . ." His gaze dipped over her too-round body outlined in the clinging clothes—top to bottom and back again, making her heart leap with embarrassment. His eyes met hers. ". . . wet."

Grace's mouth opened, but not a single word emerged.

Noah kept advancing, closer and closer, despite the way she instinctively backed up. Until he stood directly in front of her, until the power of him, the heat and the deep male scent of him touched her all over.

Her breath caught, her pulse tripped and tumbled.

"Gracie," he murmured, and he touched her cheek, looking at her in a way he'd never looked at her before, in a way no man had ever looked at her. His smile deepened, his eyes brightened. "You're going to have to lose the wet clothes."

Grace closed her eyes and wished like hell he wasn't drunk. But wishing didn't work. He *was* drunk—the fact that he'd said such an outrageous thing to her proved it—and that meant she couldn't take advantage of him, no matter what he said, no matter how badly she wanted to.

Well, damn.

Chapter Two

Even in his inebriated state, Noah knew that half of what he said and did was out of character. Or rather, it was out of character for the man he'd tried to be, to live up to his grandmother's specifications.

But for the first time in years, he felt like himself again. He was a free man, allowed to do as he pleased, with whomever he pleased. He owed Kara nothing, and after Agatha's explosion, he didn't owe her anything either.

In his typical fashion, he'd carefully considered how to handle things after being disowned. Only then had he reacted. He'd already set his plans into motion, and before long, he'd be completely free of Agatha. If they had a relationship after that, if his grandmother claimed him at all, it'd be because she wanted to, not because she needed to.

Because he lived without illusions, he was prepared for either reaction.

He hadn't been prepared for Grace. She'd thrown him for an emotional loop, giving him her unquestioning support and loyalty. As an illegitimate and late addition to the Harper family, loyalty meant the world to Noah.

Probably because he'd never had it.

Agatha had recently proven he couldn't have it from her, no matter how many different ways he bent himself—which was why he wouldn't bend for her anymore.

And he sure as hell hadn't ever gotten it from the foster parents who'd grudgingly taken him in. Only his brother— who he hadn't met until he was nearly grown—had ever given him that kind of unconditional support.

And now Grace.

Agatha had made an excellent choice the day she'd hired Grace Jenkins. Noah remembered sitting in on the interview, watching the too-plump twenty-two-year-old, fresh out of college without a single reference. She was alone in the world; her parents had passed away in an accident years before. At that moment, he'd felt a strange affinity to her. They were both alone, both stubborn and determined.

Grace had lifted her rounded chin, met Agatha's shrewd gaze squarely and listed what she considered her best qualities.

Hardworking, driven, intelligent, rational . . . and loyal.

That thought made Noah frown. He caught Grace's hand and tugged her with him toward his bedroom. "Does Agatha know you're here?"

Noah practically dragged her, she showed so much resistance. But he didn't let up. He liked the feel of her soft hand in his, and he especially liked the way she looked at him with those enormous brown eyes. They were sexy, no two ways about it. He'd always liked her eyes as much as her determination and backbone.

Noah especially liked them now.

Of course, he was beyond horny, on the ragged edge, but it was more than that. It was . . . he didn't know what the hell to label it, and at the moment he didn't even care to try. "Gracie?"

He pulled her into his bedroom and turned to face her.

She looked up at him through her lashes. Long wet ropes of twisted brown hair clung to her face and throat. She glanced around his room and licked her lips. "What?"

"Does Agatha know you're here?" he repeated.

"She knows."

Noah crossed his arms. "I bet she was none too happy."

That adorable stubborn chin of hers lifted. "I'm a grown woman, Noah Harper. I make my own decisions."

Shaking his head, Noah turned away to rummage in a drawer. "Meaning she forbade you to come here, huh?"

Grace started to inch back when he located a white T-shirt and pulled it out. He caught her by the upper arm. She was . . . very soft. Plump, as he already knew, but also soft and warm and intensely female.

He could smell her wet hair, her damp skin, and his blood burned.

It hadn't been that long since he'd walked in on Kara, but there'd been much to do, to deal with, and no time to find a woman. Knowing he was now free to indulge his true nature made it doubly hard to wait. He was so frustrated, so sexually primed after the long deprivation of his engagement and the emotional drain of ending it, he felt ready to go nuts.

But he had to remember that this was Grace, his grandmother's secretary, a gentlewoman, a very respectable and innocent woman.

I'm not used to men touching me. God, the very idea of being her first made his imagination shoot into overdrive and all his muscles clench.

"Grace," Noah said, his voice too harsh, "are you going to be in trouble for coming here?"

She lifted one shoulder. "I don't know. I'll deal with that later. Not that it matters." That ferocious, protective glimmer lit her eyes. "None of them had any right to crucify you. I couldn't stand by and let you think that we all felt the same."

"Because you don't?"

"Of course not."

"Because you know me so well?"

She stammered, then snapped her teeth together. "Noah Harper, I've known you for three years. You're like me in a lot of ways. Hardworking and proud and conscientious. You would never do anything so reprehensible as breaking an engagement without a good solid reason."

God, her faith in him felt good. It seeped into him, warming him from within, easing some of his roiling tension.

Noah prided himself on his ability to analyze situations, to calmly make sound decisions. He couldn't analyze Grace or how she made him feel.

Without another thought, Noah bent and kissed her.

Grace leaped back so quickly, she lost her balance and landed on her butt.

Dazed by her reaction, Noah frowned, bent to

haul her upright, and lost his balance, too, almost landing on her. She stiffened her arms against him until he'd regained his equilibrium and straightened back up.

"Noah, really!" Grace sputtered from her position at his feet.

Hoping to sound gentle rather than predatory, Noah stared down at her and said, "Out of those wet clothes, babe."

She lumbered upright in graceless haste and clasped her hands together over her sweater, as if to keep it on her person.

What? Did Grace think he meant to attack her? Hell, he could barely keep from falling on his face. Not that the idea of having her under him didn't appeal. It did. In a big way. But Noah doubted he was up to the performance. Gracie was the type of woman who deserved to be treated special.

She was not a woman for a quick lay.

Still, he noticed the frantic rise and fall of her magnificent breasts. Unable to stop staring, wondering how she'd look buck naked, Noah asked, "What's wrong, Grace?"

Noah actually heard her gulp. It had been a long, long time since he'd had to deal with a timid woman. He kind of liked it. Before becoming engaged to Kara—and even a few times after—women had come on to him with blatant confidence in their skills. Even Kara, though reserved in her genteel nature, had never doubted her appeal or her influence.

Grace, however, looked like a bewildered rabbit, ready to bolt if he said boo.

She hadn't looked like that earlier, when she'd vehemently defended his abused honor. Noah grinned. Yeah, he liked it; he liked her, a lot.

"There's no reason for me to change my clothes," Grace muttered, "because I'll just get wet again when I leave."

Noah was drunk, no two ways about it, but he wasn't dead. Grace felt like a balm, like a ray of warm sunshine in the middle of the storm, and he wanted her.

He waited till she looked up, then snared her gaze. Her dark eyes widened warily. "I don't want you to leave, Grace."

"You don't?"

Noah felt himself sway and squared his shoulders. "Will you stay with me, Gracie?"

Her gaze skipped to the bed behind him. "Here?" she squeaked.

That single word sounded like a suggestion, a seduction. His gut tightened. "Yeah."

Grace looked scandalized and . . . maybe full of yearning? Damn, Noah wished his head wasn't so foggy with drink. He had the feeling that dealing with Grace would prove tricky. Especially since at the moment he wasn't even sure of his own mind, much less hers. He only knew he wanted, and the wanting was somehow tied to Grace.

For now.

"Why?" Grace asked, still holding herself and still very uncertain.

"I need you."

He said it without thinking about it, and Grace appeared to melt right before his eyes. Her knees went weak and she leaned on the dresser while devouring him with her deep dark gaze. Her lush mouth relaxed, her face softened, her entire expression became one of tenderness and acceptance and love.

Noah hadn't known he was starving till he saw everything he wanted so clearly in Grace.

"Oh, Noah," she whispered.

Metering his pace so she wouldn't run from him, Noah approached her. He slung the T-shirt onto his shoulder and, still holding her gaze, began unbuttoning her sweater.

With a gasp, Grace looked down, away, everywhere but at him.

"Hey."

She swallowed and shook her head, quivering—from cold or nervousness?

"We . . . we should turn out the light."

"It's not on." But the curtains were drawn wide, and despite the rain-dark weather and low purple clouds, there was enough gray light coming through the windows that Noah could see her clearly. A good thing, since he wanted to visually explore her whole body, inch by luscious inch.

He pushed the drenched sweater off her shoulders and inhaled sharply. Her breasts were more than a handful, full and heavy and so sexy his cock strained in his jeans.

Her bra was the sturdy type, white cotton with an underwire, necessary to support a woman of her endowments. But it, too, was wet, making it transparent. Noah could see the outline of her rosy nipples showing through.

He was busy staring and trying to rein in his lust when Grace jerked away, turning her back on him and hunching her shoulders.

Because he'd drowned his anger in drink, his damn reflexes were slow, and Noah stood there a moment trying to decide what had happened. By the time he realized she was actually hiding from him, it was too late. Grace reached behind her and flapped an impatient hand. "Give me the shirt."

There was a strange quiver to her tone, what sounded far too close to embarrassment to suit Noah.

Somehow, he'd find a way to make her understand her own appeal.

He handed her the tee and said, "Get rid of the bra, too." *Yeah, all of it.* He cleared his throat, but even to his inebriated ears, he still sounded far too turned on. "You're soaked down to your skin, Grace, and I don't want you to catch cold."

And if she believed that, he'd sell her a bridge. Grace froze, clutching the T-shirt in her small fists. Then, with a contortionist's dexterity, she pulled it over her head without losing her fragile grip on the sweater. Beneath the cover of the tee she stripped out of her bra and finally removed the wet sweater—without showing Noah a single speck of additional flesh. She dropped the sweater and her bra over the arm of a bedside chair.

Noah quirked a brow, amused and also disgruntled that he hadn't gotten to see her. He felt drunker by the moment. And hotter. "Now the skirt."

Grace peeked at him over her shoulder, and he saw her cheeks were hot with color. But she had guts, his Gracie. She kicked off her shoes, then bent to pick them up and place them neatly by the door. With her bottom lip caught between her teeth, she reached beneath the skirt and peeled out of her panty hose. She folded them and put them with the shoes.

Unknowingly, she provided Noah with a tantalizing strip show that nearly did him in. His testicles tightened, and his blood surged.

Noah locked his knees and said, "Go on."

Because he was so much taller, his T-shirt hung to mid-thigh on her, half covering the long loose skirt. She'd put it on over her wet clothes and now it was damp, too. It also molded to her breasts, and the second Noah noticed that her nipples were pressed tightly against the cotton, he nearly lost it.

Grace walked to the other side of his bed, where Noah couldn't see the bottom half of her, and reached back to slide down her zipper. She watched his face while he watched her body. Her movements thrust her breasts forward, made her nipples even more noticeable. He could almost taste her in his mouth, feel the texture of her against his tongue.

In a growl, Noah asked, "Why are you hiding from me, Grace?" He had his suspicions, but he wanted to hear her say it to be sure.

She pursed her mouth and shimmied the skirt down her fleshy thighs. *Soft, silken, fleshy thighs.* Noah wanted to feel those thighs high on his shoulders, or better yet, against his jaw while he tasted her. . . .

"I'm fat."

His head jerked up, all thoughts of devouring her temporarily scattered. *"What the hell did you say?"*

Grace frowned and dropped the skirt over the footboard of the bed. Cheeks warm, her eyes soft, she faced him in nothing more than his white T-shirt and panties. Her wet hair streamed over her shoulders, her feet pressed together, she said, "You're not blind, Noah. You've known me three years."

"Yeah, so?"

"So you know I'm fat."

Anger ripped through him. It wasn't at all like

what he'd felt when confronting his grandmother and Kara and her parents. No, this was the real thing, singing through his veins, firing his blood.

Through a red haze, Noah surveyed Grace, and all he could think about was getting his hands on her. All of her. "Who says?" he growled.

She tilted her head in confusion. "No one has to say. I have a mirror."

"And I have a hard-on."

She drew back, blinking rapidly. "You . . . you're drunk."

"Yeah." He couldn't very well deny that when even now he kept swaying on his feet. "I'm also ready to combust with wanting to get inside you." There, let her deal with that honesty.

Her gaze skipped down his body to his lap, her fascination almost tangible. Damn, but Noah *felt* it like a lick of fire.

Or just a lick.

"Not," he rasped, wanting to reassure her, "that I intend to do anything about it."

Grace chewed her lips, still staring at his cock, which without his instruction flexed and strained against the rough denim of his jeans. She lifted dark eyes to his. "No?"

Through his teeth, Noah said, "You're an incredible woman, Grace. Too damn good to be bedding down with me."

That caused her modesty to evaporate posthaste. "No!" She rounded the bed in a furious stomp that did interesting things to all her bouncing parts. With a short finger jabbing at his chest, she shouted, "You're the finest man I know, Noah Harper!"

He caught and held her wrist, keeping her hand close so she couldn't prod a hole into him. "A man presently disowned by the only family who ever wanted to claim him."

Anger vibrated through her. Her hand opened on his chest, fisted in his sweatshirt. "Agatha is being pigheaded. But don't worry, I'll see to her."

Now that thought was truly alarming. "You let me deal with Agatha."

Her chin firmed. "I'll do what I think is right."

Noah scowled. "Grace, it's not necessary for you to get involved. I have no doubt my grandmother will turn around soon enough. She might not really want me in the family—"

"She does!"

"—but she needs me there all the same."

Her frown almost matched his own. "What are you talking about?"

"In the last few years, there's been a shift of power in at least one aspect." Noah felt great satisfaction as he explained, "Not only have I been in charge of all the finances, making all the decisions without influence, but the employees at the restaurant are loyal to me first, Agatha second. And she knows it."

Looking much struck, Grace murmured, "I hadn't really thought about it, but of course you're right. She's been deferring to you for so long . . ."

"Hoisting all the work on me, you mean. Especially anything that required a diplomatic tongue." At Harper's Bistro, Noah was in charge, and that gave him leverage. "Agatha tends to demand a lot for a little, and her impatience is legendary. I believe in rewarding good work accordingly."

Grace stared at him, deep in thought. "I know you're very respected. Agatha brags about that all the time."

Noah didn't allow himself to believe that. Compliments from his grandmother were few and far between. Not that he gave a damn. Not anymore.

"The fact that Agatha chose to add another chef into an already territorial mix of personnel will only alienate them more. If she doesn't quit pushing, she's going to end up with several key members of the staff walking out."

And then, Noah thought, she'd be beckoning him back, despite what her society friends might have to say about it.

He knew how to deal with his grandmother, and he would.

"Oh dear," Grace said, already jumping ahead mentally to all the complications, and likely more work such a scenario would bring her. As Agatha's personal secretary, Grace caught the brunt of his grandmother's temper and had to deal with the fallout whenever things didn't go her way. Grace had fixed more messes than Noah ever would.

Noah watched Grace's smooth brow pucker, saw her purse her mouth in contemplation. Even with all her bravado, Grace was no match for his hardhearted grandmother. Thinking that, Noah touched her cheek. She was so damn soft. All over. And it made him nuts. "I don't need you to fight my battles, Gracie."

"Standing up for what's right is never a hardship."

He laughed. "God, how did I overlook you for so long?"

He had her full attention again with that comment. Her mouth twisted in bemusement, and as if speaking to a halfwit, she said again, "I'm fat."

"Oh no." Noah cupped her face. His thumbs rubbed along her jaw, under her chin. "Round, hell yeah, just the way a woman should be. With beautiful breasts and a killer ass and the sexiest bedroom eyes imaginable. I *did* notice your eyes, Grace. I used to wonder how you'd look while having sex."

A hot blush exploded over her face and upper chest. "You did not." She said that as a denial—with hopeful undertones.

Noah was more than happy to reassure her. "Yeah, I did. I still do."

She drew several deep breaths, almost gasping, then came against him hard, embracing him and squeezing him with all her might.

For a moment, Noah held himself rigid, shocked at the feel of her, how damn right it seemed. True, Grace was overweight, at least by modern, model-thin standards. But now her ripe body was against his, wiggling as she tried to get even closer, and he felt every single generous *female* curve.

"Oh hell." Noah clutched at her, drawing her into him. Grace smelled like a woman. She smelled *hot,* and his libido rocked into overdrive. He gave up and reached down to fill his hands with her backside.

Grace squeaked and shot to her tiptoes in surprise, which only flattened her breasts against him, rubbed her belly against his crotch.

He groaned again, nearly gone, in a frenzy of lust he hadn't experienced in far too long.

With Grace.

It was a mind-boggling reality, drunk or no.

In so many ways, Grace was taboo. She worked for his grandmother, sacrosanct in her position as personal secretary. She was a marrying kind of woman, not meant for one night or even one week of hot sex—no matter how incredible he sensed it'd be. She was earthy and real and domestic and . . . honorable.

"Shit." Noah's head swam with disappointment even as his body battled with common sense.

"Noah?"

He released her to stumble to the bed, as hindered by blazing arousal as by too much drink. He dropped to the edge of the mattress and put his head in his hands, fighting with himself, struggling for control.

He couldn't use Grace for sex, damn it. No matter that it felt more right with her than he'd felt in years, certainly since his engagement.

No matter that she appeared to want him, too. He'd be everything his grandmother had recently called him if he took advantage of sweet, innocent Grace.

She sat beside him and touched his neck. Her fingers felt cool and feather light on his heated skin. "Are you okay?"

Noah knotted his hands in his hair, rebelling at what he knew he had to do.

"Shhh, it's all right," she crooned. "You've drunk too much."

Beneath the concealment of his hands, Noah's eyes narrowed in surprise. She should be slapping him, not petting him.

"I'll take care of you," Grace promised, smoothing his hair with gentle hands. "Let's get this sweatshirt off you so you'll be more comfortable."

Noah dropped his hands and stared at her with red eyes and rioting emotions.

Her sweet smile touched him in places he hadn't known existed. "You'll feel better in the morning," she assured him, and to a man like Noah, a man who'd never been coddled, her tenderness meant more than the lust, knocking the breath right out of him.

With no signs of shyness now, Grace came up on her knees and started to work on his sweatshirt. Entranced, Noah helped by raising his arms, but he couldn't stop himself from looking at her adorable dimpled knees or the way her breasts swayed inside the tee.

It was as if everything about her suddenly appealed to him. Shirtless, he sprawled back on the bed at Grace's insistent push. She stared at the snap on his jeans, and Noah wondered if she'd be brave enough to continue.

He'd about decided to spare her by removing his pants himself when she mustered up that iron resolve that had enabled her to deal with Agatha for three long years and tended to snap and zipper with competent alacrity.

Noah lifted his hips to shove the jeans down, and Grace, with only a brief awed glimpse at his lap in snug boxers, slipped off the bed to tug them away.

Voice quavering and breathless, she said, "There." Her lips were parted, her eyes glazed. "Isn't that more . . . comfortable?"

Noah was so damn hard he could have been lethal. He was surprised his boxers didn't rip under the pressure. Comfortable? Hell no, he wasn't comfortable.

But he was comforted. By Grace.

He watched her through a cloud of sensual pleasures—lust, and other emotions that were somehow more potent. "Yeah."

"Up you go." She turned down the spread for him and patted his pillow.

She was such a nurturing woman. So domestic.

Those qualities held a lot of appeal for Noah, but he wondered if they were countered by more basic desires, those of raw sexual need. Would Grace Jenkins be giving and nurturing in bed? Or would she be demanding, taking her pleasure?

While he scooted up in the bed, Noah growled, "No way in hell can I sleep, Gracie."

"Why not?"

"You'll leave." It hurt to make that admission, but damn, he didn't want her to go. Noah figured in the morning, when sobriety hit, he'd regret his actions. But for now, keeping Grace close seemed more important than breathing.

She tilted her head, her expression again hopeful—and uncertain. "I'll stay if you want me to."

Just what he wanted to hear. Noah snagged her around the waist and tumbled her into the bed with him. "Yeah, stay. Right here next to me."

"Oh!"

He snuggled her up close to his body, despite her gasp and the way she went rigid. "Relax with me, Gracie," he murmured, nuzzling her temple, kissing her hair. "Sleep with me."

He pulled her half onto his chest until her head nestled into his shoulder and her hand rested tense and uncertain on his abdomen. He could feel the wild rapping of her heart—or maybe it was his heart—and then he felt lethargy drag at him.

He hadn't slept much since he'd discovered Kara with her lover. She'd ignored his advice to take a trip and instead had turned tearfully to her parents the very next day, spurring them into an indignant rage. Agatha had gotten the news from them, rather than from Noah himself, which in part explained her fury.

She'd been taken off guard, embarrassed among

her peers, and for a woman with Agatha's pride, that was unforgivable.

Noah understood Kara's reasoning, putting all the blame on him, saving her own ass from as much grief as possible. But he was still nettled. He'd offered her an out, and instead she'd stabbed him in the back. He half wondered if her lover had put her up to it.

And why.

Grace's hand opened and smoothed over his skin, tangling in his chest hair, petting him with a kind of wondering curiosity. Making him burn. "I'll stay as long as you want me to, Noah."

Now that sounded good. *As long as he wanted.* Hell, maybe he could just keep her forever.

He pushed thoughts of Kara and her parents and his grandmother from his mind. He concentrated on Grace's touch, on her understanding. And all too soon, he felt himself drifting into sleep.

At that last lucid moment, Noah could have sworn he felt Grace's lips on his flesh, gentle, fleeting.

And then he passed out.

Chapter Three

The harsh pounding in Noah's head woke him. He opened his eyes, squinted in blinding pain, and saw nothing but blurry confusion. The room swam around him, his stomach pitched, and he went perfectly still, concentrating on not being sick.

When the roiling of his stomach subsided to mere queasiness, he put his efforts to focusing. Something white was in his line of vision, something large. Noah blinked twice until the fuzziness cleared and the object took form. Noah realized it was a bra.

He froze, staring in incomprehension.

It wasn't just any bra but a large one, made for a large woman. And surely a woman with impressive breasts.

His brain seemed a vast wasteland, and the more he tried to think, the more it pulsed.

While Noah stared at that sturdy, substantial bra, trying to figure out what the hell it was doing in his bedroom, a warm body next to him stirred.

Alarm skittered through him, and he again froze. His heart punched into his throat, and slowly, so slowly it seemed to take forever, Noah turned his head.

He found himself staring at Grace Jenkins.

Grace Jenkins with the beautiful, bountiful breasts.

Good God! She clung to him like a limpet, her smooth white arm over his chest, her small hand fisted, her fingers laced into his chest hair with a secure hold. Her head was practically in his armpit, her nose smooshed up into his side, and he could have sworn he felt her warm breath on his left nipple.

A ripple of sizzling awareness rode though his muscles, starting at his toes and ending with a crescendo in his already befuddled brain.

Damn, but Grace was smiling even in her sleep. A small, sexy, inviting smile.

What the hell was she dreaming about?

Her rich brown hair, impossibly long and thick, trailed down her back, over her shoulder, and onto him. It teased the arm he had holding her securely, his abdomen. Noah choked.

What had he done?

Like a small, chubby cat, Grace stirred again, stretching and making a sweet, feminine sound of awakening that caused all Noah's most sensitive body parts to clench in response.

It was at that moment that Noah realized her warm bare thigh was over his lap, rubbing against him.

He was stunned, breathless, appalled.

He was rock hard and getting harder by the second.

Grace blinked her sleepy eyes open and looked at him. For a long moment neither of them moved. Noah had always thought her eyes incredible, but never more so than in that moment, when she looked so drowsy and sweet and . . . happy to see him.

Heat shimmered between them. As Noah stared at her, Grace blushed a little, but she didn't look away. Even when his cock rose up and nudged her inner thigh, flexing against his will, she didn't move.

He knew he had to. "Hey."

Her lashes drifted down and she looked at his chest. Morning light blazed through the open drapes over the window, leaving long white sunbeams slanting across the bed, over their bodies.

Grace turned her face, nuzzling him, and one selective beam caught the clean line of her jaw, her small upturned nose, a long lock of tangled hair. It glinted on her stubby lashes and in her dark, mysterious eyes.

At that moment, Noah thought Grace was about the prettiest thing he'd ever seen.

But what the hell was she doing in bed with him?

Shy and hesitant, her hand on his chest opened and she touched him, brushing her fingertips over his pecs, his collarbone. Noah felt that gentle, innocent touch everywhere.

Grace smiled up at him, a smile of awareness, of complete and utter awe. "You are so warm."

An inferno. Noah closed his eyes, hoping that by not seeing her, he could distance himself enough to figure out what to do.

Her fingertips drifted across his brow, riffled

through his hair. "Are you all right, Noah? Do you feel sick? I don't know much about drinking, but I suppose you have a hangover."

He remembered guzzling one beer after another with Ben. Way too many beers. Hell, he hadn't gotten stinking drunk since before Agatha had adopted him when he was a teenage hell-raiser. He'd gotten sick back then, too, and had sworn never to do it again.

Of course, he hadn't expected anyone other than his brother to share in his drunken foolishness. But then Grace had shown up with a sort of misplaced desire to protect him. . . .

Bits and pieces of the previous night pecked at Noah's brain. A groan broke loose, and he put one forearm over his eyes to shield himself from the light, the memories, and Grace's astute gaze. Things he'd said to her, things he'd thought about, whirled inside him, making him sick with self-disgust.

He didn't like needing anyone. He *wouldn't* need anyone. But Grace . . . last night he'd considered her a lifeline.

He almost hated himself.

"I'll make some coffee," she offered while keeping her voice low in deference to his hangover.

Noah dropped his arm to watch her scamper off the bed, then immediately snatch the sheet up and around her body.

Feeling contrary and mean, he said, "It's a little late for modesty, isn't it?"

Grace blinked at him. It was an expression she often wore when unsure of what to do next. Noah had been the recipient of that look far too many times. Grace could be busily at work, animated, and when he walked in, she'd freeze while keeping her dark eyes on him warily. He knew Grace didn't fear him. Hell, he doubted Grace feared anyone.

Had she been wanting him all that time, then?

"I suppose you're right," she said at last, surprising Noah. And with a defiant tilt of her head, she flung the sheet back at him. Noah had only a moment to admire her abundant curves in the clinging T-shirt and panties before she lost her nerve and turned, all but running from the room.

The back view she provided was . . . interesting. Her long, luxuriant brown hair swished directly above her generous, heart-shaped ass. She was barely concealed by white cotton, and her haste added extra jiggle to things.

Noah heard the hall bathroom door close.

"Shit, shit, shit." His stomach lurched again, and he forced himself to breathe, to lie still until the sickness passed.

Damn it, he'd been hoping she'd tell him he was all wrong, that her sleepover had been innocent. That maybe she'd gotten drunk, too, and they'd both passed out. But he knew Grace didn't drink.

She also didn't sleep around.

The more he tried to think, the more his head throbbed. The last thing he could really remember was wanting Grace. Fiercely.

Hell, he wanted her still.

Noah threw his legs over the side of the bed—and almost lost his stomach as the bedroom spun around him. It took him a moment to recoup, and he staggered into his connecting bathroom, shucked off his shorts, grabbed his toothbrush and stepped into the shower. The first blast of cold water made his every ache intensify, and then gradually go numb.

As the water warmed, his head began to clear. He stood there, stiffened arms braced against the shower wall while the water beat down on his neck and shoulders. It was several minutes before he felt human enough to brush his teeth and wash.

First he'd have to apologize to Grace.

Then he'd just have to hope like hell she forgave him.

"Noah?"

Her voice came in through the open bathroom door. Ready to face the repercussions, Noah turned off the shower and stepped out, tossing his toothbrush into the sink. Grace, agog and scandalized, whipped around so fast she half-spilled the hot coffee she'd brought as an offering.

"Hey." Still disgruntled with the situation, Noah dried off and wrapped the towel around his hips. "Don't faint on me, okay? I feel so lousy this morning, we'd both end up on the floor before I'd manage to pick you up."

Grace knelt down to mop up the spilled coffee with a washcloth. Her back still to him, she squeaked, " 'Kay."

Noah rubbed his bristly jaw, considering her. "I'm decent, Gracie."

She peeked at him, then her eyes widened and slid over him so slowly, he felt devoured. She lingered on his abdomen until he cleared his throat.

"Grace? The towel is secure, I promise."

She nodded and gave him a tentative smile. "I thought you could probably use this." She stood and held out the now half-empty mug of coffee.

Just by being herself, Grace managed to take the awkwardness out of the quintessential "morning after." Noah nodded and gratefully accepted the cup.

"Damn, that's good," he said after his first sip. About six more cups and he might even begin to feel human. It struck Noah that for the first time that he could remember, his apartment felt like home. Kara had picked it out for him, and a decorator had thrown furniture and stuff around. He spent as little time in the place as possible because it had never really suited him.

But now, waking up with Grace beside him, having her hand him coffee with a smile and hearing her chitchat . . . it all felt right. It felt like a home should feel, even with all his tension and uncertainty about the previous night's happenings.

He liked it, but he also *didn't* like it. "You can have the shower now if you want."

"Oh no!" Grace pushed her hair behind her ears, shifting around from one bare foot to the other in typical Grace-like nervousness. "I couldn't."

Noah propped a shoulder on the bathroom wall and surveyed her as he downed more coffee. She had great legs, not real long but nicely shaped, with full thighs, cute dimpled knees and small, arched feet.

And now that he was sober, Noah could also see how her waist dipped in, adding emphasis to her voluptuous breasts and bottom. He even looked over her rounded shoulders and the curve of her belly with sensual appreciation. She reminded him of a Grecian statue: Put her in a toga and she'd be a perfect replica.

Gracie had a lot of shape—all of it sexy as hell. "You're here," Noah reasoned, pointing out the obvious. "You spent the night." *A night he couldn't remember, damn it.* "Under the circumstances, you can even use my toothbrush if you want."

Her gaze darkened more and darted to the

bathroom sink, where his wet toothbrush lay. "I, ah, I found baking soda in the kitchen and made do." Holding up a finger like a toothbrush, she demonstrated. "But thank you."

"Grace, about last night . . ."

She tugged on the hem of his shirt, trying to bring it farther down her thighs and distracting him from what he wanted to say.

"Are you feeling better?" she asked when he didn't continue. Her voice had gone all soft and sympathetic, putting Noah on edge.

It was bad enough that he'd slept with her, that he'd had all those luscious curves under him and couldn't remember a thing about it; the idea that he might have been a whiny ass, too, was intolerable.

Through his teeth, Noah said, "I'm fine."

"Good."

He needed to get back on track. By the second, Grace became more appealing. He almost wished she wasn't such a sweetheart, in which case he'd already have her panties off her and apologizing would be the last thing on his mind.

Resigned, Noah gulped down the last of the coffee. "I wanted to apologize."

"No need." Her smile now was genuine. "I didn't mind. I even . . ." She blushed. "Well, I enjoyed myself."

Noah could only stare. Grace was a lady, always. Not a priss like Kara, but just as proper. Surely more moral. Yet she'd enjoyed herself?

He heard himself say, "Well, thank God for that."

"What?"

He shook his head and decided a few admissions were in order. "I was so damn drunk, I had no idea if I'd embarrassed myself." Noah could just imagine how much more awkward this would be if he'd fallen asleep in the middle of things, leaving Grace unsatisfied.

But God, he wished he could recall her satisfaction.

Grace frowned. "You don't ever have to be embarrassed with me. Besides, you were justified."

His head started pounding again. Noah set the mug aside and caught her shoulders. "I shouldn't have touched you, Grace. Drunk or not, whether you liked it or not, that was out of line. You should slap my face, not make excuses for me."

She appeared to be holding her breath and staring at his mouth.

"Grace?"

"You didn't," she gasped out, and her breasts heaved, drawing his attention.

"Didn't what?" Noah asked, even as his brain began an erotic fantasy with those bountiful breasts as the focal point.

"Didn't . . ." She gestured between their bodies. ". . . do what you're thinking."

Noah had meant to make amends, to promise Grace it'd never happen again. He should have been relieved that things hadn't gone quite as far as he'd feared.

Instead, disappointment weighed him down.

"That's . . . good, then," he said. It was better this way, he knew that, but the feel of her under his hands, so smooth and warm, made him forget his resolve. She was close, and she stared up at him with blatant invitation—whether she realized it or not.

He wanted her now, more than ever.

"Noah," Grace murmured in a hesitant whisper, "are you saying you didn't really want me?"

The question threw him. "I want you all right."

"You're not drunk this morning?"

"Dead sober." He'd *never* be drunk again.

"Then . . ." She shifted, looked up at him. "Okay."

His knees almost gave out. Was Grace trying to kill him? He tightened his hold on her upper arms and tugged her the smallest bit closer. "Okay? What the hell does *okay* mean?"

"Yesterday you were so drunk, I knew I couldn't take advantage of you."

"You couldn't . . ." She left him speechless.

"I especially wanted to touch you. Leaving you in your boxers wasn't easy. But I promise, I behaved."

She behaved? "Grace, are you saying we really didn't do anything? As in *nothing*? As in not even kissing?"

"You don't remember?"

"Not much."

"Oh." That one word held a wealth of disappointment. "You, uh, well you did kiss me a couple of times. It was . . . really nice."

The timid way she confessed that made Noah want to kiss her again. He *had* to kiss her. As he leaned down toward her, Grace went on tiptoe to meet him halfway. He took her mouth without his usual care. But then, at the moment, he could barely think, much less summon up any finesse.

Grace's lips parted at the first touch of his tongue and he sank deep, groaning and then feeling the responsive bite of her nails on his shoulders.

Oh yeah. He *loved* the bite of a woman's nails. Her mouth was hot and sweet and his body tensed with razor-sharp hunger. "Grace . . ." He kissed her throat, beneath her ear; he drew her skin against his teeth, marking her.

"You said you wanted me," Grace admitted on a soft moan. She clung to him, her head tilted to give his mouth free access to her throat. "But I figured it was just the alcohol talking. I didn't want you to do something you'd regret this morning."

Very slowly, awareness sank in. Though it was one of the hardest things he'd ever done, Noah forced his hands to open and he released her.

Christ, he hadn't touched Grace last night in a drunken stupor, but he was about to lay down with her today, when he wouldn't even have the excuse of being drunk.

He turned away and rubbed the back of his neck. "I'm sorry, Grace."

Silence.

Noah wanted to kick his own ass. He turned to face her and saw her ravaged expression. Her face had paled, and her arms were crossed defensively.

Her pain twisted in his heart. The last thing he ever wanted to do was hurt her. "Gracie . . ."

"No, I understand." She took two hasty steps back—away from him. Her eyes glistened wetly but she didn't cry. She tried a small laugh that fell flat. "I don't know what I was thinking. Dumb."

Noah had been through the emotional wringer, and none of it had anything to do with his grandmother or his canceled wedding plans.

It all had to do with Grace. He narrowed his eyes and firmed his jaw. "What the hell does that mean?"

"I'm twenty-five." She laughed again. "I should understand these things better."

He took a purposeful step forward, crowding her, stalking her. For sixteen years he'd lived on the edge, growing harder each day in order to survive. That hardness was now ingrained in his psyche, and even his grandmother, with all her refined living and influence, hadn't been able to soften him.

He'd learned to cover it up, but he'd never conquered it, and now, with Grace standing before him, her body soft and warm and timid, he felt every single rising surge of that primitive past. "These things?"

His tone brought out her wariness. "Drunken men, sex talk, the combination of the two. It doesn't mean anything." She shrugged and again retreated. "It's okay, Noah, really. If I'd been thinking, I'd have realized . . . well . . ." She glanced up at him, then away. "I'd have known you didn't want me."

There were a thousand and one reasons why he couldn't get involved sexually with Grace Jenkins. None of them mattered in that moment. "You blind, Gracie?"

"I . . . what?"

"You know what a boner looks like?"

Her face went comically blank, then she shook her head so hard her hair whipped over her shoulders. "Not exactly, no."

Noah damn near smiled. Honest, silly Grace. She forever amused him at the most surprising times.

Noah dropped his arms to his sides and braced his feet apart. "If you're feeling adventurous, I can drop the towel and show you."

Her back straightened. Her gaze crept down his body with agonizing precision until she stared at the way his towel was now tented. "Oh."

"Whatdya say, Grace?"

She reached out and flattened a hand on the wall for support. "I need to sit down for this."

"I want you, Grace. Never doubt that."

With her eyes still south of his navel, she swallowed hard, licked her lips, nodded. "I already said okay."

"It'd help," Noah ground out, "if you'd demand an apology or something."

Grace snorted. "I'm not stupid." She forced her chin up and met his gaze squarely. "Besides, I want you, too."

Drawn against his will, Noah moved to stand in front of her. She made him feel savage, but she also made him feel protective. "Everything is a mess right now, Grace. No way can I get serious with another woman, no way do I even want to." Her big eyes were direct, unblinking. "All I want, all I really need, is sex."

"Okay."

Noah squeezed his eyes shut. "I wasn't finished."

"Sorry."

He looked at Grace and saw heated anticipation in the way her eyes had darkened and dilated, in how her cheeks flushed. In how hard she breathed. Signs of arousal, and damn but he felt them, too. The woman could make him insane.

"Grace, I'm not a refined man."

Her lips curled, her eyes got heavy. "You are the best of men."

"No, damn it!" Her faith humbled him, but he had to make her understand. "I was raised more on the streets than not. I'm hard, inside and out."

"I know." She gave his chest and arms a telling look. "Your body is . . . well, I'm speechless. You're magnificent."

His hands curled into fists; the little witch was

seducing him and he had to make her understand. "I like to work hard, play hard, and I like to fuck hard."

Her mouth slowly fell open.

"I can pull my punches in a lot of ways when it comes to dealing with others, to fitting in with my grandmother's world."

"It's *your* world, too," she insisted fiercely.

Noah wrapped one arm around her waist and covered her mouth with his free hand. "Quit trying to defend and protect me and just listen to what I'm saying."

Eyes rounded, Grace curled her hands onto his shoulders for balance, but she nodded.

"You're right that what happened last night only happened because I was drunk. No, damn it, don't start looking embarrassed again. If I hadn't wanted you all along, it wouldn't have happened. But I did, and then you showed up here and . . . I was just drunk enough to stop thinking about what I shouldn't do and start thinking about what I'd like to do instead."

"Noah." Her lips moved against his hand, igniting him. "We both want the same thing."

He pressed his fingers more firmly against her mouth. "I want sex. Hot, wet, grinding sex. I want a woman who's willing to give me her body in any way I want it. But until I get everything else squared away, that's all I want. No commitments. And God only knows how long that'll take."

She gave an exuberant nod.

Noah dropped his forehead to hers. "Grace, you don't know what you're offering."

She caught his wrist and gently freed her mouth. "I'm offering you anything you want. Anything."

An explosion of lust made him tremble. He felt

on the verge of violence, his need was so strong. "So if I tell you to get naked, to sprawl on the bed, you'll do it?"

She blanched, but after a few seconds she said, "If you're sure that's what you want."

"And when I tell you to spread your thighs so I can kiss you?"

It took a moment before she understood, and then hot color flooded her cheeks. "You don't mean . . ." Her voice was a croaking whisper.

"Yeah, I damn well do mean it. I want to kiss you everywhere, Grace, especially between your legs." Then, just to push her, he added, "I'll want you to kiss me everywhere, too."

"Oh."

She sounded intrigued.

Noah gently shook her. "I told you I don't play nice with sex, Grace!"

Her breath came in small pants as she purred, "We can play however you want."

Sweat broke out on his forehead, on his back. His muscles all rippled with tension.

Through his teeth, he growled, "I'm not going to be satisfied screwing in the dark, under the covers. I'm not going to be satisfied once a week, maybe not even once a day. When I take you . . ." *What the hell was he saying?* "Grace, I'll want to hear you yell and moan and see you squirm and feel you with my hands and my mouth and my tongue, all of you, inside and out. And then I want you to beg for more, until we're both too damned tired to move or even breathe. I want—"

She launched herself against him and kissed his chin, his neck, his chest. "Noah!"

He caught her up and headed for the bed, ready to self-combust. Grace squirmed against him, touching him everywhere, as fierce in her hunger as she'd been in his defense.

They fell across the bed together. Noah caught her mouth and plunged his tongue deep, tasting her, stealing her breath. His hand closed over her breast and they both froze, groans echoing between them.

"Grace," he rasped, feeling her taut, swollen nipple with his fingertips. Her back arched hard.

And the phone rang.

He easily ignored it—until the answering machine picked up and his grandmother's strident voice sounded over the line. "Noah, you'd better be there. Something has happened to Grace."

Something was about *to happen to Grace.*

Agatha continued. "We argued yesterday— thanks to you—and now she's not here when she's supposed to be and no one can locate her. You know she's never late, and she absolutely never misses work without notice. I'd appreciate it if you'd give me a call. If she doesn't show up soon, I'm notifying the police." The line went dead and the machine began rewinding.

Grace stiffened beneath him and Noah, feeling sluggish, levered himself up. "Grace?"

"Ohmigod, ohmigod, ohmigod! What time is it?" She twisted beneath him, looked at the clock and fairly exploded off the bed. "I was supposed to attend a meeting over an hour ago!"

Noah watched her with narrowed eyes. "Forget the damn meeting."

"I can't!" She shoved her long hair off her face and frantically began gathering her clothes. "You heard what Agatha said. She'll call the police."

"So?"

Grace looked amazed that he didn't understand. "So I'd just die if I caused that kind of fuss!"

The tee was now twisted, Grace's nipples were
ripe and pointed and Noah needed to come,
damn it. He needed that a lot.

Grace stepped into her worn, wrinkled skirt.
Apparently, despite their new agreement, she intended to leave. Right now.

Noah sighed. So much for her accommodating
his sexual whims.

"I'm dying here."

"Oh Noah." She snatched up her bra and began
struggling into it—once again beneath the T-shirt.
She looked emotionally pained and deeply sincere.
"I'm sorry. *Really.*" She turned her back, whipped
off the shirt and yanked on her sweater in record
time. She sat on the side of the bed, but when
Noah reached for her, she reached for the phone.

He propped himself on one elbow and took it
out of her hand. "What are you doing, Grace?"

"My car broke down last night, remember?"

"Honey, if I don't clearly remember coercing
you out of your clothes, you can be certain I don't
remember squat about your car."

"Oh." She tucked in her chin. "Sorry. But my
car died on me last night, which is why I arrived
here soaking wet and why you coerced me out of
my clothes."

He nodded slowly, his memory jogged. "Yeah,
now I remember telling you that."

Her brows rose high. "You're saying you made it
up?"

"I'm saying I wanted you out of your clothes.
Them being wet was a good enough excuse."

"Oh." Grace looked bemused for a moment,

then pleased. She leaned down and gave him a smacking kiss. "I'm going to love having sex with you."

He groaned, caught between tenderness, amusement and lust so hot he should have been breathing fire.

Grace rose from the bed and again reached for the phone. "I have to call a cab."

"The hell you will." Seeing she wouldn't be swayed otherwise, Noah forced his tensed muscles to bend and sat up beside her. "I'll drive you."

"But . . ." She shook her head. "Noah, I'm going to your grandmother's."

"Yeah, I gathered as much." And from what he'd just heard, no way would he let her face Agatha alone. His grandmother claimed they'd argued last night—thanks to him. No doubt Grace had been busy defending him, and no doubt his hardheaded grandmother had taken exception to her opinion.

"But Noah . . ."

"I'm taking you, damn it."

She stiffened. "Don't take that tone with me! I may have agreed to do whatever you say in the bedroom, but I never said you could boss me anywhere else."

Noah grinned as he pulled on his jeans. *She agreed to do whatever he said in the bedroom.* Life suddenly looked pretty bright.

"My little sex slave," he teased, and watched her blush. "Hell, Gracie, the bedroom is the only place I want to direct you, so we're in agreement."

She looked suspicious but finally nodded. "Okay, then."

"But," he added, not about to let her have the last word, "I am taking you to my grandmother's.

And afterward I'm bringing you back here, and we'll find out just how obedient you can be in bed."

Rather than put her off with his autocratic tone, Grace nodded. Her eyes bright with anticipation, she said, "I promise I'll try my best."

Well, hell. She had the last word after all.

Noah was too busy trying to breathe to argue.

Chapter Four

Agatha stepped around Kara, whose lashes were still damp from her most recent crying jag. Annoying, that. Agatha never could tolerate all that whining and whimpering. Of course, the girl had cause. Noah had crossed the line this time, dumping Kara so suddenly. Agatha had to find a way to make him change his mind. It'd be best for everyone, but especially for Noah.

She had to fix things.

Funny, but whenever she'd said as much to Kara and her parents, Kara had only cried that much more. Fickle girl. She probably assumed there was no chance; she knew as well as Agatha did how unbending Noah could be once he'd made up his mind about something. His iron backbone proved he was a Harper through and through.

But Noah loved the work he did, especially overseeing Harper's Bistro, and as Agatha was quickly discovering, the employees loved him. Somewhere along the road, the added responsibilities she'd given Noah had earned him respect and admiration from her associates in their social circle. They deferred to Noah, and valued his opinions.

He'd also gained the loyalty of everyone at the restaurant, from the busboys to the very temperamental chefs. Agatha would use those connections to lure Noah to her way of thinking.

She needed Grace here to help her. Grace not only kept her life organized, she was always a rock, and she had a calming effect that helped keep disasters at bay. If Grace hadn't been out of town during the confrontation, Agatha likely wouldn't have lost her temper and disowned Noah. Now she had to figure out how to get him back, get the wedding back on track and save face in the bargain.

Unfortunately, Grace had gone missing after their heated discussion. For some reason, Grace had taken grave offense at the supposed slights dealt to Agatha's hardheaded grandson.

Hillary and Jorge, Kara's parents, sat in stony silence, waiting for Agatha to come up with a solution to the problem of the canceled wedding. She loved them both and counted them as two of her closest friends, but they could be such nitwits sometimes. What did they expect her to do? Ground Noah in his room? Sometimes he reminded her of a wild animal turned into a house pet. Noah might often appear domesticated, but Agatha had to remember that most of it was a facade. Deep inside, Noah was still a creature of independence, determined to survive.

He had a stubborn predilection for doing what he considered best. Because his instincts were acute, oftentimes he was correct.

This time he couldn't be.

To herself, Agatha muttered, "Damn it, Grace, where are you?"

Jorge cleared his throat. "You're really worried about her?"

"Of course I'm worried. She's the most steadfast employee I've ever had. If she's not here, it's because something has happened to her." Agatha had already decided a pretense of worry would buy her some time and give her an excuse to contact Noah again.

Hillary, looking impatient, handed her quietly weeping daughter another tissue and turned to Agatha. "You said the two of you argued. Perhaps she's still annoyed."

"She would have called and said so."

Jorge raised his brows. "She tells you when she's annoyed with you?"

If they only knew, Agatha thought with a secret smile. Grace always spoke her mind, especially when she felt righteous. Agatha said only, "Yes, but always in the most diplomatic terms."

As if on cue, the library doors burst open and Grace tumbled in looking like a ragged weed caught in the wind. "Agatha! I'm so sorry I'm late."

Agatha stared at Grace, utterly speechless. Good God, had she spent the night in the gutter? Had she been attacked?

"Late," Agatha finally said, giving her mind a chance to work, "is a few minutes. Grace, you're several hours tardy."

"I know." Grace shoved thick handfuls of tangled hair from her face. "And as I said, I'm sorry."

Agatha looked her over. She was aware of Jorge coming to his feet behind her, of Kara and Hillary staring in mute shock. Her voice sharp with concern, Agatha snapped, "What in the world has happened to you?"

"Happened to me?" Grace blushed even as she parroted the question.

Skirting furniture and guests, Agatha approached her. A very real niggling of worry intruded. "Don't play dumb with me, young lady. It doesn't suit you at all. Just look at you. You're a wrinkled, dirty mess."

Grace brushed at her sweater—which had two buttons in the wrong holes, leaving a peek of her cleavage—and straightened her sagging skirt. Her legs were bare, her shoes water-stained. "My car broke down last night. I got caught in the rain."

"All night?" Hillary asked with real concern.

"No, actually . . ." Grace fidgeted. "No."

Agatha scowled. "No actually no *what*?"

Kara stepped up behind Agatha and placed a slim, manicured hand on her shoulder. "I think we should go, Agatha. Maybe Grace would like a little privacy with you to discuss her . . . dilemma."

Grace looked at Kara overlong, then bobbed her head. "Is the meeting over, then?"

Agatha tipped back on her old tired heels. She had never seen Grace flustered, but right now, she was bright red and rattling nonsense. "Of course it's not over. We weren't even able to begin without you here."

"Oh?"

"We were going to discuss the business aspects of the wedding."

Grace blinked. "What wedding?"

Agatha tapped one foot. "Noah's."

"But . . . I understood that the ceremony has been canceled."

Kara drew in a shuddering breath and Agatha patted the hand still on her shoulder. "There are some things that have to be resolved, Grace. But I have no idea where you have the legal files in my computer."

"Oh."

"Will you quit saying that!" Agatha snapped.

"Grace?" Jorge stepped forward. His handsome face was stiff with concern. "Are you all right?"

Agatha realized they now surrounded her, and Grace didn't like it. Her chin lifted and she crossed her arms over her ample bosom. "I'm perfectly fine, thank you." She made to move around them. "I'll just open those files right now."

"No point," Jorge said, watching her closely. "At least not until we know if the wedding is truly canceled or not."

And then, from the doorway, a rough-edged voice intruded. "The wedding is definitely off."

Everyone whirled to face Noah. Agatha felt a mixture of supreme annoyance and grudging pride. Noah wouldn't hide from animosity. Noah didn't hide from anyone.

After all, he was her grandson.

"What are you doing here?" Agatha asked, even as Hillary put a protective arm around her daughter.

In a flash, Grace was at Noah's side. Or rather, she stood in front of him.

Agatha's brows lifted. "Grace?"

"He brought me here. Remember, I said my car broke down?"

Jorge looked between the two of them in confusion. "And you called *him* rather than Triple A?"

"Last night?" Hillary clarified, and there was a load of speculation creeping into her tone.

Noah shoved his hands into his pockets and leaned into the door frame. He looked at Grace, from all appearances as curious about her reply as the rest of them.

Grace stiffened. "I went to see Noah last night."

The silence in the room was so thick, Agatha almost choked on it.

Grace forged on. "My car broke down a few blocks from his place and I got soaked getting there."

Kara held herself protectively and walked away to a window, staring out at the sunny afternoon sky. Agatha noticed that Noah's gaze never wavered from Grace; he was oblivious to Kara and her upset. Just as he appeared oblivious to her parents. All his attention, all his focus, was on Grace.

It was almost . . . intimate, the intensity with which he watched her secretary.

"My God." Agatha looked at them both, then narrowed her gaze on her grandson as everything became crystal clear. Mortification and outrage struck her hard. "This is too much, Noah! Far, far too much."

Lazily, he looked away from Grace to meet her insinuation. But before he could say anything, Grace took an aggressive step forward.

"Don't accuse him of anything!"

There was nothing diplomatic in Grace's tone this time. Aghast, Agatha said, "You're denying you spent the night with him?"

Grace pinched her lips together. Both Hillary and Jorge stiffened. Kara turned to face them, her eyes rounded.

"Look at you," Agatha continued, determined to take charge of the awkward situation. "You haven't even brushed your hair. And your clothes look as if they spent the night on the floor."

Noah made a sound, but amazingly enough

Grace raised a hand to quiet him. He grinned—the rogue—and fell silent.

Through her teeth, Grace said, "I did spend the night, yes."

Everyone spoke at once, Jorge furious, Hillary scandalized, Kara whining.

Agatha shouted, "Enough." She glared her discontent at Noah, and in a quieter but no less furious tone, she said, "That's low even for you, Noah. Grace is a nice young woman, too good for you to use that way."

Grace sputtered, she was so furious. "Too good for him?" Somehow she managed to stand two inches taller and said in a low voice laced with significance, "I should be so lucky as to draw his notice."

Noah reached forward and tugged on a long lock of Grace's hair. "You got my notice, Gracie, and you know it."

Agatha suffered a surge of protectiveness toward Grace. How could her grandson toy with her that way? Grace was in no way used to men and their flirting, and she surely wasn't used to a man like Noah.

"Are you using her to punish me, Noah?" Was Noah capable of such a thing? Agatha could never underestimate him. "Is that it?"

Grace stiffened further. "Noah didn't use me."

"We're leaving," Jorge announced, and Noah politely stepped out of his way. Hillary clutched her daughter close and dragged her toward the door.

Grace threw up her arms. "You've got it all wrong."

And as Kara and her parents continued to

march out, she added loud enough to rattle the windows, "*I* used *him!*"

Everyone froze, not even daring to breathe in the wake of that awful disclosure.

Then Noah choked, and to Agatha's astute eyes, he looked near to laughing. She considered booting him, but he was such a hard young man, she'd probably break her ankle. She wasn't nearly as sturdy as she used to be.

"So," Jorge demanded in austere tones, "this is the reason you broke off with my daughter? Because of an . . . assignation with *Grace*?"

"Nope," Noah replied, calm to the point of indifference.

"*No.*" Grace agreed, horrified by such a conclusion.

"Then why, damn you?" Jorge asked.

Noah briefly glanced at Kara, and with a twisted smile said to her father, "I have my reasons, and I'm sure Kara could explain them to you. But Grace had nothing to do with them."

Hillary, trembling in her anger, squeezed Kara closer. "I don't believe you. It's obvious to one and all what you've been doing. It's . . . disgusting."

Agatha had to figure out what was going on before things got completely out of hand. She didn't want Grace insulted, or her integrity called into question, but she had to admit it all looked very suspicious.

"You two wait here," she ordered Grace and Noah. She approached Jorge and Hillary with no idea of what to say. Damn, she hated to be put into these kinds of predicaments and Noah knew it. She avoided scandal and gossip by taking iron control of every situation. Yet she'd never really been able to control Noah. On occasion, he allowed her the ruse of control. But they both knew the truth.

Once they were well away from the library, Jorge muttered in low, angry tones, "This is incredible, Agatha."

Hillary added, "He should be horsewhipped."

Agatha considered that suggestion. "You know, Kara, it seems to me Noah's just sowing some last-minute wild oats." She made sure neither Noah nor Grace—*Grace!*—could hear her. The idea of the two of them together was so farfetched she was still a little shocked, and a lot disbelieving. There had to be another explanation. "I understand that's typical of young men."

"He's thirty-two," Kara pointed out, and to Agatha, Kara seemed far calmer than her parents.

"True. But he's led a restricted life."

Hillary made a rude sound at that. "Agatha, please. Before you took him in, he ran wild. There's nothing restricted in that."

"Without money? Without familial support? Think about it, Hillary. He was all alone in the world. That can be very restrictive."

"I suppose," Hillary reluctantly agreed.

Deep down, Agatha respected Noah, too. It was impossible to know him for long and not respect him, she thought. "I think you should fight for him, Kara."

Jorge drew up short before the front door, the epitome of the insulted father. "My daughter does not have to fight for the likes of him. She has her choice of successful men."

"*The likes of him*, Jorge?" That was an insult Agatha couldn't accept because it reflected badly on her. "Noah comes from my family, from my blood, and that's as good as it gets. Or are you try-ing to denigrate me now?"

Jorge relented. "No, of course not, Agatha. It's just that this is all very difficult. I don't like the idea of my little girl chasing any man."

"Kara needn't be blatant about it," Agatha soothed, when what she really wanted to do was smack Jorge. "Kara could visit the restaurant more, perhaps flirt with a few other men. That might spark Noah's jealousy."

Hillary and Jorge started to object, and Kara cut them both off. "That's a wonderful idea, Agatha. I'll give it a try." She hugged Agatha tightly, ab-surdly pleased by the suggestion.

Heart in her throat, Agatha returned Kara's em-brace. As weak-willed as Kara might be, Agatha adored her, and she badly wanted her for her granddaughter-in-law. Kara was sweet and kind and gentle, and she had an enormous heart. She also went out of her way to make her parents proud—unlike Noah, who seemed to take berserk delight in tweaking Agatha's temper.

Together, they would give her incredible great-grandchildren, and Noah's future would be set.

"All right, then. We still have a little time before the wedding. Not much, but maybe it will be enough. For now, we won't make any announcements."

Jorge looked stiff enough to crack. "We can give it two weeks. But then guests will be arriving if we don't tell them the wedding is off."

"Two weeks," Kara repeated.

Agatha watched from the doorway as they went out to Jorge's sporty Lexus convertible. Hillary was already tying a scarf around her fair hair, while Kara sat in the backseat, her face lifted to the sun.

Something didn't add up; there was more going on than the obvious.

Agatha shook her head and turned away. She could hear Grace and Noah talking. Now to face down them both.

Sometimes it was hell being the matriarch.

Grace propped her hands on her hips and said, "No." She wasn't about to relent on something so important, regardless of what Noah thought about it.

Noah had claimed he only wanted to "direct" her in the bedroom, but Grace had her doubts about that, based on his autocratic behavior so far.

"Grace . . ." Noah warned. His silky dark hair hung over his brow and his blue eyes glittered with menace.

"No what?" Agatha asked as she reentered the room.

Grace dismissed Noah's silent warning and rushed up to Agatha, determined to make her understand. "No, I won't let him take the blame for this." Noah had accepted enough blame lately. No way would Grace knowingly add to it. She sucked in a breath, braced herself, and blurted in all honesty, "Noah was drunk and I took shameful advantage of him."

Agatha tripped to a halt in her sensible tan pumps. Her faded blue eyes were first disbelieving, then hot with incredulity.

Noah laughed, raised his arms as if to say, "What can I do?" and dropped into a creaky leather chair, at his leisure. He stretched out his long legs, now clad in comfortable, clean, and pressed khaki slacks. He laced his fingers together over his abdomen and watched Grace.

Grace swallowed hard, as always affected just by the sight of him. She'd watched Noah dress that morning, had seen him in nothing more than a towel, felt his big, strong body pressing down on her.

She shivered with the memory. Noah was so gorgeous, so incredible. He was hairy, but not too much so. Muscled just right. Warm and hard and tall and strong . . .

Next to him, even with his beard stubble and red eyes, Grace felt like a limp, dingy rag. A pudgy rag.

She mentally dug in, determined to do what she knew to be right. She couldn't be distracted with thoughts of sex. "It's true, Noah, and you know it."

He shrugged. "It's true I was drunk."

"Mourning your hasty decision about Kara?" Agatha quipped. Her tone was far from pleasant. In fact, Grace would have categorized it as deliberately provoking.

Noah didn't seem to notice. "Celebrating, actually."

Agatha drew back. For a brief moment she looked hurt. "Why, Noah?"

He met her level gaze. "Sorry, but I told you, that's private."

Grace moved to stand in front of him again, wishing she could somehow protect his heart. To most people, Noah probably looked stubborn, and as durable as a granite cliff.

To Grace, he appeared vulnerable and chivalrous, and she wished with all her heart that Agatha would tell him she understood, that she believed in him and trusted his judgment. She wished Agatha would show him that he was loved.

Her wishes were in vain.

Agatha took them both in with a shrewd glance. "If only you'd kept this unseemly little liaison private. You hide your reasons for publicly humiliating a family we've counted as close friends for too many years to count and flaunt an indiscretion."

"Unseemly?" Grace sputtered in indignation.

Agatha ignored her. "However, since you didn't keep it private, you've ruined Grace, probably along with any chance you had of reconciling with Kara. I hope you're ready to deal with the consequences."

Slowly and with a good dose of menace, Noah pushed to his feet. "I don't want to reconcile with Kara. And as to Grace, I—"

Without conscious thought, Grace took his hand. It was large and warm, and despite his being the grandson of a very wealthy and influential woman, his fingertips were rough from outdoor work and play.

As they locked fingers, Grace saw Agatha take note of the telling gesture. "Noah did not ruin me," she said, struggling for a calm she didn't feel, "even though I was more than willing to be thoroughly ruined."

"Grace Jenkins!"

Noah stared at the ceiling, but his shoulders trembled with silent laughter.

"It's true, Agatha. *I* went to his house. *I* knew he was drunk, but still I stayed. And *I* was the one who—"

Grace's words were cut off by Noah's big hand. He pulled her back into his chest and with a hold

on her hand and mouth, held her securely. He
even rocked her a little.

She liked it. When she tipped her head back to
see him, he winked.

To Agatha, he explained, "Grace is a little dis-
traught at having missed the meeting. She takes
her work very seriously."

"You don't have to tell me that," Agatha replied
sharply. Her gaze narrowed in challenge. "Then
again, under the circumstances, it hardly matters,
does it?"

Grace stilled at those shrewd, cutting words.
With her free hand, she reached up for Noah's
thick wrist and gently pried his fingers from her
mouth. Tension had invaded him; she felt it and
wondered that Agatha didn't also. "What are you
talking about, Agatha?"

Agatha sniffed and patted at her silver hair.
"You've shown a distinct lack of morals, Grace.
The Callens are friends, very dear friends."

"I know that." Grace's heart thumped and her
stomach tightened.

"Of course you do. You've worked with them,
through me, many times. We deal with them so-
cially and through business on a regular basis. I'm
sure you can see how awkward this would be for all
of us." Agatha turned away to stride to her desk.
She didn't go to the chair but chose instead to
perch on the edge, her ankles crossed and her
head lifted in challenge. She was a tall woman,
quite slender, and even at seventy-eight, she had
an imposing air.

Noah held Grace a little tighter. She felt his frustration and his growing anger. "What would be
awkward, Agatha? Spell it out."

"Why, Grace working for me." Agatha straightened a paper, moved a pen. "She's involved herself in this sordid little contretemps, and unfortunately, there's no way to extricate her now. It would be an insult to the Callens, and to Kara especially, to keep her on."

Grace sank into Noah, grateful for his support since her legs had turned to rubber. "I'm fired?"

"Bullshit, Agatha," Noah all but shouted over Grace's head. "You better rethink this."

"Watch your mouth, Noah! I won't tolerate that language in my house."

"I'm fired?" Grace asked again. They both ignored her.

"And I won't tolerate you using Grace against me."

"You're the one using her," Agatha challenged, "to embarrass Kara, and to hurt me."

"No one is using me." Again, she was ignored.

"She'll be better off taken out of the equation." Agatha glanced at her nails. "Or are you going to tell me that you really care for her?"

Grace bit her lip, then almost tripped when Noah took an angry step forward. Because she was in front of him, she had to move, too.

"You couldn't find a better secretary and assistant if you paid double Grace's salary and you know it, Agatha."

"I'll make do." She glanced up. "I'll have to, since I have no intention of further insulting your fiancée."

"*Ex*-fiancée," Noah ground out.

"I'm really fired?" Grace couldn't quite grasp it. She'd never been fired in her life. Of course, she'd never had a man of Noah's appeal hugged around her either. Yet he was there, all but holding her up. Indignant on her behalf.

Agatha gave Grace a pitying look. "I'm afraid so, dear. I'll give you two weeks' pay, of course."

Well hell, Grace thought.

Noah forcibly set Grace aside and confronted his grandmother nose to nose. Agatha was tall, but Noah towered over most men. He made his grandmother seem diminutive in comparison. She didn't back down. She glared up at him with the same blue eyes, only hers were faded with time.

"Fine." Noah's smile was not a nice thing. "You're on your own now, Agatha."

Despite Agatha's usual bravado, her face paled. "What does that mean?"

"It means I'm finished. I know you put on that little show of disowning me, but you haven't had your hand in the actual day-to-day work in years. I figured you'd be calling in no time, looking for a way to make me keep things running for you. Odds are, I'd have done it, too. But not now."

Agatha scowled, and Grace saw her eyes darken with a measure of guilt. Obviously, Noah knew how his grandmother's mind worked.

"You have no interest in Harper's Bistro, is that what you're telling me?" Agatha tried to brazen out the situation, but Grace saw the worry in her eyes, and it bothered her. She didn't want grandmother and grandson growing further apart.

Though Grace knew it wasn't true, Noah said, "I have no interest in any of your businesses."

"They were *our* businesses."

"Maybe—before you disowned me and fired Grace. But I'm sure you remember how to keep it all running. The boards for all the charitable organizations will welcome you back, I'm sure. They barely accepted me as your representative anyway. And Lord knows you'll have no problem finding an informed escort to take you to the political functions fast approaching."

Agatha looked more furious by the moment. Furious—and panicked. Grace wondered if Agatha even realized how full her social calendar had become. She had a lot of obligations pending, and without Noah to assist her, she'd either have to start canceling or be busy every night.

"And the restaurant," Noah continued, "well hell, Agatha. You started it, so I have no doubt you remember how to keep it running."

Agatha thumped her fist on the desk. "You've hired all new people! And you've repeatedly ignored my suggestions on schedules and pay and . . ."

"So now's your chance to change things your way. Have fun. Just don't come to me when it all blows up in your face." Noah turned and caught Grace's hand. "Let's go."

Grace was forced to skip along beside him or be dragged. She felt sick at heart, seeing the enmity grow between them. She'd wanted to mend things, not make them worse.

Agatha hadn't been on her own in too many years. She was older now, and despite her assurances to the contrary, her age had caught up to her. Grace kept track of everything for her, and handled all her day-to-day affairs. She knew that Agatha often napped, that she had prescribed medications to take.

Grace had an awful feeling Agatha would be lost without the two of them, and a worse suspicion that she'd never admit it.

Until it was too late.

"Agatha?" Grace said over her shoulder, hoping against hope that Noah's grandmother would say something profound to stop it all.

"You need me," Agatha insisted loudly with only a slight ache in her tone.

Noah just laughed and paused briefly to stab her with a look. "I got along without you for sixteen years, Agatha, and that's when I was a boy. I'm a man now. Believe me, I know how to take care of myself."

"You'll miss the restaurant," she predicted.

Noah grinned without humor. "Not as much as it'll miss me." He jerked the front door open and pulled Grace down the steps.

"Enough!" Grace complained in the middle of the walk, tugging her hand free.

Noah turned to her, his frustration and impatience a palpable thing. *"What?"*

Grace unnecessarily dusted herself off and peeked back to see Agatha hovering in the doorway. "I'm not a sack of potatoes to be toted about, Noah Harper. For all you know, I might have wanted to stay."

"You're fired," Noah reminded her. "What would you stay for?"

He had her there. When Grace looked at Agatha again, admitting defeat, the older woman shut the door with a snap. Grace sighed.

"Let's go, Gracie." Noah stood there with his hands on his hips, the sun behind him gilding his tall, solid form and making Grace's heart beat double-time. "I can sure as hell think of better things to do today than hang around my grandmother's walkway."

Grace shaded her eyes against the glaring afternoon light and wrinkled her nose. "Yeah? Like what?"

In an instant, the air changed, became more charged around her. Noah's pale blue eyes suddenly appeared hot rather than cool, intimate rather than annoyed. His gaze lingered on her mouth, her breasts, the tops of her thighs. "Like putting you into bed—after I strip you naked."

"Oh."

"The first time is going to be fast, Grace; I can't help that. But I'll make it up to you the second time. Or the third. I promise."

Second or third?

His jaw locked, his shoulders bunched. In a voice rough with need, Noah asked, "Are you going to keep to your agreement, Grace? Will you do everything I tell you to and give me everything I want?"

Grace sucked in a deep breath of humid air. The previous night's storm had left everything clean and fresh. New and ripe with promise.

The late spring sunshine suddenly felt sweltering hot, the sidewalk baking beneath her feet. She rushed forward and caught Noah's hand, and now it was she dragging him toward his car.

"Let's go, Noah," she said, in lieu of an answer. She didn't wait for him to open the door of the Land Rover, but instead quickly seated herself. "We've got better things to do," she agreed, "than hang around your grandmother's walkway."

And, Grace thought as Noah climbed behind the wheel with a grin, if she was naked, Noah would be, too. Oh boy. He'd touch her, but she'd get to touch him back. And more.

Under the circumstances, it was easy to forget

about the family strife, the loss of a job she loved, and the sight of Kara Callen with huge wounded eyes.

Grace could only think of Noah and imagine what he might want from her, and how quickly she could give it to him.

Chapter Five

Noah held on to Grace's arm as they entered his apartment building. Graham smiled at the sight of them, but his smile faded when he realized Grace still wore the same ruined clothes of the night before.

"Afternoon, Graham."

Graham nodded. "Mr. Harper." And then, with a bit of concern, "Ms. Jenkins?"

Grace blushed hotly and growled some incoherent complaint to Noah. She'd wanted to stop at her place and change. When Noah had told her that he couldn't wait that long, she'd promised to just grab clothes to bring along. He'd nixed that idea, too.

He needed her beneath him in a bad way. Never in his life had he experienced such a driving urgency for a woman, and at the moment it felt like he'd explode if he didn't sink inside Grace's soft, welcoming body.

"No visitors, Graham," Noah announced in passing, and Graham nodded, wearing his best poker face.

"Noah." Grace sounded as though she was strangling. "Why don't you just paint a big red *A* on my forehead, for heaven's sake?"

He grinned. Grace was more prickly than usual, and Noah hoped part of that mood was caused by sexual frustration. She wanted him, but he'd deliberately kept her from knowing what he'd ask of her. He'd hoped to heighten her anticipation, and help her forget some of her nervousness.

"Gracie, you're the one who announced to all and sundry that you'd taken advantage of me. What difference does it make if Graham knows your intent?"

She mumbled again and punched the elevator button.

Making no attempt to hide his good humor, Noah asked, "What was that, Grace?"

The elevator doors slid open and he allowed Grace to yank him inside. As the doors shut behind them, she glared, and her brown eyes smoldered. Indicating her clothes, she said, "I'd at least like to look presentable while ruining my reputation."

The baby-fine hair at Grace's temple drew him, and Noah reached out to touch it. Her hair was incredible, and quickly becoming an object of sexual obsession. He could already imagine how it'd feel spread over his shoulders and chest while she loomed above him, giving him her breasts to taste and tease. And then on his abdomen when he urged her soft mouth lower and lower . . .

His hands shook and he curled them into fists. "It's not too late to change your mind, Grace." Noah offered her the out even though it pained him to think of calling a halt now, when his body burned for her. He hadn't shaken with lust since he was sixteen, but now he trembled with the need to have Grace.

Her annoyed frown changed to one of worry and her eyes darkened. "What are you talking about?"

"Your reputation, honey." He continued to toy with that soft curl, wrapping it around his finger, rubbing it with his thumb. "You know, you can claim that little scene at my grandmother's was stress-related or something. Odds are, everyone will quickly forget about it, and Agatha would probably even give you your job back." He shook his head. "Everyone is a little disbelieving that you want me anyway."

"You have that backward, Noah," she said gently, "but either way, no, I'm not changing my mind. And neither are you." She stepped up against him and went on tiptoe to kiss his chin.

Noah was so primed, he froze at the sensation of her mouth brushing his hot skin. "Grace . . ."

She caught his head in her hands and brought his mouth down to hers. Her kiss was tentative at first, tender, but they quickly became lost in heightened breathing and urgency. Grace tasted so good and felt so right. Her small hot tongue licked against his, and Noah lost it.

He had Grace off her feet, pinned between his body and the elevator wall in the next heartbeat. A ding signaled their arrival, and with an effort, Noah pulled back the tiniest bit. His mouth touching hers, his hand cupping her cheek, he whispered, "You're sure, Grace? And before you answer, think about it, because once we get into bed I'm not positive I'll be able to stop."

Her eyes were heavy, her lips parted. She offered no hesitation. *"Yes."*

Noah let out a strangled breath. Thankfully, the hall was empty as he made record time rushing her to his apartment door and then inside. Late afternoon sunlight poured through the open balcony doors, making lamps unnecessary.

Noah caught her hand and said, "To the bedroom, Grace."

He wanted to race her there, but he could feel her nervousness, so instead he spoke to her as they walked at a very discreet pace. "Do you want to know what I'm going to do to you, Grace?"

She peeked up at him, then away. A pulse throbbed wildly in her throat. "Yes."

Her voice was so low he barely heard her. He felt like smiling but didn't want her to misunderstand his happiness for amusement at her expense. They stopped next to the bed and Noah turned her to face him. "First I'm going to get you out of your clothes. All your clothes."

Her magnificent breasts rose and fell with deep breaths. "Are you sure you want to do that?" She fretted, looking toward the wide wall of windows where yet more sunlight flowed into the room and across the bed.

Very slowly, Noah tackled the tiny top button on her sweater. "Absolutely. You're a sexy woman, Grace. And," he added, when she started to shake her head, "I don't want to hear a word about weight. I have no idea where you got the idea you were too heavy."

Her mouth dropped open and she momentarily forgot that he was disrobing her. "I've always been overweight. Even when I was a little kid."

"That's nonsense."

"It is not. Everyone knows I'm overweight."

"Who?"

She shrugged. "My parents, friends, relatives. Even Agatha."

Damn his grandmother. "You're kidding. What the hell did Agatha say to you?"

"Just that I should try to eat less and exercise more. She offered me use of the pool and the gym equipment in my off hours, and whenever I'm there through lunch, she orders Nan to cook low-fat foods."

Noah opened the last button and pulled Grace's sweater open. She turned her head away, but Noah caught her chin and lifted her face. "No, Grace. Don't hide from me."

"I'm embarrassed."

"And here I thought you were excited." He eyed her breasts and murmured, "Your nipples are puckered."

Her shoulders slumped. "I am excited," she admitted in a tiny voice, "but it's not easy for me to stand here in front of you like this. At least last night you were drunk, and probably not seeing straight anyway."

"Grace, look at me."

If anything, she ducked her head even more until her long hair fell like a curtain, hiding her expression.

Gently, Noah lifted her hair over her shoulders. He loved her hair, but he didn't want anything to shield his view of her body. "This is the bedroom, Gracie, and you agreed to follow my every instruction, remember?"

Her blush intensified. "I remember."

"Good. Then look at me and keep looking at me." Tentatively, her gaze locked on his, filling him with primal satisfaction. "That's right. I like your pretty eyes, Grace. They turn me on." Knowing she watched his every move, Noah reached behind her and unhooked her sturdy bra, then pulled it away. Without the support, her full, heavy breasts rested softly against her chest.

As Noah examined her, weighing her in his palms, cuddling her, his testicles tightened and his heart pounded. He had big hands, but Grace filled them to overflowing. Her small, tight nipples were flushed a dark rose, and he rubbed his thumbs over her, making her quiver and gasp. He liked it that she watched him, that she saw the lust darkening his face.

Noah smiled. "I want you to forget anything my grandmother told you. You're lush and curvy and one hell of a temptation, Grace Jenkins. Seeing you like this makes me nuts. Seeing you completely naked will be even better."

"Clothes hide a lot."

"Too much." It'd take time to reassure her, but already Noah felt on the verge of coming. He wanted to be as slow and easy as he could, but he wouldn't be able to wait much longer. "Hold on to my shoulders while I get your shoes off."

Noah crouched down, and Grace obediently braced a hand against him as he removed her shoes, tossing them aside with her discarded sweater and bra. Before she had time to anticipate his next move, he trailed his fingertips beneath her long skirt, up her smooth, soft thighs, and hooked his fingers into her panties.

Grace yelped.

Absurdly pleased with her, Noah said, "Relax, Grace." And he tugged the underpants all the way down. Like her bra, they were white cotton, devoid of any decoration. "Step out of them."

She did, and Noah stood again, hugging her

close. Her breasts were a bountiful cushion, further inciting his lust. Noah jerked off his shirt, wanting to feel her against his bare flesh. "Kiss me, Grace."

She immediately stretched up and took his mouth. Noah clutched her ample backside, palpating and stroking and enjoying the feel of her naked flesh beneath the fabric of her skirt. But only for a little while, then he needed more. He pulled his mouth away.

"I have to get this off you, Grace. Right now." The zipper caught, his impatience exploded, and Noah jerked hard, ruining her skirt.

"Noah!"

"I'm sorry, Grace," he rasped, already lost. "I can't wait."

She paused, blinking nervously.

Praying she'd understand, that she was ready, he said, "I need you, Grace."

"Oh." She smiled. Her beautiful brown eyes were soft, full of understanding, acceptance... love.

No. Noah shoved the skirt down, over her hips, but one look at Grace's sweet belly, her rounded thighs, the dark brown curls over her mound, and he was a goner.

"Ah, God, Grace ..." He turned with her onto the bed and sprawled out over her, pinning her with his weight. He took her mouth with voracious hunger—and Grace matched him, her hands now gripping his shoulders, her hips lifting into his.

Noah sucked at her tongue, gave her his own. He trailed wet, eating kisses over her throat, her shoulder, down to her breast until he felt a swollen, turgid nipple against his lips, and then he drew it deep, sucking hard.

Grace nearly lurched off the bed with a whimper of surprise and delight. Noah held her still and feasted off her. He moved from one breast to the next, unable to get his fill, wanting more and more of her until her nipples were red and throbbing and Grace writhed mindlessly beneath him.

Absorbing the smooth, silky texture of her skin, he stroked one hand over her body. He luxuriated in the softness against his rough palm, plump hills and dipping valleys and the reverberation of her racing heart.

The curve of her belly charmed him, and Noah had to kiss it, too. While he indulged in that, he wedged his hand between her thighs.

She was hot, nice and wet.

"Grace, damn."

She stretched, tipping her head back, moaning. Noah slid his fingers over slick lips, opening her for his entry. Grace was remarkably small and tight, even on his middle finger. He was barely inside her and her muscles were clamping down on him, squeezing him, and he just knew when he felt all that sensation on his cock, he'd die with the pleasure of it.

"Tell me how this feels," he muttered, and pressed deeper into her.

"Noah . . ."

He could smell her, her scent intensified by her excitement, and he reared back to look at her. The sight of his dark hand between her pale thighs, his fingers now shiny wet from her, was a great provocation. Noah bent and kissed her thigh. "How do you taste, Grace?"

She moaned again, her eyes squeezed shut, her thighs tensed.

Noah nuzzled closer while rhythmically fingering her, just barely in and out, bringing her closer and closer, getting her ready. Grace's shyness was long gone and her thighs fell open, letting him see her, all of her. Her pink flesh glistened, and her small clitoris looked tempting and ripe.

Noah licked her.

"Ohmigod."

"Mmmmm." He stroked with his tongue, flicked . . . sucked.

"Noah." Her hands settled in his hair, urging him on, holding him to her.

Noah pulled his finger out, pleased with her groaning protest, then forced a second finger into her. He knew she was a little uncomfortable with the snug fit, but he said only, "It'll make it easier for you, Grace. You're so damn small."

"I'm big," was her automatic, nearly incoherent wailing reply.

Noah raised his head and gave her a tender look. She was flushed, damp with perspiration, open and yielding and hot.

Sweet, amazing Grace.

He caught her ass with his free hand, lifting her a bit. "Yeah, here you're a luscious handful, Gracie. And here." He rubbed his cheek over her breasts, kissing each puckered nipple in turn.

"But not here, babe." He worked his fingers into her, out, in deeper again. "Here you're small and tight and you feel so good, I can't wait anymore."

He raised himself up and quickly unfastened his slacks. With a small cry, Grace jerked up next to him and began helping, pushing his slacks down, struggling with his shoes and socks.

Seeing her bottom, the graceful line of her

back, only added to Noah's frenzy. When at last he was naked, she started to crawl on top of him. Her eyes were vague, smoky with need.

Noah held her back. "I need to get a rubber, Grace."

She looked blank, and Noah laid her on her back. Her dark hair spread out in a silky mass across his white sheets, her chest heaved. "Don't move, honey. I'll only be a second."

He yanked the nightstand drawer open and located a full box of condoms. He ripped one small silver packet open with his teeth and, with Grace's fascinated observation, he slid it over his straining erection. "Now."

"Yes, please." Grace held her arms out to him, and that was enough. More than enough.

Even as he used his knee to spread her legs wide, Noah again wondered if this would be Grace's first time. The idea seemed amazing; she was in her mid-twenties, as sexy as a calendar pinup, and beyond willing.

Yet she didn't act experienced.

Normally that'd be enough to bring out his protective instincts, to help him conquer any lust so he could be gentle and patient.

This time it only fueled his need. He felt like a caveman, but he wanted to be Grace's first. Just the idea of taking her virginity made him near to howling with primal urges.

"Noah," she whispered, moving beneath him, squirming to get closer, to pull his weight down onto her.

"Easy, babe." He opened her with his fingers so the head of his cock could wedge in. Her muscles flexed, her nails bit into his shoulders. "Look at me, Grace."

Lips parted, face flushed, she stared up at him—and Noah thrust hard.

They both gasped, Noah with indescribable pleasure, Grace with shock and discomfort. He caught her hips and kept her from retreating while he fought the urge to move, to pound into her. His whole body went taut at the moist, hot clasp of her body, slowly accepting him, easing around him.

Grace panted, her eyes now squeezed shut. He heard her swallow, saw the strain on her face.

God, he felt like a total bastard, but pulling back was beyond him. He fought himself and managed to hold still with an effort. Sweat dampened his shoulders, his brow. Striving for gentleness in the middle of savage need, Noah lowered his head to kiss her open mouth, then the bridge of her small nose, her brow.

"It'll be all right, Grace," he promised. "Just try to relax."

She nodded, but it seemed she held her breath.

Noah kissed her again. Damn, how could he get hit by tenderness in a maelstrom of lust? The combination of the two was devastating to his senses, keeping him off balance.

Everything about Grace had him floundering. He was used to gauging himself, to thinking through his every action so there'd be no regrets later. But in fast order, he'd coerced Grace out of her clothes and into his bed.

He hadn't given either of them much time to ponder all the ramifications.

To buy himself some time to adjust, Noah

teased her. "You're not very good at this obedience stuff, Grace. You're so tense, I'm afraid you'll break."

"I'm . . . trying."

An emotion expanded in his chest, nearly smothering him; he kissed her again. "Then keep those gorgeous bedroom eyes open, baby. Okay?"

She nodded.

"Can you feel me, Grace?"

She groaned. "You're inside me. Of course I can feel you."

"Tell me," he urged. Maybe talking would help her to relax so that she could enjoy this. "What does it feel like?"

As Noah asked that, he kept himself rigidly still except to tease her ear, her temple, with light, barely there kisses.

"I feel . . . *full.*"

"Yeah." That one word had the effect of a lick along his spine.

"You're a big man, Noah."

Not unusually, but she wouldn't know that—and Noah wasn't up to explaining. He said only, "All over."

"I feel hot, too."

"You're the hottest woman I've ever met, Grace Jenkins."

Her breath came a little faster. "It feels a little slick—"

Now Noah was the one to squeeze his eyes shut. "Getting slicker by the second." Her virginal opening pulsed around him, milking him, pushing him.

Grace squirmed, trying to adjust, and said, "Noah, kiss me again."

He complied, thrusting his tongue past her lips

the way he wanted to thrust into her sex. He took her mouth roughly while making gentle sweeps of her breasts and hips with his hands. "Grace," he ground out, "I'm going to die if I don't move soon."

Her legs lifted around him, hugging him tight. "Then Noah, move."

With a raw sound of power, Noah tipped back his head and slid deep, pulled out, slid deeper. With each stroke, her body accepted more of him while she tensed and panted and finally, Noah couldn't take it anymore.

He considered himself a good lover, a patient and considerate lover. But with Grace . . . she pushed his buttons and he had no control. Not now. Noah buried himself hard and deep and shuddered with an incredible, draining climax that seemed to go on and on.

Vaguely, he heard his own loud groans, the soft touch of Grace's hands on his shoulders and chest, and the gentle kisses to his throat. When he collapsed against her, she wrapped herself around him and held on.

Long seconds ticked by before Noah's senses returned. He was aware of Grace's heartbeat galloping against his chest, her breath static in his ear.

Sluggish and replete, Noah turned his head beside hers and kissed her shoulder. He liked the way she tasted, sort of warm and sweaty and womanly. He kissed her again, this time lingering, his mouth open and slow and thorough.

She looked at him, eyes heavy and dark with arousal. Her mouth quivered with unfulfilled lust, her whole body still warm with need.

Damn, she was something else. A lady through and through, smart and sweet and independent.

And a firecracker in bed.

Feeling like the luckiest man around, Noah smoothed a fingertip over the corner of her mouth. "I'm sorry."

She stared at his smile intently. "You don't look sorry. You look . . ."

His smile widened. "Satisfied?"

"I don't know." And then, with a hint of worry, "Are you?"

Noah laughed, content from the inside out. "Grace, you were so damn good, you drove me over the edge."

"I did?"

He nodded. "That's why I came so quick. And I am sorry, sweetheart. I'll make it up to you."

"It's all right," she said, still all breathless and trembly.

"The hell it is." His grin lingered as he moved to her side and propped himself up on one elbow so he could gaze down the length of her bare body.

Grace in his bed, still hot and flushed and *ready*, was a real treat. He'd be happy visually exploring her for an hour or so.

But Grace needed more than that right now.

Holding her heavy gaze, Noah reached for her breast and carefully pinched one pink, distended nipple. She shuddered and he said low, "Shh. Lie still. I'll make you feel good, Grace."

"What will you do?"

He met her worried eyes and taunted softly, "Whatever I want to. That was our deal, right?"

Though she nodded, she looked ready to swoon. It hadn't taken Noah long to realize that Grace enjoyed giving in to his sexual demands. It turned her on—not that she seemed to understand that.

Grace's particular brand of inexperience, curiosity, and sexual daring blew his mind.

Noah pushed his tired body up so that he was propped against the headboard, then removed the condom and dropped it into the wastebasket at the side of his bed. Grace watched with fascination, giving special attention to his cock, which still glistened and was quickly becoming hard again. Amazing.

"Come here, Grace."

She gave him a questioning look even as she scooted up.

"Right here," he said, and patted his lower abdomen. "I want you to face away from me. That way I can play with you all I want."

She went very still, her expression worried and hesitant. "I don't know how much more of this I can take, Noah."

That was pretty up-front for a virgin. "Trust me, Gracie. You can take plenty." Noah reached for her. "And you will."

She whimpered in a mix of excitement and dread. But she didn't fight him when Noah arranged her to his satisfaction, her back to his chest, her soft legs draped wide over his muscular thighs, her hands at her sides, palms flat on the mattress. With his mouth touching the side of her throat, Noah said, "Now don't move, Gracie."

She moaned in anticipation. Noah cupped both her breasts, pulling gently at her swollen, sensitive nipples. "Most women," he told her, speaking above her panting breasts, "can feel this even between their legs. Can you?"

She nodded shakily and whimpered again.

"Feel good?"

With a broken gasp, she murmured, "*Too good.*"

"No such thing, sweetheart." Noah kissed her throat, determined to make her first experience memorable. "Let's just spend some time doing this, okay? I love your breasts."

Her back arched and he warned, "Be still now."

"I . . . I can't, Noah!"

"Yes you can." He opened his mouth on her shoulder, then closed his teeth down carefully on a muscle—and tugged at her nipples, tweaking, rolling.

Grace's fingers knotted in the sheet and her groan was deep and ragged. Noah took his time, teasing her and teasing himself until they were both breathing roughly. His erection nestled between Grace's firm bottom cheeks, snug and warm. He wanted to enter her this way, he decided.

Hell, he wanted to enter her every way, in every position imaginable.

He heard her give a soft sob, shaking uncontrollably, and he smoothed his hands down her body to her belly. "Open your legs wider, Grace."

She quickly obeyed.

"Mmmmm," Noah said, staring down the length of her sprawled body and touching her with just his fingertips. "Damn. You're really close, aren't you? Do you see how swollen your little clitoris is?"

She gasped as he thumbed her, her hips jerking hard.

"You keep moving, Grace," he playfully chastised. "Hold still."

"*I can't.*"

Noah pushed two fingers into her. He entered easily now because she was so wet, but still he felt her flinch. "You sore, baby?"

"No. Yes. A little." She strained against him. "You're big."

"Especially for this little virginal opening, huh?" He held his breath, waiting for her reply, his fingers buried deep inside her. She was stretched taut around him, clenching his fingers in quick spasms. Noah felt certain Grace was a virgin, but he wanted to hear her admit it.

He wanted to know that she was his.

Her head pressed back into his shoulder and her buttocks squirmed against his erection. "Yes."

Savage emotions surged inside him. He hooked his free arm under her breasts and hugged her tight. It took him a moment before he could speak, and then he whispered, "Do you want to come now, Grace?"

"Please."

He pulled his fingers from her body and, using both hands, tweaked her nipples again, leaving them damp and ultrasensitive in the afternoon air. "Bend your knees," he directed softly, "and spread your thighs as wide as you can."

She did, but Noah helped her, opening her legs more, moving her so that her feet were flat on the mattress at either side of his knees.

She was wide open, vulnerable, *and willing*. "Now try to hold real still, sweetheart," Noah murmured. "I know it won't be easy, but do as I tell you."

He opened her sex with one hand and with the other he began rhythmically petting her, using his fingertips to rasp up and over her clitoris, gently, purposely, again and again.

Every so often he dipped between her lips, gathering and spreading her moisture, altering his movements to keep her from coming too soon. He wanted the pleasure to build and build until Grace totally lost it.

He wanted to know that he'd pushed her over the edge and given her a mind-blowing orgasm.

It didn't take him long. Minutes later, Grace was crying out, panting. She couldn't hold still and squirmed against him in blind carnality. Her head rolled on his shoulder, and Noah felt her soft, silky hair all over his chest. "You ready, Gracie?" he asked, knowing he was beyond ready himself. He kissed her temple.

Grace answered with a rough moan.

"All right." Feeling like a world conqueror, Noah concentrated his touch just right. Grace's heart thundered, she stiffened, and then, with a harsh cry, she broke.

"That's it, Grace," he encouraged, almost as wild as she. "Hell yes. You can move now, honey. Any way you want to."

She did, countering the stroke of his fingers, crying and shuddering and lifting her hips in frantic rhythm. Noah loved every second of it, her eagerness, her lack of inhibition.

When her body finally went lax and boneless against his, Noah cupped his warm palm over her mound, gently holding in the feelings for her.

Choking on unrecognizable emotions, he whispered, "Christ, you're beautiful, Grace."

She turned her face so that her cheek nuzzled his chest and mumbled an incoherent reply. Noah carefully turned her, then lowered her to her stomach beside him on the bed. Other than a deep sigh, she didn't move. He reached over her for another condom, rolled it on, then knelt behind her.

"I'm going to take you again, Grace," he told

her as he looked at her naked back. "God knows I shouldn't be hard again this soon, but you affect me."

The fingers of her left hand fluttered, as if giving permission. If it hadn't been for that small movement, Noah might have thought she slept, she was so still.

He shook his head, delighted with her, then picked up a fat bed pillow, slid his forearm under her to scoop up her hips and shoved the pillow beneath her until she was practically on her knees.

Having her bottom in the air pulled Grace from her lethargy real quick. Alarmed, Grace looked back at him. "Noah, what . . ."

He held her still with a hand flattened on the small of her back. Seeing her so provocatively posed made Noah's muscles cramp. With a groan, he laid down over her and easily pushed into her body.

"Tell me if I hurt you, honey." Though Grace was wet and tender, she was unused to physical excess, and Noah knew it was too soon to be taking her again; he just couldn't seem to moderate himself around her, not his thoughts, not his emotions, not his sexual need.

Still, she quickly got into his cadence and within ten strokes Noah was ready. He drove harder, faster, enjoying the slapping sound of his abdomen on her behind, the way her back arched and her hair flowed around her shoulders.

Just as he felt the churning pleasure start, Grace tensed and she, too, came with a long, low, lazy moan.

They collapsed together. The position was awk-

ward, but neither of them was anxious to move.
And that suited Noah just fine.

He couldn't remember the last time he'd felt so
sexually satisfied.

Amazing—and somehow special—that he'd
found that satisfaction with Grace.

Chapter Six

"**A**re you hungry?"

Grace bestirred herself, trying to gather her numb wits. Little ripples of unbelievable pleasure continued to pulse through her body. Places she'd never before noticed, very private places, were tingling. Her heart felt heavy and full to bursting.

Noah had made wild, passionate love to her. Her mind could hardly grasp the fact of what had just happened, what she'd done—with Noah.

Oh God, she wanted to hug this moment to her and keep it forever.

She drew a deep breath and became more aware than ever that Noah was a warm, hard weight pressing onto her back. Because he hadn't withdrawn, he was still a part of her, still inside her body. They were connected, and for Grace it was so much more than just physical. She loved him so much, it almost hurt.

His breath, more relaxed and even now, teased her ear, and his body hair tickled her prickling flesh. It was wonderful.

And then she realized something else.

Her big backside was propped up with a pillow!

She froze, picturing how she must look, and there was a moment of real worry, of acute embarrassment. But then she shook off the worry and mentally shrugged. Really, she should have at least blushed, but it had been too incredible to regret in any way.

She could easily get used to this sex slave business.

"Gracie?" Noah leaned up and brushed her long hair to the side so he could kiss her nape. Goosebumps rose in the wake of his mouth.

She shivered in bliss. "Hmm?"

"You hungry?" He stroked his hand down her side to her waist, lingering, exploring.

Her waistline wasn't trim and toned, but Noah didn't seem to mind. In fact, he appeared to be luxuriating in her skin, opening his big hand wide and kneading her. Not that she was an expert, but she liked to think she could recognize disgust if she witnessed it. And Noah was far from disgusted. He sounded almost . . . tender.

"Grace?" He kissed her again, then again and again, lingering here and there, tasting her. Her toes curled as he licked a sensitive spot on her nape. Grace sighed and squirmed against him.

"Oh no you don't," Noah scolded. "No more tempting me to unreasonable levels of lust. We need nourishment, woman." And to punctuate that, he gave her hip a swat. "What would you like to eat?"

Grace was actually famished, but since she was overweight, she denied it. Eating in front of others always made her feel self-conscious. "I'm fine."

His lips were still touching her skin and Grace felt his grin. He must enjoy kissing her, she reasoned, since he did it so often.

She definitely enjoyed it.

"You're better than fine, baby." He put a tingling love bite on her shoulder. "Hot. Sexy as hell. You're a regular wild woman."

"Me?" *Now* Grace blushed—more with pleasure than embarrassment. No one had ever accused her of being wild. As to that, no one had ever called her sexy either. "All I did was lay there."

"And moan and gasp . . . and come." Noah nibbled his way down her spine until he rested on her legs, pinning her in place with his chin touching her bottom. Then he added in a gruff voice, "I loved it."

Grace smiled in contentment. "I loved it too. I had no idea sex could be so . . ."

"Explosive?" He gently bit one buttock, then kissed the small sting.

"Yes." She wiggled again, getting more comfortable beneath him. Thoughts swirled through her mind, and she asked, "Noah?"

"Hmm?" He wedged a hand under her breast and held her while he continued to nibble on her behind.

Grace had never in her life imagined any man kissing her there. It would take a little getting used to.

She cleared her throat. "Will I get a turn to touch you?"

Noah went still a moment. "Now that I've come twice, yeah. I think I can muster up the control for that." He bit her again, a soft love bite, then rolled to the side of her with a groan. "But first we have to go eat. I'm starving."

Without Noah covering her, Grace felt more on display than ever. Suffering a distinct lack of coordination, she scrambled to get off the pillow, then sat up at the side of the bed and eyed her clothing. It was now well past wearing, in her opinion. The zipper on her skirt was ruined. Her sweater was baggy.

She heard the bed creak and turned to watch as Noah stood and paced naked to the closet. He pulled out a white oxford shirt and handed it to her.

Grace eyed the proffered shirt. "Umm . . ."

Grinning, Noah caught her hand and pulled her upward. Grace could do little more than look him over. She was inexperienced, no denying that, but she knew Noah was a gorgeous man with a body that would excite any woman. There was no fat on him, just muscles over more muscles, sleek skin, long bones, and masculine angles.

While he stuffed her arms into the shirt, she looked at his wide shoulders, flexing with casual strength as he moved. He was a dark man, and crisp black hair covered his chest, his legs, his forearms. Grace wanted to stroke him everywhere.

There was even a narrow, silky trail of sexy hair that angled down his body and bisected his abdomen. It swirled around his navel, then continued downward to his groin, where it grew thicker.

His penis was soft now, and Grace stared, thrilled, enraptured, curious. She wanted to touch him, but he'd already finished buttoning up the shirt and turned away.

His backside was muscled and sexy, too, as were his long hard legs. Even his big feet were appealing to her.

Noah strode to the dresser and pulled out two

pairs of boxers. He tossed one pair toward her and they hit Grace in the chest.

By reflex, she caught them and then stared at the expensive, silver-and-black-striped silk underwear in confusion.

"Put them on, sweetheart. If you stay bare-assed there's no way in hell I'll be able to keep my hands off you."

Grace looked up at Noah. The implied compliment was wonderful, but she had a bigger thought on her mind. "You wear silk underwear?"

Noah laughed. "Those were a gift."

"From who?" Agatha surely didn't buy her grandson underwear.

Gently, Noah asked, "Do you really want to know?"

Oh. She shook her head even as she suffered a stab of jealousy. She couldn't imagine Kara being risqué enough to purchase men's underwear, so it must have been one of the other women always vying for Noah's attention.

Women of all ages gravitated to him. The ladies who attended the same social functions were forever eyeing Noah with lewd intent, as were their secretaries and housekeepers. Even waitresses and clerks gave him double-takes and tried to catch his eye.

Grace knew Noah well enough to realize he hadn't been swayed from his commitment to Kara. He was too honorable to cheat on a fiancée, but now . . . now he was a free man again.

He could have his pick of women.

Watching her, Noah said, "I prefer good old cotton." And he added with a teasing wink, "Like you."

Grace's face flamed. She knew her underwear

was utilitarian to the point of being outright ugly, but since no one had ever seen it before she'd never cared.

She could only imagine what Noah's other lovers had worn. Kara, she knew, would own the finest, most delicate lingerie money could buy. And being that Kara was slender and toned, she would have looked stunning in it.

Grace frowned in thought.

As if he'd read her mind, Noah said, "We should go shopping. I'd love to buy you some lingerie."

Mortification rolled over Grace, nearly taking her breath away. Never, not in a million years, would she stuff her overweight, overblown body into some slinky little concoction meant to entice. Just the thought was appalling.

She'd seen underwear models plenty of times. They were tall and willowy, not lumpy with large breasts and hips and a barely there waistline.

Grace shuddered in telling reaction, then thrust her chin in the air. "You said you only wanted sex," she reminded Noah. And, Grace told herself, all she could realistically hope for was that Noah would want it with her for a while, before he decided to take advantage of his newfound freedom to seek out more attractive companionship.

Noah paused, then stepped into his snug cotton boxers. They hugged his hips and thighs and . . . his sex. Grace couldn't help staring. She wondered how it would feel to cup him through the cotton.

Noah stared at her with a closeness that bordered on scrutiny as he approached. "Let me help you get these on, Gracie."

Grace pulled back, clutching the silk boxers to her chest. "I can manage."

His blue eyes heated and his lush lashes lowered suggestively. "We're still in the bedroom, sweetheart."

Grace, softening at the endearment, looked around. "So?"

"So in here what I say goes, remember? And I said I'm going to help you dress."

Grace propped her hands on her hips. "I think you're using our agreement to unfair advantage, Noah."

He cupped the back of her neck, drawing her a tiny bit closer. "But," he said, his voice warm and rough, "if I told you to go down on your knees right now, you'd do it, wouldn't you, Grace?"

An image of her kneeling before him, her mouth even with his boxers, filled Grace's mind. Her toes curled in delicious expectation, and her stomach flip-flopped, leaving her breathless. She licked her lips and bobbed her head in ready agreement. "Yes."

"Good. That's what I thought." His rough-tipped fingers rubbed her nape, then he lowered his arm and held out his hand in undeniable demand. "Now give me the boxers."

Grace held on to them. "Do you want me to, you know, go down on my knees?" *Please, please, please.*

He flicked the end of her nose and treated her to a half-smile of blatant satisfaction. "Not just yet."

"But . . ."

Noah wrestled the boxers from her, bent to hold them, and said, "Step in, Grace."

And like an obedient little sex slave, she did.

Grace merely nibbled on her cheese sandwich and corn chips, even though they were delicious and she felt ravenous. Having sex had really worked up her appetite.

Of course, since she was sitting on Noah's lap—as he'd insisted—hunger was her *second* most prominent urge.

The dual assault of embarrassment and wantonness was new to her. She was embarrassed because, really, she was too big to sit on anyone's lap. Not that Noah was complaining. No, he just kept touching her and kissing her, and that was what accounted for her wantonness.

She'd led a sexually repressed life, but now all those feelings, so long buried, were bursting free. Her previous state of virginity hadn't been so much by deliberate choice but because no man who'd appealed to her had ever shown an interest.

Noah appealed to her in a big way—he always had—and he appeared fascinated with her body, which she took for interest. It amazed her, but Grace didn't want to question it. She just wanted to enjoy it while it lasted.

"Open up." Noah enticed her mouth with a pickle chip and Grace obligingly accepted it. Pickles had never tasted so good.

"I should have taken you out someplace nice to eat," Noah grumbled. He reached for a frosty can of cola and took a healthy drink, then offered it to Grace.

"This is nice." Better than nice. They were in Noah's living room, cuddled together in a large cushioned chair. Music played from the stereo. The sun wasn't quite as bright through the patio doors now, but a nice breeze wafted in, bringing with it the scents of spring.

Grace could feel the hard strength of Noah's muscled thighs beneath her, the heat of his solid chest behind her. And he was being so affectionate.

"Besides, I don't have anything here to wear. Somebody," she said, eyeing him so he wouldn't misunderstand, "was too unreasonable to let me stop and pick up a change of clothes."

Noah cupped her breast through the white shirt. "Not unreasonable, Grace. Too horny."

Grace laughed. She couldn't remember ever having so much fun. She even liked it that Noah drank straight from a can, just as she did when no one was around to see her. Though she'd never have admitted it to anyone, she liked the metallic taste and hated the way ice watered down the pop.

She also liked sharing the can with Noah, drinking where he drank.

Noah was different from most men of his station. He had money now, and he'd learned how to spend it, but it never seemed that important to him. His life wasn't about money or acquisitions. He was . . . more real than that.

He cared about others, and it showed.

Noah teased her throat with a knuckle. "Want me to send someone over to your place to pick up some of your stuff?"

"No!" Grace patted her mouth with a paper napkin and relaxed against his shoulder. "I don't want anyone rummaging through my things, Noah."

Noah stared at her, then nodded. "All right."

As Grace watched, his bright blue eyes heated. He looked at her mouth. "Did you want the rest of your sandwich?"

Sensing the change in his mood, Grace shook her head. "No." At the moment, food was the last thing on her mind. She felt a solid ridge suddenly

pressing up against her bottom, and the knowl-
edge that Noah was again aroused had a similar effect on her. Her breath caught and her nipples
puckered. "But I would like the rest of you."

His gaze shot to hers, and a slow smile spread
over his handsome face. "You want your turn to
tease, Gracie?"

Grace fought her blush and nodded. "Yes."

"What will you do?" he asked low, and shifted to
bring her closer, turning her so that she was more
or less cradled in his arms. He touched his nose to
hers. "Tell me."

Heart fluttering, muscles going liquid, Grace
whispered, "I was thinking—"

A knock at the front door made them both twist
around. Noah frowned, then looked back at
Grace. "I'm waiting."

"Um . . ." She eyed the door. "Aren't you going
to answer that?"

"Hell no." He playfully kissed her throat. "I've
got a sexy broad on my lap and she's about to tell
me all the wicked acts she wants to inflict on my
poor body. All things considered, I don't give a
damn who's at the door."

"But . . ."

Noah cupped her head and tipped it up, then
kissed her hungrily. Against her lips, he said, "Hey,
I'm on pins and needles here, Grace."

The knock came again, this time more impatient.

"Uh . . ."

"Ignore it. Or better yet, let's go back in the
bedroom where I'm in charge and I'll make you
forget all about the damn door."

Noah began to stand with Grace held in his

arms, and she squealed, pushing him back in the seat and laughing out loud. "Okay, okay! I'll tell all."

Suddenly the lock on the door clicked, and a second later, the door swung open.

Their laughter died a startling death. Noah and Grace both stared.

Kara, impeccably dressed, her hair neatly styled, stepped in. She dropped her key in her purse, closed the door, and turned. The second she saw Noah and Grace her mouth fell open. "Oh dear."

Noah plopped back in his seat with a furious scowl. "What the hell are you doing here, Kara?"

Face hot with embarrassment, Grace started to scramble off Noah's lap. But as if he'd anticipated her move, he laced his arms around her middle and held her tight. Unless she wanted to indulge in a scuffle—which she'd obviously lose—there was no way for her to remove herself.

That being the case, Grace was forced to improvise.

It was awkward, but she pinned on a bright smile and greeted their unexpected guest. "Hello, Kara."

"I knocked." Kara looked at Noah, then Grace, and back again. One brow arched high. "Twice."

"We ignored it," Noah rudely told her. And with a sarcastic smile: "Twice."

"I assumed you weren't home." Kara frowned and folded her arms. "I was going to wait for you."

Both Noah and Kara sounded hostile, and Grace couldn't bear it. There'd been enough hurt already. "We were just . . . having brunch. Would you like a cheese sandwich?"

Noah choked on a laugh and squeezed Grace in a warm hug. "She didn't come here to eat, Grace."

Kara stared at Grace. Her attention went from their mostly naked appearances to the way Noah held Grace on his lap, pressed close to his chest. Amazingly, Kara looked more confused than angry or hurt by their intimate embrace.

"No," Kara agreed, "no, I didn't come to eat." She cleared her throat and gave Grace a pointed look. "Noah, could I speak to you, please?"

Grace again tried to leave Noah's lap, and Noah again restrained her. "It's a bad time, Kara."

"Noah," Grace hissed through her teeth. And then, in a whisper, *"Let go."*

Without her discretion, Noah said, "I don't want to let go, Grace. We have unfinished business."

Grace smiled at Kara, then reached behind herself and gave a small, vicious tug to his chest hair. He yelped, released her to rub at the sting, and she all but sprung off his lap.

Trying to brazen it out and act as if she hadn't just assaulted his body, Grace said, "I'll just go get dressed and—"

Noah caught her hand, bringing her to a halt before she could take a single step away. He looked ... displeased. "You don't have anything to change into, remember? Your skirt is ruined."

Grace pondered how successful she might be at strangling him. Probably not very, considering how thick his neck was.

Kara rubbed her forehead. "This is ridiculous, Noah. I only need a moment."

He stood next to Grace. "I'll give you a call tomorrow."

"It's important."

"Yeah? So is this."

Face red with growing annoyance, Kara said, "I need to speak with you *now.*"

Noah started to reply as heatedly and Grace, feeling like an interloper, squeezed his hand. "Noah, be reasonable."

He turned his dark frown down to Grace. She should have been intimidated by that ferocious expression, Grace thought, but instead she smiled and nodded encouragement. Amazingly, Noah softened.

He sighed and shook his head at Grace. "Fine, whatever. You want to talk, we'll talk." And then, firmly: "But Grace stays."

Like a ton of bricks landing on her head, Grace suddenly understood that Noah needed her at his side. He wasn't just twitting Kara, trying to be mean-spirited because of whatever had transpired between them. He'd been through hell the last few days, facing down more than one accuser. Regardless of how he tried to pretend it didn't matter, she knew that he had to hurt.

And now he wanted Grace's support.

Grace was more than glad to give it.

She pulled her hand free but didn't move away from his side. "Kara, why don't you sit down? Can I get you something to drink?"

Kara strode to the sofa and perched on the edge of the seat. Her smile was chagrined when she said, "You're turning into quite the little hostess, Grace."

Unsure if Kara was mocking or sincere, Grace smiled. "Thanks."

Grace started to sit in another chair, but Noah caught her by surprise and hauled her back into his lap. "Let's get this over with, Kara."

Grace wanted to box his ears, but more than that she needed to reassure Kara. It was obvious she was on edge, her hands shaking, her eyes clouded with worry. "I won't repeat a word, I promise."

"And I trust *her,*" Noah added, making a direct jibe at Kara.

Facing defeat, Kara sighed. "All right." She clasped her hands together on her knees, not happy with the situation but understanding that she had little choice. "Your grandmother suggested that you're flirting with Grace just to get my attention. To maybe make me jealous."

Noah snorted.

Grace's reaction was a bit more volatile. She nearly swallowed her tongue. "But . . . that's absurd! I'm not the type of woman who'd make anyone jealous."

For some reason, that made Noah snort again, and the squeeze he gave her forced the breath right out of her.

He was back to looking annoyed again.

Kara nodded. "I realize that it's not true, of course." And then hesitantly, "Is it?"

To Grace's relief, Noah dropped the antagonism. "Kara, I wish you well, I really do. But beyond friendship, my interest in you is over. I'm not even sure it was there in the first place, at least not the way everyone assumed."

Kara stared down at her hands, but she didn't deny that.

"Is that all you wanted?"

"No, of course not." Kara looked between the two of them. "Agatha wants me to visit the restaurant more, to try to regain your attention. I agreed just to appease her and my parents. But I didn't want you to think I was . . . chasing you."

She flicked a glance at Grace and licked her lips in a show of nervousness. "You've been very kind about all this, Noah, and I didn't want to cause you any more . . . discomfort. But the idea . . . well, it seemed like it could benefit us both."

Noah raised a brow. "You think?"

Kara's obvious nervousness grew. "I'd like to be there, you know that."

At first, Grace didn't understand that cryptic comment, but Noah seemed to. He said, "Yeah, the restaurant is your favorite hangout, isn't it? I wish I'd figured out why a little sooner and saved us both some time. But hey, I never claimed to be real swift."

Suspicion dawned, but Grace had a hard time reconciling it to what she knew. Could there be another man involved? Could any woman look at another man when she had Noah?

It was hard to believe, and Grace decided to give it more thought. But first she frowned at Noah. "Of course you're swift. You're a brilliant businessman." And to help Kara along, she added, "Everyone likes hanging out at the restaurant, especially since you added the live entertainment."

Noah looked at Grace and chuckled. "Yeah, there is that."

Kara flushed with guilt, then forged on despite her discomfort. "It would appear to my parents as if we're trying to work things out. Then, after a while, they'd think we'd both tried but we just couldn't resolve our differences. We'd both win."

"That'd just drag out the inevitable, Kara, and you know it. You have to tell them the truth sooner or later."

Kara closed her eyes. "I'm not ready yet."

Noah shook his head in disgust. "Fine, whatever. You can hang out at the restaurant all you want. It's no skin off my nose."

"Oh, Noah, thank you!" Her whole face brightened. "I was hoping you'd take that attitude."

"Doesn't matter to me," Noah continued with a
shrug, "because I won't be at the restaurant."

"What! Why not?" Kara appeared momentarily
panicked. "Please don't tell me you're taking a
leave of absence right now. It's the worse timing
imaginable . . ."

"Agatha disowned me, Kara. You were there."

"Oh, that." Kara waved her hand in dismissal.
"You know she didn't mean it. She was just disappointed that we wouldn't marry and was lashing
out. It didn't mean anything. Surely you know
that."

Idly, as if he wasn't even aware of it, Noah
stroked Grace's arm. Grace felt his hurt. The idea
that his grandmother could treat him so callously
and yet have it mean nothing was a painful fact to
accept. She patted his hand on her arm, hoping to
offer him a measure of comfort.

"Lashing out at me was fine, Kara. But she also
fired Grace."

"But . . . why?"

"She's afraid you'll be offended by Grace's presence."

Grace added, "She thinks I'm the *other woman.*"
Secretly, Grace was titillated by that awesome assumption, not that she'd admit it to anyone.

Kara groaned. "But that's absurd!"

Grace started to nod in total agreement, and
Noah went tense. His hold on Grace tightened
once again. "What the hell is so absurd about it?"

Sensing that she'd angered him, Kara went
blank and then started talking rapidly. "Um . . .
maybe I could talk to Agatha . . ."

"Won't do any good," Noah said. "Agatha has

her own reasons for doing things, and no one is going to change her mind."

Kara acknowledged that with a nod. "Grace, I'm sorry."

Grace shrugged. "I'll find another job. It's okay."

"No, it is not okay," Noah insisted. "I'm done. I won't be returning to Harper's Bistro at all."

Kara deflated with uncharacteristic drama. "But Noah, if you're not there, I won't have any reason to be there."

"No reason except the truth."

Grace watched as Kara colored. So, it was someone at the restaurant? That would explain why Kara wanted to be there.

Grace thought of all the men who worked the different shifts, but none of them measured up to Noah. Andrew, the maître d', was a handsome, stately man, but he was gentle and courteous in the way of a favorite uncle. He wasn't the type to make a young woman's heart flutter. Besides, he was married.

There was Enrique Deltorro, "the bull," a forty-year-old Latin musician Noah had hired to play live music during the dinner hour. But he was an outrageous flirt, flamboyant, with an earring and chains. And he was with a different woman every night. Even if the age and appearance didn't matter, Grace couldn't imagine Kara putting up with the variety of women.

And the chefs—well, the chefs were the envy of every restaurant in town, that much was true. They were as educated, as sophisticated as Kara, but again, Grace couldn't quite picture them appealing to a young, attractive woman. They ranged from short and portly to tall and razor thin.

The wait staff, however, mostly consisted of young, handsome men. Grace had heard them referred to as "studs" many times. They were smart, fun, outgoing. But were they Kara's type? And what was Kara's type? What man could possibly have lured her away from Noah?

Kara spoke again, drawing Grace from her ruminations.

"Noah," she said in a plea, "my parents barely accepted you, and you're related to Agatha. I don't dare try to push them any farther."

Noah smirked. "I'm the lesser of two evils, is that what you're saying?"

Kara's dark blue eyes were big and sad. "I'm sorry, but yes, you know you are."

In an instant, Grace lost her temper. Every ounce of pity she'd felt for Kara went out the patio doors. "That is the most ridiculous thing I have ever heard."

She sat stiffly on Noah's lap, all but huffing, her hands curled into fists. "Noah is a wonderful catch and your parents should have been thrilled to have him. In fact, I'm sure they *were* thrilled."

Noah didn't try very hard to hide his grin. "It's all right, Grace," he soothed. "I've always been well aware of what Hillary and Jorge thought of me."

Grace whirled on him. "It is not all right. It's outrageous." She pointed a stiff finger at Kara. "She was darn lucky to have you!"

Kara gulped.

Belatedly, Grace realized the insult she'd dealt and turned to Kara with a frown. "I didn't exactly mean . . ."

"I know what you meant, Grace. And I agree. Noah is a wonderful person. The very best, in fact." Kara looked at Noah and found her first

smile since her infelicitous arrival. "She's very defensive of you."

"Yeah."

"Well, you appear to enjoy it. I'm surprised."

Noah shrugged, nearly toppling Grace from his
lap. She didn't appreciate them speaking about
her as if she'd left the room.

Just to make sure Noah was aware of her feelings, she deliberately elbowed him as she stood.
"I've contributed more than enough to this conversation." An escape seemed her best bet, before
she humiliated herself further. "I think I'll call to
get my car towed."

Noah stood, too. "What's your hurry?"

The man could be so obtuse. Did he think she
enjoyed being in the middle of a conversation between him and the woman he'd been engaged to
for so long? She didn't say any of that, and replied
instead, "I need to get home so I can shower and
change."

"You can shower here."

"Noah!" Red to the roots of her tangled hair,
Grace stomped back up to him and grumbled
under her breath, "You have a lot to learn about
discretion."

He rolled his eyes. "You're the one who just told
me how swift I am."

Grace supposed it was hard to be taken seriously
when she wore one of his enormous shirts and a
pair of striped silk boxers.

Thank God Kara hadn't commented on the
clothing, though she'd certainly made note of it.

Kara also stood, and though she still appeared
worried, she grinned. "I think Noah has been very
discreet. And Noah, I really do appreciate it."

Then, to Grace, "Please, don't rush off. I'm leaving now anyway. I have a few things to figure out."

Noah put his fists on his hips and regarded Kara. "You should give your folks a chance. They might be more understanding than you think."

"The same way Agatha understood you?"

"That's different."

"I don't see how. They all had the same expectations."

"That we'd marry and live happily ever after?" He made a rude sound. "I'm beginning to think they wanted the marriage more than you or I ever did."

Grace stared at Noah, wondering what he was thinking. He wore his most enigmatic expression, so she couldn't really tell.

Kara hooked her purse over her arm and smoothed her sleek, short brown hair. "Be happy, Noah."

He slung an arm around Grace's waist, hauling her close. "Yeah, you, too."

"At the moment," Kara whispered, "that seems pretty impossible."

She turned away and Noah said, "Kara?"

"Yes?"

"My key?"

With a rueful smile, Kara removed the apartment key from her purse. "I suppose I won't be needing it anymore. And," she added, sparing a glance for Grace, "I'm sure you don't want any more awkward interruptions."

"You've got that right." Noah accepted the key, then curled his fingers around it.

Grace waited until Kara had left before jerking away from Noah. He pulled her right back.

"Noah!" She pushed at his hard chest without much success. "In case you missed it, I'm angry."

"Why?" He bent and kissed her throat, nipped her ear.

"You embarrassed me." How could he not realize that?

"What?" He tipped back to give her a look filled with endearing confusion. "The shower remark?"

"It was totally uncalled for."

"Showering with you is very called for." He kissed her again, and Grace felt her resolve quickly melting away. She didn't really blame herself because this was all too new, too unexpected for her. Even in her dreams, Noah had never been this attentive, this attracted. It was enough to rattle even the most levelheaded woman.

"Noah," Grace complained, albeit without much intensity, "I really do need to go home."

He dropped his forehead to her shoulder with a groan. "Why?"

"I have to check my messages, get my car looked at, shower—*in my own bathroom*—get into my own clothes. And I have to get a good night's sleep so that first thing tomorrow, I can find a job."

"You plan to go job hunting tomorrow?"

There was a note of disappointment in his tone. Had he wanted to see her again? "Noah, I live on my income. No, I won't starve overnight. I'm sensible about saving for a rainy day. But I can't take unemployment lightly either, so finding a job is a priority." And because she wanted to make him her priority, she said, "I'm really sorry."

He considered her for a long moment, then finally nodded. "I understand. I have some things I have to work on anyway."

Grace got a sick feeling. "Oh?"

His grin was lopsided, charming. "Yeah. I've gotta find a job, too, remember?" He chuckled at her surprise, then hugged her off her feet. "Did you forget you weren't the only one fired?"

"Oh, but surely . . ."

"No, don't say it, Grace. I'm not going back to work for her. If Agatha and I are ever going to get along, if there's to be any type of family atmosphere, then she has to know she can't manipulate me like this."

Grace hated to admit it, but Noah was right. Because Agatha knew he loved the restaurant, she thought she could use it to control him. "She's going to be hurt."

"She'll get over it. I know my grandmother. Besides, she'll probably enjoy getting involved again. She stepped aside because she thought it was the thing to do, not because she thought I could do any better."

"You have done better, though. As her personal secretary, I'm privy to all Agatha's private information. I know she has far more assets now than she did before you took over. Her stock has nearly doubled, Harper's Bistro has improved its reputation and doubled its profits, and all her property investments are thriving—thanks to you."

"Hey, don't give me too much credit, Grace. I've had Agatha relentlessly tutoring me on business since I was sixteen."

Grace reached up and cupped Noah's face. True, Agatha had taught him the basics, but he'd gone far beyond that with instincts and savvy and good common sense. It was amazing that he was still, even under the circumstances, willing to share the credit with his grandmother. "You're pretty special, you know that, Noah?"

Just that easily, the fascinating heat was back in his eyes. He started to bend down to her—and another rap sounded at the door.

Noah groaned. "What now?"

Chuckling, Grace said, "Maybe Kara forgot something. You did take her key."

Before Grace could protest, Noah strode to the door, glanced out the peephole, and opened it.

In a flash, Grace leapt behind the couch. Because there was a sofa table situated there, and she was far from petite, it was a tight fit. "Noah! We're not properly dressed."

"It's just Ben," he told her, "and he's seen my underwear before."

"Not on me, he hasn't!"

Grace heard Ben laugh, and she peeked over the back of the sofa at him. He didn't look any the worse for his night of drunken revelry. In fact, he looked really good—like he always did.

His black hair was wind tossed and his equally dark eyes were smiling. He wore a white polo shirt with an open collar that showed a generous amount of sexy chest hair and contrasted sharply with his tan. The shirt was tucked neatly into faded, snug-fitting jeans.

Ben grinned, showing a dimple in his left cheek and strong white teeth. "Hi Gracie."

"Ben." At this rate, Grace expected to burn herself up with embarrassment. "If you'll just turn your back, I'll escape to the . . ." She drew to a verbal halt, unwilling to admit that her clothes were scattered over Noah's bedroom floor. "I'll dash down the hall and dress."

"I dunno," Ben teased. "I'm awful curious now. You say you're wearing Noah's underwear?"

Noah, the rat, just grinned. "She looks real cute in them, too."

"S'that right?" Ben started toward the sofa.

Grace's heart did a somersault at his feigned approach. "Ben Badwin, you turn your back right now!"

Ben stopped and turned to Noah. "She's screeching. I never heard Grace screech before."

"Yeah." Noah nodded, watching Grace thoughtfully. "But then, she's had a rough night."

"Noah!" The two of them together were enough to fluster any woman.

He winked at her. "Get your mind out of the gutter, honey. I was talking about Agatha firing you."

"Oh."

Ben nearly strangled on his laughter this time.

"You think it's funny," Grace challenged, still cowering behind the furniture, "that I'm without a job?"

Ben's expression froze comically. "You mean the old witch really did fire you? You're kidding!"

"She really did," Noah told him, then he walked to Grace. "Come on out, Grace. Ben won't peek."

"Scout's honor," Ben agreed, and he finally turned his back.

Grace scooted out and felt Noah's hand on her backside as she did so. She glared at him, and he said, "Just helping."

"Yeah, right." She turned to march down the hall. "You both need a swift kick."

As she headed into Noah's bedroom and closed the door hard, Grace also thought how similar the brothers were—in looks and in warped senses of humor. Before she'd finished pulling on her wrinkled, damaged skirt, which thankfully still had a button at the waistband, she was smiling.

Chapter Seven

Ben waited until he knew Grace was almost out of sight, then he peeked. He just couldn't help himself. It was enough of a shock that Noah was apparently interested in Grace, even sexually involved with her. But it was doubly intriguing to think of Grace bouncing around in boxers.

He'd only gotten a glimpse of her bare legs, her voluptuous body buried beneath one of Noah's white shirts, when Noah shoved him.

"You told her you wouldn't look."

"Yeah, well, I was never a Scout." Ben eyed his older brother. "What the hell's going on, Noah?"

"I told you all of it last night."

"You sure as certain didn't tell me about Grace. I remember she stopped by—I wasn't too drunk to recall that." He propped his hands on his hips. "But now I'm wondering if she ever left."

"None of your business, Ben." Noah strode toward the kitchen and placed a door key on top of the fridge. Ben followed him.

"She's a nice girl."

"Real nice," Noah agreed. Then, with the gravity

so much a part of him, he added, "Grace is unlike any woman I've ever known."

Ben pulled out a kitchen chair and sprawled into it. "You got anything to drink?"

"Didn't you have enough last night?"

Grinning, Ben said, "I had too much, if you want the truth."

Grunting in agreement to that, Noah asked, "Want me to put on coffee?"

"Yeah, and make it strong. I've still got something of a hangover, so maybe the caffeine will help." He rubbed his temples. "Remind me never to drink with you again."

"Ditto." Noah went through the cabinets while Ben considered the situation.

He studied Noah, and noticed that he looked more relaxed now than he had in recent months. Even after getting rip-roaring drunk, he looked . . . more peaceful.

He also looked bigger. His brother was a prime specimen, a fact that made Ben proud. But now he looked . . . enormous. "Is it my imagination or are you getting bigger?"

Noah shrugged as he measured coffee into the strainer. "The last few months I've spent more time in the gym, taking out my frustrations on the heavy bag and anyone who'd volunteer to spar."

"Sexual frustration?" It was a rhetorical question because Ben had warned Noah all along that Kara wasn't the type of warm, open woman a man wanted to be tied to. Not that he was an expert on marriage, and not that he was in any hurry to leg shackle himself. At a tender twenty-nine, Ben figured he had years before he had to worry about it.

But he knew damn good and well that, if he ever

did marry, it'd be to a woman who gave him one hundred and fifty percent—in bed and out.

"It doesn't matter now." Noah spoke in an off-hand manner that didn't fool Ben at all.

His suspicions grew. "What did you mean about Grace being different?"

His back still to Ben, Noah grumbled, "What is this? Twenty questions?"

"Just curious."

"Some things aren't any of your damn business."

"So you got something private going on with Grace?" That goad got to Noah, and he turned to Ben with a fierce frown.

"Grace is genuine. Up front." His frown turned thoughtful, and he folded his arms. "You know, I almost want to say fearless, but that's not the right word."

"What about honorable?"

Noah paused, then nodded sharply. "Yeah, that suits Grace." He grinned. "And she's protective."

"Of you?"

Noah dumped water into the coffeemaker, switched it on, and then pulled out his chair. "Yeah. It's the damnedest thing. Grace doesn't mind giving me hell, but she takes exception any time someone else tries to."

"She's the mothering sort." Ben had noticed that about Grace almost from the moment he'd met her.

He could still recall the day Grace had sought him out. She'd met Noah from working with Agatha, and when Agatha had confided that another grandson had been discovered but not claimed, Grace's sense of fair play had been outraged. She'd looked him up and presented herself at his hotel, and Ben had thought she was about the sweetest thing he'd ever met. Guileless to the point of leaving herself vulnerable. Ben felt protective of her, and strangely, she'd acted protective of him.

Ben had picked up on that right off.

He sometimes had the feeling that Grace wanted to protect and nurture everyone. It was an integral part of her nature.

Noah said, "She doesn't seem to realize that I don't need coddling, that I can take care of myself."

Ben lifted his brows. "Coddling is nice every now and then. My mother loves to coddle."

"Yeah. Brooke is great."

Ben nodded. Unlike Noah, he'd had a wonderful mother to take care of him while growing up. Ever since they'd learned of Noah, Brooke had been trying to mother him, too. He'd resisted her efforts.

Evidently, he wasn't resisting Grace.

Of course, Grace could be pretty determined once she'd made up her mind. Grace thought that Noah had missed out on a lot because of his upbringing. Ben, however, hadn't missed having a father at all; if anything, he felt disgust for the man who'd provided his seed and nothing more. Because of that, Ben was very careful about taking risks. He never had unprotected sex and thought men who did were unconscionable.

"It's no wonder Grace seems different to you," Ben said finally, "considering the type of women you knew growing up." From everything Ben had learned, prostitution, drug addiction, and other forms of desperation had colored the lives of most of the young ladies Noah had associated with before meeting Agatha. It made Ben sick at heart whenever he thought of the environment Noah had grown up in.

And it made him beyond thankful that they'd finally met, that he now had a brother who seemed a part of him. Noah was, without doubt, the finest man Ben knew.

The coffeemaker sputtered to a halt and Noah stood to fill two mugs. "It's more than that. You're right that Grace isn't anything like those women. But she's not like the women in her social circle either."

"You mean Agatha's social circle?"

Noah handed him a steaming cup. "Whatever. I don't know any other woman who would have put up with cheese sandwiches for dinner while wearing my boxers."

Ben laughed so abruptly, he nearly spit his coffee across the table.

And then Grace marched in.

She'd brushed out her long hair and put on her ruined skirt and shoes. She still wore Noah's white shirt, hanging loose over the skirt to mid-thigh. It was an odd, mismatched outfit, yet it somehow looked adorable on her.

She folded her arms over her ample breasts and looked at both of them before settling her gaze on Noah. "I hope you don't mind, but I'm going to borrow your shirt. I need to have it dry-cleaned now anyway, and I need it to cover my ruined zipper. And I'll need a bag or something to carry my pantyhose and my sweater home. There's no way I can wear them."

"What about your bra? Are you wearing it?"

Ben sat back to enjoy himself. He'd never

known his brother to deliberately embarrass a woman before. Just the opposite; Noah had a gallant streak toward women and kids that ran a mile wide. But Ben had to admit, flustering Grace was downright fun, so he didn't blame Noah much.

Grace's jaw dropped, then snapped shut. She set her mouth in a mulish line, but she didn't take the bait. With slow, precise enunciation, she said, "I'm going to call a cab."

Noah sat up straight. "Hell no. I'll drive you home."

"I don't need you to drive me home, thank you very much."

"I'm doing it anyway."

"Noah." She glanced at Ben with what looked like an apology for Noah's bad manners. Ben winked at her.

Grace sighed. "Noah, you have company."

He scoffed. "It's just Ben. He doesn't want you to take a cab either."

Luckily, to Ben's way of thinking, Grace didn't ask him to verify that. Personally he didn't know what Noah had against a cab, but he didn't want to disagree with him and he didn't want to get pulled into their squabble.

"I'm ready to go and I'm not a child," Grace stated. "I can make it home in a cab just fine."

"No."

Grace looked distinctly stubborn about it. *"Yes."*

Noah looked more than stubborn. "No way, Grace."

They made an amusing couple, to Ben's way of thinking. Noah needed someone like Grace. She was a woman who wouldn't be pushed around but who would put herself in the line of fire to protect those people she cared about. Her feminine strength was a match to Noah's strong, take-charge personality. And Grace—well, bless her heart, she didn't hesitate to speak her mind. Noah always did appreciate an honest woman—and as to that, so did Ben.

Noah's phone rang, making it impossible for Grace to continue to argue. Noah shoved himself out of his seat and snatched up the receiver from the wall. Since it was on the opposite side of the kitchen, he had his back to Grace. He barked, "Hello?"

Grace glared at his back, and for a moment there, Ben thought she might actually stick out her tongue. But she showed great restraint and instead dropped into the seat he'd vacated.

She picked up Noah's coffee cup without realizing how telling her actions might be and took a sip.

She immediately plunked it back down and shuddered. "Good God, who made the coffee? It's awful."

Ben toasted her. "We were both in need of the caffeine kick."

Grace's expression softened as she pushed the cup out of reach. "Feeling the effects of last night's drinking binge?"

"When I first woke up this morning, I thought my eyeballs had fallen out. It's taken me all day to begin feeling human again."

Grace smiled. "Hopefully last night taught you something."

Ben scrutinized her, appreciating how she looked in Noah's shirt. "Yeah, it taught me that all the fun happens after I leave."

She blushed and frowned at him at the same time.

Noah's voice rose, drawing their attention. "For the last time, it's not my problem, Andrew. No, and that's final." He hesitated and then growled, "I told you, I'm fired, so there's nothing I can do. Call Agatha and tell her what's going on. She's the one who hired the new chef, anyway, not me."

Grace looked at Ben, appalled, and Ben winced. "Trouble at the restaurant?"

"I was afraid of that." Grace watched Noah with a worried frown. "Agatha insisted on hiring a new chef. I interviewed him last week, and I told Agatha he wasn't the most even-tempered man I'd ever met." She glanced at Ben. "He was actually a rude, snooty jerk. But Agatha only cared about his reputation with food, not his personality. It sounds like he's ready to start work."

Ben grinned. "Perfect timing on his part. He's arrived right in the middle of chaos."

Grace didn't see the humor in the situation. "Agatha needs Noah, but he's right that she lords his interest in the restaurant over him. I don't know what to do."

Ben propped his elbows on the table and regarded her. "Do? You were fired too, Grace, so it seems to me it's not your problem."

She shook her head. "I know how you feel about Agatha, Ben. But you're all family. It's not good to have this level of discord."

"Agatha thrives on discord."

"She's afraid of losing control."

Personally, Ben didn't think Agatha Harper was afraid of anything, but since he knew Grace was fond of her, he held his peace. "I have a suggestion."

"On how to patch things up?"

He snorted. "Hell no. I meant that I'm leaving

in just a few minutes anyway. I have some things to do, and if you want, I'll give you a ride home."

Noah hung up the phone in time to hear Ben's comment. "I'm driving her home."

Grace stood. "No you're not. You need to go to the restaurant."

Noah glowered down at her. "Like hell I will. I don't work for Agatha anymore, so it's not my problem. Let her deal with it."

"This has nothing to do with what's happened between you and Agatha." She touched his chest and gave him a solemn look. "You'll go for all the employees who are loyal to you, all the friends you've made there. You owe it to them to explain things, Noah, to help them understand."

Noah's frown darkened even more. It was an interesting thing to watch, because Grace didn't back down one bit. If anything, she stepped closer to Noah. She lifted her hand from his chest to his jaw.

Ben watched in awe.

"Think about it, Noah. Do you want any of them to act so stupidly that they get fired by Agatha, too? You told me Andrew was perfect for the job as maître d', and that he's supporting aging parents as well as his own wife and kids. And you said Enrique was thrilled to be hired as the entertainment, that he saw this as his chance to settle down."

Noah made a rude sound. "Yeah, well, I'd like to reevaluate that assessment. Enrique is a hound dog who'll probably always run around."

Grace seemed to be considering that comment, though Ben doubted she understood Noah's sentiments. Finally she shook her head and went on with dogged determination.

"Well, then, what about Greg and Dean and

Michael? They're working their way through college on tips. If they get in trouble, who else will hire them for so much money, and work around their school schedules, too?"

Noah rolled his eyes and looked at Ben. "Did you know Grace was such a pushy broad?"

Grace let loose with an indignant gasp.

"Yeah," Ben said, grinning at her, "I'd gotten that impression. At least over things she considers important." And Ben had no doubt that Grace considered Noah very important. She didn't want him to have any regrets.

Grace turned away in high dudgeon, ready for a grand exodus, and Noah pulled her back around and into his arms. Ben watched with interest as Noah treated her to a very passionate kiss that had her groaning softly, then clutching at him.

Deciding he was too young and too single to witness such outrageous displays of affection, Ben gave them privacy by walking out of the kitchen. He was still a little staggered by the idea of Noah and Grace as a couple. And he couldn't help but worry about Grace. As Noah said, Grace was unique and needed special care. He hoped Noah remembered that.

But the idea was growing on him. They complemented each other, and it was plain that Noah found Grace very sexy. Ben had never seen his brother look at Kara the way he looked at Grace.

Two minutes later Grace and Noah joined him. Noah's smile was the epitome of male contentment, and Grace was warmly flushed.

"She's going to ride home with you," Noah announced.

"And," Grace muttered, "Noah is going to go to the restaurant and smooth things over."

"A compromise?" Ben asked, and damn if he didn't feel almost as satisfied as his brother. Grace was not only a gentle, intelligent woman, she was also a reasonable, calming influence—just what his brother needed right now after all the hell he'd been through.

Except that Noah claimed he was done with the idea of matrimony. And Grace, with her big heart and bigger innocence, was definitely a marrying-type woman.

Ben frowned in concern. He didn't know how it'd all work out, but he trusted Noah to do what was right. And in the meantime, he'd just enjoy the show.

Grace was relieved to have made it to Ben's truck without running into anyone besides Graham. "I appreciate the ride," she told Ben.

He pulled out into the traffic and nodded. "Not a problem. I was heading out anyway. I just stopped by to check on Noah, to make sure he hadn't continued drinking this morning."

"You know Noah better than that."

"I know he was madder than hell last night. What I didn't know," Ben teased, "was that you stuck around to . . . soothe his savage temper."

Grace refused to blush again. "I hope you didn't cut your visit short on my account."

"Nope. I've been running an ad for a new waitress in the bar. I have to be at the hotel in an hour to do two interviews. Wish me luck that one of them will suit, because I'm getting desperate."

"You're hiring someone?" Grace liked Ben's small hotel at the opposite end of town. It was plain but clean, with around twenty units situated in a *U* around a built-in rectangular pool. There was a game room with two pool tables and a small bar that served drinks and soup and sandwiches.

"Yeah, one of my employees quit without notice, leaving me in the lurch. I've gone through three women since, but none of them are working out."

"How come?"

"Let's see—the first one kept coming on to me."

Grace laughed. "Oh, and I can see what a terrible problem that'd be!"

"Actually, it was," Ben said, summoning up a look of mock insult. Then, more seriously, "I make a point of not dating employees at all. It can lead to legal complications. Only this one lady wouldn't take no for an answer."

Fascinated, Grace twisted in her seat to face him. "What did she do?"

Ben rolled one shoulder and gave her a quick look. "You really want to hear this?"

"Yes." Grace had always considered Ben a real ladies' man. The idea of him turning women down intrigued her.

"Well, somehow she got it into her head that I had money, like she thought I owned the hotel free and clear or something. She thought I'd make good husband material and showed up in my room one night. I found out later from some of the other employees that she intended to screw my brains out, figuring after getting a taste of what I'd been missing, I'd fall madly in love."

Grace bit her lip. Ben made it sound like the most ridiculous idea in the world—and he was right. Sex and love often had nothing in common. But she wouldn't feel guilty about having sex with Noah. He was her dream come to life, and she intended to enjoy every moment.

Grace cleared her throat. "I guess since you live at the hotel, it'd be easy for a woman to sneak in on you?"

"Easy enough," Ben agreed. "Everyone who works for me knows where my suite of rooms are, especially since they're off limits."

"What did you do when you found her there?"

He flicked a glance at Grace. "I hadn't turned on the lights before falling into bed. It had been a very long day and I was already half asleep."

"Ben?"

"I didn't know who it was," he said in his defense. "I reacted on instinct."

"You threw her out of the bed?"

"Yep, tossed her right out onto the floor. She didn't like that much." He grinned, as if it were a favorite memory. "She protested, causing a real racket. But I protested more, and before we were done half the hotel knew what was going on. Being the lady was naked, she was doubly pissed by my lack of interest, and she finally left."

"Naked?"

He laughed again. "No. She pulled on her dress first. But she had to face a crowd in the hall. Thankfully, that was that."

Grace shook her head in disbelief. "I've led such a sheltered life."

"Yeah, I imagine you have."

His quick agreement bothered her. She hadn't been *that* sheltered. She understood about the world. "What about the other two?"

"One stole from me. I caught her red-handed, trying to stick a bottle of whiskey in her purse. The other was continually late."

Grace wasn't really a brazen person, but she did

need a job, and this seemed like too good a situation to pass up. "Can I ask what you pay?"

"Base pay isn't that high, but the average tips are great." When he quoted a figure for Grace, she was stunned.

"No kidding? Just for serving drinks?"

"It's not as easy as you probably think, Grace. Weekends and evenings can get really busy. Some of the customers can be a real pain. The trays get heavy, the crowd gets impatient . . ."

"What are the hours?"

As if just catching on to her line of questioning, Ben said, "Oh, no, Grace. Really. You wouldn't be interested."

"Why not?"

"*Why not, why not?*" he muttered. "Well, the hours are late on the weekend, for one thing."

"I can adjust to that."

He groaned under his breath, "Oh, God." Then louder, "Grace, really, men come on to the women all the time, and . . ."

She laughed. "I hardly think *I'd* need to worry about that, Ben. Men don't come on to me." Then a thought occurred to her, and she wanted to shrink into the car seat. "Um, that is, unless you only want someone sexy and skinny for the job."

"No!" He looked away from the road to glare at her. "Damn it, I didn't mean that at all." He pulled up to a red light and stopped. Twisting in his seat to face her, he said, "Besides, you *are* sexy."

Grace ignored the outrageous compliment since he'd been more or less coerced into it. "I wouldn't expect any favoritism, Ben, but I'd love to apply for the job."

"Grace . . ." Ben sounded almost desperate,

then he rushed to say, "How can you date Noah if you're working every night?"

"We're not dating."

He looked at her again, this time incredulous. "That's not the impression I got." The light turned green and he eased forward.

Grace wondered how to explain. Surely assignations with a sex slave—she really did like that term—weren't considered dates. She wasn't positive about it, because really, she'd never had sex before, much less been a slave about it. She hadn't even had all that many dates. But she felt certain there was a difference.

Of course, there was no way to explain all that to Ben. "We're not dating," she insisted.

And Ben said, "Noah isn't going to like this."

"Noah isn't my boss." Except in the bedroom. "So if that's your only objection, then I take it I can fill out an application?"

Ben ran a hand through his hair, leaving it standing on end. He locked his jaw and groused, "Yeah, sure. Why not? Come in tomorrow afternoon for a trial run, say around noon?"

"I'll be there! And Ben?"

Sounding sickly, he said, "Yeah?"

"Thank you."

Agatha paced, uncertain what to do. She detested her current loss of control over this insane situation. It seemed the older she got, the less impact she had on others. Intolerable. Since reaching adulthood, she'd always been able to keep her small world in tact, in her own manner of orderliness.

Except for her son. Pierce had rebelled at every turn. She'd loved him, yet he'd often been a disappointment. At times, he'd even been an embarrassment.

Agatha sighed and took another turn around her desk—a slow turn, because her arthritis had been acting up lately and all this ridiculous excitement was wearing on her. Getting old was hell.

A large oil painting of Pierce, done a year before he'd died, hung on the far wall. Agatha braced herself against the pain of failure and looked at it. Her son and her older grandson had the same magnificent coloring. Handsome devils, both of them. Equally bullheaded. Each determined to do things his own way.

There was a huge difference between the two, though.

While Noah often insisted on doing things his own way, he was prompted by an inborn pride and strength of character that left Agatha awed.

Pierce had been self-destructive and self-centered to the point that he didn't care who he hurt in his campaign to live free and unencumbered by social restrictions. While Noah also disdained the watchful eye of society, he sought out responsibilities, for himself and for others.

Many of her friends were wary of Noah because of his background, because he was edged in a darkness they couldn't comprehend. A barely leashed power emanated from Noah, gained from a life of poverty and abuse. No, her friends didn't understand Noah, but they all respected him.

Agatha turned away from the painting. She'd given Pierce everything, probably too much. He'd been spoiled and contemptuous of his duties.

Thanks to her son and his lack of conscience,

Noah had grown up with nothing. Agatha pinched the bridge of her nose and fought off stupid tears of pity. Noah neither wanted nor needed them. He was strong in a way his father had never been.

He was stronger than she could ever hope to be.

What Noah needed was the guidance she'd given him: a head start into financial success, and a sound foundation for the rest of his life, so that even after she was gone he'd be accepted. She wanted his future secured. Matching him with Kara would have accomplished so much, but Noah seemed determined to ruin that.

Maybe he was a little like Pierce after all.

Agatha straightened and marched to her desk. No, Noah was his own man. She'd find a way to get things back on track—for his sake. She'd lost Pierce, but she wouldn't lose Noah. She'd do what she had to do, and he'd understand that it was all for his own good. Eventually.

Chapter Eight

Noah entered Harper's Bistro, pausing just inside the ornate double doors with the intricately etched glass panels. He peered around at the familiar faces, cursing himself for being foolish enough to be there. He could think of a dozen things he'd rather be doing at the moment, and they all had to do with Grace being naked.

Damn, she had a great body. Her breasts were beautiful, not to mention her nipples. They were velvety pink and ultrasensitive, and it didn't take much more than a soft suck to get her going.

"Shit," Noah muttered under his breath, aware of a tightening in his groin. He had to get his mind on safer ground, and fast.

Safer ground happened moments later when Andrew rushed up to him. He was in his midthirties, and based on how the women flirted with him, Noah assumed he was handsome, too. He had an easy way about him that drew in most people.

"Damn, I'm glad to see you, Noah." Andrew's impeccably trimmed brown hair was mussed and his normally calm manner was harried. "It was bad enough a few hours ago, when everything started, but now it's gotten impossible. I have customers getting upset because they haven't gotten their food yet, but no one is cooking. Every so often you can hear them arguing in the kitchen. At first the assistant chefs kept it going, but I gather things have gotten ugly in there. Some people have given up and gone home."

"Damn."

Andrew nodded. "I, uh, I lied and said there was a problem with the ovens. The customers didn't look like they believed that, but I took their names and told them they could have a meal on the house when they returned. That helped."

"Good thinking." Noah clapped him on the shoulder and started through the restaurant toward the kitchens. He should have entered that way, but since he was already there, he'd wanted to see if everything was going as it should. Grace had evidently gotten to him, made him feel responsible for things that were no longer his to deal with.

He saw Kara seated discreetly at a corner table, neatly tucked away from prying eyes. She'd changed clothes and now wore a simple black dress and heels.

Around her throat was the pearl choker Noah had bought her on her last birthday. He still couldn't get over what a fool he'd been.

She must have felt his gaze because she looked up, locked eyes with him, and straightened expectantly. Noah merely nodded to her and kept going.

He hoped like hell Kara knew what she was doing, but at the moment she was the least of his concerns. He passed Greg, Dean, and Michael all huddled together, looking like a group of fretful old ladies rather than healthy, athletic college men. When they saw him, their expressions brightened.

Dean, the oldest at twenty-two, stepped forward. "What the hell are we going to do, Mr. Harper?"

The waiters Noah had hired were young men with big dreams, working their way through college. He'd offered them higher wages than they could earn in almost any other part-time job, but he demanded a lot in return. So far, he hadn't been disappointed.

Now he scowled at Dean, and included the other two in his look. "Standing here looking guilty isn't going to help. Go out there and offer everyone a free drink as an apology for the delay. Tell Deltorro to start his performance early, to distract them from the time. And regardless of how irate anyone is, be polite."

They all bobbed their heads.

Get it over with, Noah thought. "While you're all three here together, I want to give you some news."

"Another raise?" Michael asked, half joking, half hopeful.

Noah was grim. With him out of the picture, no one would be getting another raise for a while. Agatha was tight with the purse strings, and she'd always bitched at the salaries Noah paid. There was even a chance she'd hire in cheaper help now that Noah had forced the responsibility onto her.

"Whether or not you get any more raises won't be up to me," Noah explained. "I got canned yesterday, so now you'll be dealing directly with Agatha Harper, the owner, or whoever she hires in my place."

Dean sputtered in shock. "Fired! But . . . I thought your grandmother owned the joint."

"And it was my grandmother who fired me."

"Why?" Greg demanded.

They were a loyal lot—and Noah admitted to himself that he'd miss them. "Personal reasons. Nothing you need to be concerned with. But," he said, cutting off more questions and protests, "you do need to be concerned with the customers. So get out there and start offering some drinks."

They grumbled, casting looks at each other, but finally started off. Noah was proud of each of them.

Dean started to hurry away, too, but Noah detained him with a hand on his arm. When Dean looked up, Noah said, "Lose the swear words."

Dean flushed. "No one heard me."

"I heard you."

Dean hunched his shoulders. "Sorry."

"Just watch it from now on. Always remember that there are ladies in the room." With that, Noah strode away. He could hardly believe Grace had talked him into this. Agatha was well seasoned enough to deal with her own messes.

But the second Noah pushed through the metal doors into the kitchen, a fat, raw carrot came zinging past his head. It hit the wall next to his right ear with a soft, slightly wet thud, then dropped to the floor and rolled up against Noah's shoe. He stared at that carrot in stark amazement and fast-churning fury.

He was not in the mood for such foolishness.

His stride purposeful, his look mean, Noah stalked forward while the two chefs—one he'd hired, the other brand new—backed up in horror.

They each bumped into the metal work center, rattling dishes and toppling spices.

A morbid hush fell in the normally bustling room.

The assistant chefs, who had retreated out of the line of fire, stared wide-eyed with anticipation.

Noah stopped directly in front of both chefs. His jaw was locked so hard it took him a moment to get the words out. And then he said, "You're fired. Get out now."

Benton, the chef Noah had hired, sputtered indignantly. "You can't fire me! We have a full house."

Noah pierced him with a glare. "You're not cooking anyway, Benton, so you're useless to me and to the restaurant." He turned to the new chef. "You'll be paid for your time and trouble."

"You," the man intoned, pulling his arrogance around him like a shield, "did not hire me."

"Doesn't matter. I've been put in charge of dealing with you tonight. If you want to take it up with someone else later, fine. But not now." Noah turned to the assistant chefs. "Get to work. Have the orders prepared and on the tables in fifteen minutes flat or you're all fired, too."

In a flash, men and women began scurrying here and there. Pots and pans rattled, knife blades connected with cutting blocks, dishes clanked.

Satisfied, Noah turned to leave. Benton kept pace beside him until Noah halted at the doors.

"This is not my fault, Noah." He gestured to the other chef with stark accusation. "This, this . . ."

"Chef?" Noah supplied with a sharp dose of sarcasm.

Benton's round face turned red. "He barged in here and tried to take over."

"I was hired as the head chef," the man declared.

Noah shook his head. "You both remind me of kindergartners on the playground, fighting over a ball. Grow up already."

Benton again stopped him from leaving. "I'm really fired?"

Carefully masking his triumph, Noah eyed him. "Unless you want to get cooking, right now, without another single conflict. I won't have the reputation of the restaurant damaged over a temper tantrum."

Benton sent a smug look at the new chef and turned back to the countertop. He nudged an assistant aside, saying, "I'll do this. Get to work on the vegetables."

The new chef stepped forward. "I'm Jean Crispin. A young lady, Grace Jenkins, hired me. I intend to call her about this outrage immediately."

"Tough for you," Noah told him. "Grace is no longer in a position to hire anyone. If you have a gripe, take it straight to Agatha Harper. She's Grace's former employer and owner of Harper's Bistro."

A fresh hush fell over the kitchen while everyone absorbed the impact of Noah's statement with shocked disbelief. Since he had their attention, Noah decided to get his own announcement out of the way.

"You all might as well know, this is my last night." Actually, this trip was on borrowed time, thanks to Grace's interference and do-gooder tendencies, but he saw no reason to explain that to anyone.

"Here on out," he added, "you have a problem,

you call Agatha Harper directly. If you need her number, get it from Andrew."

Mouths fell open, eyes bugged, but no one said a word.

Feeling vaguely uncomfortable with the watchful silence, Noah turned and walked out. The finality of the moment filled him with mixed sensations.

He wanted Grace, and that sensation was the strongest and most alarming of all.

As Noah headed for the front doors, nodding to regulars and giving casual greetings along the way, the sounds of a guitar began filling the dining room.

He paused, glancing toward the center of the floor, where Enrique Deltorro eased into a soft, romantic ballad ripe with subtle suggestion and teasing heat. The tune was enhanced by his Spanish accent.

He was dressed in black jeans and boots with an open-necked gunmetal gray silk shirt. Several silver chains hung around his neck. His overlong hair had been tied back, and a diamond stud gleamed in one ear. He sat on a stool with a microphone in front of him, his guitar held gently in his arms. The audience loved him.

Deltorro was one hell of an entertainer, Noah had to admit. The restaurant's young, female clientele had grown swiftly with Enrique's performances. He had exceeded Noah's expectations and then some.

Black eyes gleaming, Enrique tipped his head at Noah.

Noah folded his arms and waited until Enrique transferred his gaze toward a table full of young ladies. They were all dressed to the nines, and with

Enrique's attention, they appeared ready to swoon. At the mature age of forty, Enrique Deltorro—the Bull—still exuded enough sex appeal to draw plenty of females, even those half his age.

Dean and Michael and Greg were alternately watching the show, taking drink orders, and sparing covetous glances at Kara. They had always admired her, and Noah had no doubt lustful thoughts often plagued their young minds.

Kara was lovely, no two ways about it. On top of that, she was genuinely nice, if a bit too proper. Looking at the waiters now, Noah accepted that he wasn't the only man who'd fantasized about turning Kara into a wild woman.

After making love to her just once, those fantasies had been long gone.

Kara had seldom visited the restaurant without an escort, either himself or her parents or a friend. So her solo appearance tonight was enough to draw speculation. But she also looked very melancholy. She wasn't just alone. She was . . . lonely.

Noah did his best to ignore that fact. Her moods no longer concerned him.

Andrew stood straight and silent at his podium in the restaurant's entrance. He had a fixed expression on his face, and when Noah followed his gaze, he realized it was Kara the maître d' watched so intently.

Damn, did she have everyone's attention tonight?

Kara, her face softly lit by a fat candle in the center of her table, idly toyed with a napkin. She was either unaware or uncaring of being eyed by several men.

Noah considered approaching her but changed his mind. There was no point to it. She was old enough to make her own decisions, and in his opinion, it was past time she started doing just that.

Andrew stopped him before he could make his escape. His gaze speculative, he said, "Kara looks beautiful tonight."

Noah gave him a lazy look. "Kara always makes a nice appearance."

"True, true."

Noah started to leave again, and Andrew added, "It's none of my business, but—"

"It's none of your business."

Holding up his hands, Andrew said, "Fine. I understand. No problem."

"Glad to hear it. And if you should run into any problems, take them up with Agatha."

"But . . ."

"I mean it, Andrew." Noah made sure there was no way for Andrew to misunderstand. "I've told the others, and I'll make calls tomorrow to anyone who wasn't here tonight. I'm totally out of it, and I won't take it kindly if you or anyone else tries to drag me back into it again."

"Right. Got it." Andrew hesitated, then said, "I hope we'll at least see you around?" His gaze flashed to Kara and back again. "You know, just as a friend."

"Maybe. We'll see." Noah glanced at Kara, too. She was turned in her seat, watching him.

Refusing to be drawn in by her lost act, Noah coldly turned away—and caught Enrique's narrow attention. With a sound of disgust, Noah looked around and realized Greg and Dean and Michael were also peering at him.

He had no idea what they all expected of him,

but whatever it was, they were doomed to disappointment.

Annoyed at himself, Noah walked out. Once in his car, he tried calling Grace on his cell phone, but her number was busy. Then he decided not to call her at all. He'd see her again in the morning, and that was soon enough.

He'd make it soon enough—even if it felt like forever.

Grace snatched up the phone on the fourth ring. Her hair was soaked, leaving rivulets of water trailing down her back, her legs, and onto her small decorative rug.

Because she'd raced straight out of the shower, she was a bit breathless when she said, "Hello?"

"I was just about to hang up, young lady."

Disappointment seeped in. Though it was late and she'd seen him only a few hours earlier, Grace had hoped it might be Noah calling just to tell her good night. How dumb. The man had better things to do than spend his every thought on her.

"Hello, Agatha." Grace tried to infuse a little enthusiasm into her voice. She wasn't overly successful. "Sorry, but I was in the shower."

"Well, that's better than what I was beginning to imagine."

"Oh?" A touch of caution struck Grace. Anytime she dealt with Agatha, she had to be on the alert. "What did you imagine?"

Agatha huffed. "After that lurid display you and my grandson put on, you have to ask?"

Grace frowned and refrained from replying. She'd have been happy with a phone call from

Noah, yet Agatha thought he might still be with her? That was too ridiculous.

"Is he there?" Agatha asked impatiently.

"Noah? No, he's not."

A long pause filled the line, and then Agatha sighed. "Grace, we must talk."

The towel Grace held around herself wasn't substantial enough to ward off the evening chill of her apartment. She shivered and started down the hall to her bedroom with the portable phone caught against her shoulder.

She wondered if Noah was still at the restaurant. Had he worked things out? If Kara did in fact have a lover there, would Noah attempt to confront him?

That thought filled Grace with worry. Noah could more than handle himself physically; that wasn't a concern. But she knew he'd regret causing a scene.

"He's using you, Grace."

The bald, blunt statement made Grace stall just inside her bedroom and scattered every other thought away. Her stomach cramped. She drew a calming breath. "This isn't your business, Agatha."

"Don't you take that attitude with me, young lady. He's my grandson and you're my employee—"

"Ex-employee." For the first time, Grace took pleasure in pointing out that fact. With equal pleasure, she tacked on, "I think I've found a new job."

A heavy silence, fraught with disappointment, filled the line.

"Agatha," Grace said gently, "you did fire me, remember?"

"Of course I remember," she snapped. "I'm not so old that I can't remember what happened hours ago."

"True. You're still sharp as a tack—except where Noah is concerned."

Because she knew Agatha well, Grace could easily imagine the way she was now pacing in her anger, how her spine would be rigidly straight, her mouth tight.

"If anyone is acting blind about my grandson, it's you." Agatha's tone trembled with annoyance. "He's using you, Grace, and you're letting him, when I always thought you had more sense than that."

"He's not using me."

"You know what he did to Kara, and he genuinely loved her."

"I know what you know," Grace replied, "that he broke the engagement. But he wouldn't have done that without good reason."

"Whatever his reasons, they're moot at this point. He's with you on the rebound. But you're too naïve, too . . . well . . ." Agatha's voice rose. "Grace, you won't hold his interest long."

"I know what I'm doing," Grace said. She had no illusions, despite Agatha's assumption of her naïveté.

"On the contrary, you don't have a clue. You just told me how sharp I am. Well, you're right. I'm sharp enough that I've noticed you never date. Doesn't matter what time I call, you're always at home alone. I doubt you were ever that popular in school, either, were you, Grace?"

Taking a firm grip on the phone and her own insecurities, Grace admitted, "No."

Agatha softened. "I want you to be happy, Grace, I really do. But my grandson is out of your league. And I'm not just talking about your weight, dear."

Grace wanted to curl in on herself. She had no idea what to say to Agatha.

"You're not homely or anything like that, Grace."

Dryly, Grace muttered, "Thank you."

"But . . . I'm going to be blunt here."

"Yes, Agatha, don't hold back."

"Noah is used to beautiful women who present themselves perfectly. Far as I can tell, you've never had a manicure or been to a salon. You don't know how to dress right and your hair . . . Oh Grace, *your hair.*"

Grace held herself silent. What could she say? It was all true.

She reached up and tugged on a long, thick lock of sopping hair. It was slightly tangled—just as it had been the entire time she'd been with Noah.

Only once in all the time she'd spent at his apartment had she even thought to brush it out. He'd seen her this way, pretty much a mess.

Yet . . . it hadn't seemed to Grace that he cared.

"You're a lovely person, Grace, and you're very sweet."

Grace wrinkled her nose. *Sweet.*

"But you need to find a man more on your own level."

Grace briefly wondered what level Agatha referred to. Probably something subterranean, where all the homely, overweight, unpopular people hung out.

When Grace didn't answer, Agatha asked impatiently, "Are you still there, Grace?"

"Yes."

"I don't mean to be cruel, Grace."

Hoping to use that as a means to end the conversation, Grace said, "That's great. I appreciate your restraint, Agatha, so maybe we should—"

"But Noah has to be my number-one concern."

Resigned, Grace sighed and dropped to the edge of her mattress. She stared at her feet. Agatha evidently had a lot to say and there'd be no dissuading her.

"Noah will be happy with Kara as his wife. He'll have everything he didn't have growing up. Respectability, stability, all the luxuries and comfort money can buy. And he'll have the influence necessary to make his own way."

Personally, Grace felt Noah already had those things, just not in the abundance Agatha apparently deemed necessary. She made a noncommittal sound.

"*You* can't bring him those things, Grace."

Grace held the phone away from her ear and stared at it. Did Agatha think she had dreams of marrying Noah? Well, dreams, yes. But reality? Grace was a very reasonable, logical person, and marriage to Noah defied logic.

She loved him, and she, too, wanted what was best for him. For now, she was his sex slave.

It worked for her.

Replacing the phone to her ear, Grace said, "You know, Agatha, you should really be saying all this to Noah."

"You think I should tell Noah that you have no fashion sense? Don't be absurd."

Grace almost laughed. Almost. "I'm sure Noah has come to that realization all on his own. No, I meant that you should be telling him how you have his best interests at heart. Disowning someone isn't the nicest way to get that across."

"He'll be back," Agatha said, "and then we'll talk."

On her terms, Grace assumed, shaking her head at the older woman's stubbornness. "I hope it won't be too late then."

"What does that mean?" Alarm caused Agatha's voice to rise again.

"It means that Noah is a man full of potential, and more than capable of making it on his own. He has a fast mind and a lot of energy, and he's proven that he knows how to make money grow. He's a natural leader, and all your business associates know it. Once word is out that he's no longer working for you, how long do you think it'll be before others try to hire him?"

It was Agatha's turn to fall silent. After a moment, she asked, "You're suggesting that Noah would betray me?"

"I'm saying Noah isn't a man to sit around mentally or physically idle. He likes a challenge, and he likes to stay busy. He's going to be working, and if you want him working for you, you'd better rethink a few things."

"Grace Jenkins, that sounds like a threat!"

Grace shook her head, all but fed up with the conversation. "Agatha, how could I threaten you? I don't even work for you anymore." The more she said it, the easier it got. "And as you've just pointed out, I don't carry any influence with Noah. All I'm trying to do is point out a few things you might not have considered."

"I see."

Grace could almost hear Agatha's mind working.

"You were always good at that, Grace."

"Thanks." Personally, Grace thought she'd been a fantastic secretary. But Agatha had fired her easily enough.

"That aside, Grace, you have to understand. If Kara—who is beautiful and elegant and comfortable in any social setting—is having difficulty maintaining Noah's interest, how in the world do you think you can compete?"

Rather than repeat herself, Grace said, "I really need to go, Agatha. Was there anything else you wanted?"

"I want you to stay away from my grandson."

Because she had no intention of doing any such thing, Grace said, "Your wishes are duly noted. Now I gotta run. Good-bye." And she hung up with Agatha in mid-protest.

Grace tossed the portable phone onto the bed and turned to her dresser. The triple mirror reflected her image back at her, and Grace winced.

She stood frozen for a moment, staring at herself then on impulse, she flashed the towel open. Seeing her own fleshy body made her wince again, and she quickly covered back up and turned away.

Throughout the years, she'd tried a few diets and exercise programs. She hadn't been overly triumphant with any of them. She'd lose ten pounds only to regain them right away. Since her high school days she'd weighed about the same, fluctuating only five pounds or so. Sometimes she weighed more, sometimes less. She always weighed too much.

Her doctor claimed it to be her natural weight and pronounced her fit.

Fit was not the same as sexy. Or desirable. Or popular. But, Grace decided, she liked herself, she really did.

And Noah seemed to find her desirable, so she wasn't going to beat herself up over a few insensitive remarks by her *former* employer.

That decided, Grace indulged in a secret little smile while she took underwear and a sleep shirt from her dresser drawers.

She might be overweight and ordinary, but people, even Agatha, were labeling her as the "other woman." That insinuated she possessed a certain amount of feminine wiles, didn't it? People credited her with the ability to steal Noah away from Kara, and darn it, it was . . . fun. Complimentary. Grace's smile widened into a grin, and in the next moment she chuckled.

Grace Jenkins, femme fatale.

It was almost as exciting as being a sex slave.

What a strange twist her common, boring life had taken, thanks to Noah. He might not want her for more than a plaything, but to Grace, that was pretty darn special, and more than she'd ever dared hope for.

Chapter Nine

Kara watched her lover as he moved, so smooth, so sexy. Her heart sank a little when he flirted with other women, when he teased and touched.

Her stomach fluttered in the way it had when she'd been young and had sneaked off to the carnival. Riding the roller coaster without permission had filled her with the contrasting sensations of guilt and fear and excitement.

The guilt now was stronger, of course. It pushed at her, almost smothering; she'd hurt so many people.

At the same time, she felt daring and brave and sexier than she ever had in her life. How could she possibly regret that?

But the fear . . . God, the fear was the worst. What would her parents do if they found out? What would dear Agatha do? Their disappointment would be unbearable. They expected so much from her, because all her life, she'd been the perfect daughter, the perfect lady.

With her lover, everything was different. She wasn't proper, but she was alive. With him, her body sizzled and burned, her heart expanded. He made her sweat and cry and laugh. He made her *feel.*

Which was probably why she'd stupidly fallen in love with him.

Kara drew in a shuddering breath and pondered all the awful possibilities. What if he didn't really care for her as she did him, if he was just using her as a novelty, a woman normally out of his range?

She squeezed her eyes shut, fighting back panic. Dear God, if he didn't really care for her, she didn't know how she'd cope. No man had ever made her feel this way. No man had ever treated her as he did, a little coarse, a little rough.

She shivered, just remembering the base, carnal things he'd done to her—the things he'd relished doing. He'd wallowed in the unwilling responses of her body, licked at her sweat, at her belly, between her legs.

Kara gasped and looked around her. So many of the employees were watching her, wondering why she was still there when Noah had left. She'd witnessed signs of pity, curiosity, and even some interest.

Yet her lover ignored her. Oh, she understood it was necessary. By her own insistence, they couldn't allow anyone to know of their involvement. But it still hurt. She wanted him to herself; she wanted to taste him again, to have him devour her.

In a rush, Kara grabbed up her small leather purse and rose to her feet. People stared, but she managed to politely ignore them. Enrique watched her go. Greg and Dean nodded her way. Andrew rushed to get her wrap.

She kept her head high and a reserved smile on her frozen face. "Thank you, Andrew."

Andrew looked as stiff as she felt. "My pleasure."

Without a backward glance, she walked out. This was difficult, and bound to get more so. But what could she do? She loved him, and for once she wanted to follow her heart rather than her parents' expectations.

For once she wanted to be a woman, not just a lady.

Grace was in the middle of applying a light touch of makeup when her doorbell rang. She had exactly one hour to finish and get to Ben's hotel for her job interview. She was strangely excited.

"Coming," she yelled when the doorbell rang yet again. She closed her compact and headed for the door. Her long sleep shirt was wrinkled from a night of tossing and turning in between erotic dreams. Her flannel pants dragged the floor, almost hiding her thick gray socks. Her heavy hair, contained atop her head with a cloth-coated rubber band, wobbled as she bent to peek through the peephole.

Noah stood there, looking impatient. "Open up, Grace."

She straightened with a jerk. Elation hit her first; she'd missed him so much!

Bemusement quickly followed because after Agatha's painful phone call, she'd really planned to try to look her best when next she saw him. The clothes she wore, not to mention the mess of her hair, were about as far from her best as she could get.

Trying to improvise, Grace called through the door, "What are you doing here, Noah?"

The question must have thrown him because he pounded on the door so hard it about stopped her heart. "Open up," he said again, this time with some annoyance.

Giving up, Grace turned the locks and pulled the door wide. "Hi." Her smile came easily. No matter what, Noah still made her heart lift and her body tingle. He looked especially good today in casual black slacks and a soft gray pullover. The dark colors made the pale blue of his eyes more noticeable than ever.

He'd never been in her apartment before and he started to automatically look around. But his gaze got caught on her, instead. He went still as he quietly scrutinized her body, starting with her piled-up hair and ending at her thick socks. Obviously amused, one side of his mouth kicked up and he said, "Hey."

"You want to come in?" Grace asked, a little unnerved by that hot stare. It made her jumpy and needy, and truth was, she didn't have time for that right now. She had an appointment to keep.

Noah stepped in and closed the door behind him, then leaned on it. His gaze did dart around her uncluttered living room but came right back to her. "You look cute."

Cute, in Grace's estimation, was not a term reserved for women who tipped the scales the way she did. Cute referred to "little" things or people. "Um . . . thanks."

He still watched her. "Come here, Grace."

Grace knew what that look in his eyes meant, especially when accompanied by that husky tone. She cleared her throat and asked, "Why?"

"Come here," he countered, "and I'll show you why."

Damn, damn, damn. The man was far too tempting. "Noah," she complained, even as she found herself inching forward, "you have lousy timing."

He stalled and his eyes narrowed. "You have another date?"

She scoffed at that. "No. I have to finish getting ready. I have a job interview today at noon."

Noah had started to reach for her, but at her announcement, he dropped his hands. "A job interview? Where?"

"I don't want to tell you where yet. I may not get it, and then I'd be embarrassed."

He looked surprised by that admission and finally pulled her to him. Hugging her close into his chest, Noah said, "You don't ever have to be embarrassed with me, Grace."

"I know I don't have to be, but I still would. I want this job. It's sounds like fun and I think I can make enough money there."

Noah tipped her back to see her face. "When do you have to be there?"

"Noon."

He rubbed his hands up and down her back, stopping to squeeze her waist beneath the large shirt. "We've got an hour."

"Now stop that!" Grace swatted at him, then settled her hands flat on his chest. She could feel the steady thumping of his heart. "I have to be there in an hour, but it's a half-hour drive and I'm not even dressed yet. If I'd known you were coming over . . ."

"Sorry. I finished some errands early." As if they'd been lovers for months instead of days, he leaned down and kissed her forehead. "I should have called first?"

"No, I don't mean that." The last thing Grace wanted to do was discourage Noah from seeing her. She smiled. "Let it go on the record right now that you're welcome to drop in any time. I just wish I didn't have to go. Now that you're here, I want to be here, too."

"How long will you be?"

"I'm not sure. He said something about a trial run, so he may work me a few hours or something."

"He?"

Grace blinked at the particular tone infused in that one word. Surely that wasn't possessiveness she heard. More likely it was mere curiosity. "The person who would hire me. He owns a business—a nice, respectable business—and he needs a new employee."

"I see."

He still looked disgruntled, and Grace patted him. "I am sorry, Noah." And then, feeling a little shy, she added, "I missed you."

"That right?" His smile relaxed and his look became lazy. He leaned down and touched his forehead to hers. With his breath brushing her mouth, he whispered, "Did you think about me last night, Gracie? About what we did?"

"Yes."

"Me, too."

She gulped. "I'm thinking about it right now."

"Good." Using the edge of his hand, he tipped up her face. "Then how about a kiss to tide me over until I can get you naked again?"

Grace wrapped both arms around his neck and pressed her mouth to his. Noah let her have her way, bending enough to accommodate her but not taking the lead. It was wonderful, as she'd known it would be.

Noah tasted hot and exciting, and when she slipped her tongue into his mouth, he made a rough sound of pleasure that shivered down her spine and into her heart.

Pulling back the tiniest bit, Noah whispered, "You know, if I took you into the bedroom, the decision would be out of your hands."

The fog left Grace's muddled brain slowly, and she frowned. Maybe this sex-slave business would be more complicated than she'd figured on.

Noah pressed her, saying, "Right, Grace?"

She scowled, wondering if he'd be cad enough to take such an advantage. "I suppose," she muttered.

He grinned and kissed her again. "Good thing I'm a generous task master, huh? At least, when I need to be." He patted her behind and stepped back. "But my patience isn't unlimited, woman. When *can* I see you?"

Both relieved and shamefully disappointed, Grace said, "I'm not sure. Do you . . . do you want me to maybe call you when I find out?" She hoped Noah didn't take that as an intrusion on his privacy. This relationship business, even if sexual rather than romantic in nature, had invisible lines that couldn't be crossed. Grace just didn't have enough experience to know what those lines might be.

Noah didn't even blink. "You've got my cell phone number, right?"

Relieved, Grace nodded. "I've got the numbers for anyone who ever had contact with Agatha." She didn't mention that she knew his home and cell phone numbers by heart. "I'll let you know as soon as I know."

Noah started to leave but hesitated at the last second. He turned back to Grace, cupped her face gently in his large, hot hands, and kissed her witless. "I like your hair like that. I like it down, too. And Grace, I love how you look at me."

Grace stared at the closed door for several moments after Noah had gone. She couldn't remember ever being so happy.

Ben watched Grace work and had to shake his head in wonder. Damn, he never would have believed it, but she was perfect. Her smile, genuine in nature without an ounce of flirtation, did incredible things to every guy in the room. From five months old to eighty-five, they all responded to her. Grace somehow lit the place up, made it seem happier, more relaxed.

Better.

Ben had no illusions. He was prosperous enough with his moderate, spotlessly clean hotel. He offered quiet, efficient service, so the rooms almost always stayed booked. And because he was located right off the expressway, the diner drew a lot of passersby, including regular truckers who stopped for breakfast and lunch.

Ben was happy with how things were going, but his clientele didn't include elite vacationers booked by upscale travel agents. More often than not, those who checked in were financially tight at best, on the shady side at worst. His spacious and orderly parking lot was filled with dusty, rusty, aged vehicles, and the luggage that passed through his doors often looked like it'd been through a war.

But he liked these people, and he related to them.

Luckily, this was his quiet crowd, a mix of truckers and families who'd stopped for lunch and not much drinking, so they rarely got out of hand. In fact, lunch tended to be subdued to the point of morbid.

Today people were chatting and laughing—*responding to Grace.* Her enthusiasm was infectious, and even his old balding cook, Horace, whistled while frying cheese sandwiches. Grace had struck an immediate rapport with the surly cook merely by admiring his tattoo. It was a naked woman, shown from the back, with her legs wrapped around his biceps. When Horace flexed his arm, the woman's ass wiggled.

Horace had done plenty of flexing for Grace, and she'd been genuinely enthralled each and every time. The bond was forged.

She had a similar effect on everyone.

And Grace loved it. Her pretty brown eyes were alight with pleasure as she went from one task to the next without pause. Ben continued to watch her, and he continued to be amazed.

He could see what Noah found so attractive— inside and out. How he'd known her so long and never noticed amazed Ben.

Rushing up to him moments later, Grace said under her breath, "A six-dollar tip!" She squeezed the money as if it were gold rather than a few crumpled bills, and then she stuffed it into her apron pocket. "Do you believe that? And I only served him a deluxe burger and fries. Amazing. I *love* this job, Ben."

Then she was off again, warmly greeting a

young couple who had just come in, waving to acknowledge a man in a booth who wanted more coffee. She was a bundle of inexhaustible energy and generosity.

Ben had to hire her, no way around it.

He had hoped there'd be an excuse to gently turn her down. There'd been the slight possibility that she'd confuse or forget orders. Or that she'd be put off by the familiarity of some of the customers who couldn't seem to remember that this was the enlightened age of equality between the sexes.

But not Grace. She didn't take offense at anything, but she did get her point across. When one wizened old man had called her sweetie, she'd patted his wrinkled cheek and said, "Sure thing, pops," and then put an extra scoop of ice cream on his apple pie. The old guy had been so infatuated, he'd nearly slid off his bar stool.

There was only one hope left, and that was in the uniform each waitress was required to wear. Ben had never seen Grace in a skirt above her knees, so perhaps she'd balk at the semishort tan dresses, covered only by crisp white utility aprons. They were serviceable outfits, but they also had a vague resemblance to something out of a fetish catalogue. A few of his younger waitresses went so far as to wear heels with the dresses. Somehow he knew Grace wouldn't.

Ben snagged Grace as she started back to the kitchen. "A moment, Gracie."

Her cheeks were flushed, her long hair held back in a ponytail that swished around the small of her back. "Okay, but can we make it quick?" she asked. "I've got orders piling up."

Conscientious to boot. Ben just knew Noah was going to kill him for hiring Grace, but what else could he do? He drew a breath and bit the bullet. "You've got the job. Can you start tomorrow?"

Her eyes widened, her mouth opened, and then she let out a loud, uncharacteristic *whoop* and threw herself against him for a hearty hug.

Touched, unable not to smile, too, Ben returned the tight embrace. Grace was soft and warm and he liked hugging her. She made him feel good. "It's just a job, Gracie."

"Oh, no. It's a fun job, and everyone is so friendly, and I like this so much more than sitting in the library taking notes or doing correspondence or putting things on the computer for hours on end. That was so boring and so . . . lonely."

Ben scowled. Agatha had near worked Grace to death and had never given her the appreciation she deserved.

He wouldn't make the same mistake.

Squeezing her again, Ben said, "Well, you've certainly impressed me. Customers have been hanging around longer just to talk with you."

She pushed back from his chest to blink at him. "They have?"

With his arms looped casually around her waist, Ben grinned. "You didn't realize? Hell, Grace, you're a hit. A lot of truck drivers stop in here for coffee and sandwiches, and most times they look miserable. They've been on the road for hours and they're tired and lonesome. Today, in less than an hour, you had them all smiling."

"I did?" She sounded so hopeful.

Ben gently turned her. "Look around, Grace."

Her attention went from one booth to the next, one bar stool to another. She gripped her hands in front of her. "They all look . . . happy."

"Not usually, but yeah, today they're lighthearted." He leaned down and kissed her ear. "Cuz of you, Grace."

She turned back to him with a blush. "Wow."

It amazed Ben that she hadn't noticed her effect on the customers, that she had no real idea of her appeal. "Noah won't be happy about you working here."

In typical Grace fashion, she drew herself up. "Well, whyever not? This is a great place."

Great. Ben shook his head. "I've been robbed twice, Grace. In the evenings, when people drink more, fights sometimes break out. No one has ever been seriously hurt, but there've been some minor scrapes, some black eyes. The cops have been here five times in two years. Noah is the protective sort. He grumbles about *me* being here, so I can only imagine what he'll have to say about me hiring you."

As if that idea were inconceivable, Grace patted his chest and said, "Don't worry. Noah and I don't have that kind of relationship. He won't bother himself about where I work, I promise."

Her naïveté blew Ben away. What did Grace think, that Noah was just playing with her?

Come to think of it, *was he?*

Ben didn't think so, but everything had happened so fast, he couldn't be sure what his brother thought. The idea of anyone using Grace didn't sit well with Ben. He'd have to have another chat with Noah, to let him in on Grace's perception of their relationship. Hopefully, Noah would set her straight.

"What hours will I be working?" Grace asked, interrupting his musing.

"Unfortunately, it'll vary and include some weekends." Noah was going to *kill* him. "Let me take you on a rundown of things."

Trying to block his brother's potential reaction at having his new relationship derailed with weekend work, Ben escorted Grace to the kitchen where she turned in her orders. While the food was being prepared, she followed him to the quiet backroom with the pop and coffee machines, where she could take her breaks, and where the schedule was posted along with a time clock.

"I'll have a time card for you tomorrow, so don't forget to clock in and out. I'll write in the hours you worked today. For the rest of this week, you'll be replacing Rose, so go by her schedule. You can finish out her time today if you want."

"That'd be great!"

Still bemused by her attitude, Ben chuckled. "Great, huh? All right. I post the new schedule on Thursdays, and the week starts on Mondays. Any problems, let me know right away."

Grace pulled a pencil and order pad out of her pocket and jotted down her hours. To Ben's amazement, she didn't look at all taken aback by the later days, but he made a mental note to try to give her as many evenings and weekends off as possible.

"Got it."

Folding his arms over his chest, Ben looked her over. She was full-figured, with a lot of curves. "Grace, what size do you wear?"

Grace's head shot up and she blanched. "Excuse me?"

He cocked a brow at her startling reaction to a simple question. "I have to get you a uniform."

Rather than answer, she bit her lip. For the first time since she'd arrived, she looked unsure of herself. Ben didn't understand. He'd expected her to not like the uniforms, but he hadn't expected her to look stricken over the prospect.

After a few seconds of heavy silence during which Grace fidgeted and didn't meet his gaze, she asked, "Do you have any in stock?"

"Yeah." Keeping his gaze on her, Ben tipped his head toward a storage closet. "The previous owner had just ordered in a bunch when I bought the place from him. They're hanging in there."

Visible relief washed over her features.

It didn't make sense. She'd been so sure of herself, diving into every duty with gusto, as if she'd been waiting tables for years. Yet now she looked timid.

"Grace, I can get you a new one in a week." Hell, he'd even let her lower the hem if she really wanted to. "There's no reason for you to keep a worn, already used uniform."

"Oh, I don't mind." She darted toward the closet.

Ben frowned. "Grace . . ."

She rummaged around a moment, continually peeking back at Ben, then turned with three neatly folded uniforms in her arms. "Um, mind if I take these home to try on? I'll return any that don't fit tomorrow."

Ben gave up. "Yeah, sure, help yourself. Take as many as you want. The women all have at least two for a change."

The cook yelled out that the orders were ready,

and Grace rushed to put the uniforms with her purse on a top shelf. On her way past Ben, she paused to treat him to a fat, glowing smile. "Thanks again, Ben. This is just the best job ever."

Ben stood there until Grace was out of sight, then scrubbed his hands over his face. The best job ever? Jesus. Working for Agatha must have been worse than he'd imagined if Grace thought being a waitress was a good job. But then, Ben would rather slave naked in a coal mine than lift a finger for his grandmother—a grandmother who wouldn't claim him.

The kitchen phone rang, and a moment later Horace shouted, "Ben, phone's for you!"

"Got it," Ben called back, and lifted the extension in the break room. "Hello?"

As if he'd summoned her, Agatha Harper grumbled at his greeting, saying, "You should teach that awful man some manners. He shouted in my ear."

Ben didn't show his surprise, or point out Agatha's own rudeness in not identifying herself. Not that she needed to. Ben knew that strident, heartless voice oh too well. "What do you want, Agatha?"

She sniffed at his surly tone, and Ben felt the weight of an awful foreboding. "Agatha?" he asked again, now with a dose of caution and mixed demand.

"I need your help."

Ben took her words like a punch in the lungs. It hurt, damn it, and knocked the wind right out of him. Wheezing, more than a little incredulous, Ben rasped, *Excuse me?*

"You heard me, Benjamin Badwin, and I'm not saying it again."

Ben remained speechless, though Agatha did not. "Be here tomorrow for lunch," she commanded. "Eleven will be perfect, so don't be late."

Ben drew one careful breath, then another. His brain felt blank, his muscles cramped, but he heard himself say with just the right amount of contempt, "Sorry, Aggie, I have to work."

She gasped. "I've told you not to call me that."

"Yeah, I told you not to call me. Period."

Once, long ago, Ben had looked forward to maybe getting to know his grandmother. He'd seen her as a form of assistance to his mother, a way to lessen her load in raising a child alone.

But Agatha's insistent belief that her son had been a saint and his mother had been too free with her love, had ruined any chance at a relationship. Agatha had dealt her first insinuation against his mother minutes after they'd met, and Ben had permanently made up his mind. He loved his mother too much to tolerate any slurs against her, subtle or otherwise.

Ignoring much of his rudeness, Agatha said, "Surely you can take one afternoon off."

The numbness receded, went away. "No, I can't." Ben sounded more like himself, stronger, thank God. "I know it's tough for you to remember, Agatha, but I'm in that lower class of people who have to work for a living. I can't afford an afternoon off."

As if speaking through her teeth, Agatha said, "I'll pay you to show up."

Fury shot through him, making his heart race. "This'll come as a shock, Aggie, but I can't be bought."

"Damn it, Ben, I need to see you!"

For the first time that Ben could remember, his grandmother sounded desperate. He didn't like her, had no respect for her, but damn it, he couldn't bear the faint hint of fear in her tone. He was used to her being an indomitable harridan, not a frail old woman.

Ben squeezed the receiver so hard, his hand hurt, but it made no difference. He wanted to refuse her, he really did.

Instead, he gave up with a sigh of disgust. "I can make it next week, maybe Sunday."

Even through the ringing in his ears and her efforts to disguise it, Ben could hear Agatha's relief. Her breath was shaky, broken. "Good. That'll be fine, then. Remember, eleven o'clock."

And she hung up.

Well, hell, was Ben's first thought, followed by loathing at his own weakness.

He couldn't imagine what Agatha could have possibly meant by her statement. *I need your help.* Ben shook his head, still muddled. Agatha Harper needed no one, least of all a grandson she didn't claim.

With precise movements, Ben replaced the phone on the hook and turned away. He needed to call Noah, and he needed to get some paperwork done. He did not need to give his grandmother another thought. Whatever she wanted, it wouldn't matter in the long run. Nothing could change the past. Hell no. Never.

Damn it.

Agatha stared at the phone on her desk, aware that her hands were shaking despite how tightly she clasped them together. That had been harder than she'd anticipated. Ben was always so . . . defensive. So difficult. Unlike Noah, she knew Ben would never meet her halfway.

She jerked around and paced across the library. The room, the whole house, seemed lonely and empty and dark without Noah or Grace around. She couldn't think in so much quiet. She couldn't sleep either.

It wasn't right.

But she had plans to fix everything. Noah was only being stubborn, and once she made him see reason, Grace would return to work, too. Everything would be back to normal. She'd see to it.

For lack of anything better to do, Agatha reached for the ornate teapot arranged among delicate cups on a tray on her desk. It was empty.

Nan, her housekeeper, was off to the grocery store, so Agatha would have to wait until she returned. She'd instructed Nan to prepare a very special lunch for Ben, and that had required additional supplies.

The lunch was delayed but not canceled. Ben would show up at the end of next week. That'd be soon enough.

In order for her plans to work, Agatha needed Ben's cooperation. She meant to give him a taste—literally—of what he could expect once he aligned himself with her, which included the very finest cuisine.

Agatha turned and started back across the eerily silent library.

Or better yet, her thoughts continued, why not take advantage of the propitious timing of this little crisis and play generous? She could at last acknowledge Ben as part of the family without denting her pride. Ben would understand that Noah's best interests motivated her, rather than any imagined weakness.

It wasn't as if she'd ever wanted to deny him, anyway. But Ben hadn't been an easy child. Agatha had met him when he was fourteen, with a chip on his shoulder the size of a mountain. Even at that young age, he'd had no qualms about denigrating his father.

He'd denigrated Agatha in the bargain, telling her in no uncertain terms that his life was full, his mother a saint, and there was nothing Agatha had that he wanted.

Ben would have been an embarrassment, throwing their good name into the dirt with deliberate contempt and disrespect every chance he had. Agatha had been left with no recourse but to deny any relationship.

Noah hadn't done the same. He was so protective of Ben, it was as if they'd been raised together, as if Noah had always filled the bill of big brother. She and Noah couldn't discuss Ben without arguing, so they'd silently agreed not to.

Grace was a different story. She was as welcoming of Ben as Noah was. The two of them often made her feel guilty, and she didn't like to waste her time on guilt.

She'd done the right thing, damn it. Then. Now, however, it was time to alter the situation. Now Ben would be a benefit to her.

Agatha was proud of her new plans and how she'd set them into motion, but there was little satisfaction without someone to share it. She was too old to be alone.

Soon, soon, she'd have it all set to rights.

Soon she'd have her family, including sweet Grace, back with her—where they all belonged.

Chapter Ten

Though he knew he was almost an hour earlier than they'd agreed on, Noah leaned on the doorbell. He was ridiculously anxious to see Grace.

He was also tight with growing arousal, but amazingly enough, it wasn't just sex he wanted. Oh, he wanted that, all right. Bad. Again and again. But he also wanted to talk with her, to hear her laugh and watch her fuss and find out how her job interview had gone.

He wanted to be with her.

It was a novel feeling, one he'd never experienced before.

When Grace had called him earlier to say she'd be home at six and he could come over at seven, she'd refused to say much about the job, other than that she'd gotten it. According to Grace, she didn't want to jinx herself. She'd sounded happy—and her happiness had felt like the sun shining down on his miserable head.

He'd spent the day separating his finances completely from his grandmother's. He'd withdrawn his name, his power of attorney, his influence, from all her accounts and business dealings. She was on her own.

God, he needed Grace.

Noah gave up on the doorbell and banged his fist on the door. He was normally a patient man, but since first touching Grace, impatience had been riding him hard.

Two seconds later the door was jerked open. Grace, bundled beneath a light blue, thick fleece robe far too warm for the weather, gave him a mutinous look. Her hair was in a ragtag ponytail and long, twisted strands had escaped. They hung around her ears, her temples, giving her an enticingly mussed look. She blew one long strand away from her eyes and glared at him.

His heart raced at the sight of her. "Hey."

Her rounded chin lifted. "You do seem to have a problem with knocking politely, don't you?"

"Ringing your doorbell didn't work, so I figured a polite knock wouldn't either." Noah took in the way she clutched the top of the robe to her throat, how tightly it was belted. He couldn't wait a single second more and leaned in to kiss her full on her angrily pursed mouth. "Why the robe, Gracie? Were you in bed?"

Giving Grace no choice but to move out of his way, Noah pushed his way in. Her apartment was as tidy now as it had been earlier. But unlike his place, hers was warm and welcoming, even cozy.

Noah was beginning to think any place would feel like home when Grace was around.

She closed the door and made to move past him. "No, I wasn't napping. I was just . . . I'm changing from work."

"Grace," Noah teased, eyeing her bare feet

peeking from the bottom of the long robe, "are you naked under there?"

Using two fingers, he reached for her right lapel, meaning to take a quick peek. Grace gave a horrified squeal and darted away, rushing down the hall.

What a reaction, Noah thought with amusement. He was suspicious about what she had to hide, and feeling challenged by her retreat.

Wearing a huge grin, he went after her.

"Grace," he called to her retreating back while watching her ponytail bounce, "you are naked, aren't you?"

"No!" she yelled back, and picked up her pace, obviously intent on losing him. But her apartment was small, the hallway short, and his legs were far stronger than hers.

Grace almost made it into the bedroom where Noah felt certain she would have slammed the door in his face, but he managed to get inside first. Grace whirled around, flushed with guilt and something else.

Noah flattened his hand on the door and shoved it closed.

They stared at each other, Noah with anticipation, Grace with nervousness.

When he slowly smiled, she colored.

Trying to sound reasonable, Grace said, "Noah, if you'll just wait in the other room, I'll finish changing and be right out."

She looked as though she actually expected him to obey that polite command. Noah shook his head.

"Sorry, Gracie, I don't want to wait." He touched her chin, then idly looked around her bedroom. Her furniture was all painted white, including her four-poster bed. There was a plush white comforter on the bed with numerous velvet pillows in pale green and various shades of blue scattered about. The curtains over two smallish windows were the same soft shade of green.

As he'd always assumed, Grace was a tidy woman with very little clutter anywhere. He did notice several fat candles, half burned down, sitting atop every surface, and fresh flowers on a nightstand.

He turned back to Grace. She was watching him, waiting and alert. "And I sure as hell don't want you to put clothes on."

Grace sputtered, clutching that ragged robe for all she was worth. Her brows pulled down in a frown. "I'm afraid I have to insist."

Excitement unfurled in Noah's gut, as raw and fresh and real as any he'd ever experienced. He'd forgotten how fun it was to chase, to meet a challenge, especially a sexual challenge. Primal instincts rose, demanding he gently conquer her.

Grace watched him with her big brown eyes unblinking. Her smooth cheeks went hot with some emotion, and the pulse in her throat fluttered wildly.

Deliberately keeping the inflection from his tone, Noah said, "We're in the bedroom, Grace."

Those beautiful eyes of hers widened. Her lips parted. "But . . ."

With supreme satisfaction, Noah reminded her of their deal. "You can't insist in here, sweets. In here, in any bedroom, you do just what I want, remember?"

He reached out and brushed the knuckles of his left hand over her breast, and even through the layers of material he felt her nipple pull tight. Grace shivered, but she didn't pull away. "Be a good little sex slave," he murmured, "and drop the robe."

Grace stifled a soft moan. "I'm not . . . little."

Noah grinned. There wasn't much rebellion left in her tone and that fueled him all the more. "Next to me, you're small and female, and Grace"—he hardened his voice—"I want you to lose the robe so I can look at you."

Her hands tightened on the material until she was nearly strangling herself. "But I'm not naked underneath."

"No?" She didn't say anything else, so Noah teased, "What are you wearing, Grace? More of that soft cotton underwear?"

Grace cleared her throat. "If you really want to know . . ."

"Oh, yeah. I insist on knowing."

"Well . . ." The color in her cheeks darkened. "It's a stupid uniform for work. I was trying some of them on, trying to find one that fits, but this one is definitely too tight."

Heat churned in his stomach, settled in his groin. He suddenly felt very full and very ready. "Let me see."

"You'll laugh," she whispered.

"No way. Not a chance." Still she hesitated, and Noah made himself sound stern when he said, "Grace, you agreed to the bargain—"

"Oh, all right!" she nearly yelled, and her face burned. Her movements were jerky, uncertain, as Grace stripped the robe off her shoulders, balled it up and threw it at Noah. It hit his chest and dropped to his feet. Noah ignored it.

Damn, she looked hot.

The uniform, if something so short and snug could be called a uniform, looked vaguely familiar, but Noah couldn't place where he'd seen it before. He was certain he'd never seen it look quite like that on any other woman. It was so tight, it squeezed Grace's generous hips and ass and pulled across her thighs, her belly.

She hadn't been able to get it buttoned over her breasts. Three buttons shy of being decent, the bodice gapped open to frame a truly magnificent cleavage. It looked as if her breasts might pop free at any moment if she dared to breathe. Noah hoped they would.

"Walk around," he instructed, unable to take his gaze off her.

Grace slapped her arms around herself and scowled suspiciously. "Why?"

If she thought he might laugh, she was sadly mistaken. He was liable to drag her to the floor at any moment, but he sure as hell wouldn't be laughing. "I wanna see you move in that thing."

"Noah . . ."

He lifted his gaze, giving her a look, and Grace started mumbling to herself. She took a tentative step to the side of him and Noah said, "Around the bed. Go to the window and back."

"I feel incredibly stupid," she complained, still holding herself, still stiff.

"I feel ready to self-combust."

Whipping around, Grace stared at his crotch. Her look was so startled, so hot, his cock twitched and stretched another half an inch. Grace inhaled with surprise . . . delight. "Oh, my."

"That's not helping, Gracie."

Watching over her shoulder for Noah's reaction, Grace took two more steps. She was still a little uncertain, but her movements were more fluid.

"You have such a great ass."

Very slowly, her lips curled. Noah watched the confidence bloom inside her. "Thank you."

"Any time, babe. I only speak the truth." He couldn't stop staring. "Now walk toward me."

She did, even adding a little sway to her hips that made him want to smile, too.

"You can't wear this dress to work in." Noah's possessive nature rebelled at the idea of any other male seeing her like this. The material was drawn so tightly, he could visually trace the outline of her nipples, the cleft of her bottom, even the plump rise of her mound. The outfit didn't conceal so much as it enhanced and decorated.

Grace started to laugh, but it was a breathless sound. "Of course not. I can't even inhale in this dress, much less work." She strolled closer, and then stopped in front of him.

"Trouble breathing, huh?" Noah drew one long fingertip along the line of her cleavage, up, down, up again. "Does this help?"

In a very tiny, trembling voice, she whispered, "No."

"What about this?" He reached up with both hands and found her nipples through the stretched and clinging material. Using fingers and thumbs, he tugged.

"Noah . . ." Grace groaned, stumbling into him. She wasn't wearing a bra, and Noah wondered if she had panties on. He'd find out for himself in a moment. He rolled her nipples gently, flicked with his thumbnails. "Shhh. Stay still, Grace. Let me see just how well this dress fits."

"I'm trying."

He caught and held her nipples. "Is that better?" His own voice had gone husky with arousal.

Grace closed her eyes and shook her head.

"Then let's try this."

Her eyes snapped open to watch him warily while he unbuttoned yet another button. The material parted, straining open over her large breasts, and before he could release it the next button popped free. Noah could see the inside edges of her nipples. They were puckered tight and flushed darkly.

"Grace," he chided with mock seriousness, "you're excited. Here I am trying to help you, and your nipples are stiff little points."

With the dress open, she breathed hard, her chest rising and falling.

Noah worked the bodice open more to completely expose her. Her breasts were held captive by stiff material, pushed together, lifted high. "Is that uncomfortable, Grace?"

"Not . . . not too much. At least now I can breathe a little."

Noah couldn't stop staring at her. She made him feel breathless, too. "You're beautiful."

She squeezed her eyes shut.

"Grace?" He caught her nipples again, and this time she could feel the rough texture of his fingertips. He played with her, tormenting her. "You *are* beautiful. I hope you know that."

She reached for him in a rush, but Noah stopped her. "No, I'm not done yet. Now Grace, I know your skirt is tight, but I want you to open your thighs for me."

She looked down at the constricting material. "I can't."

"Then I can't touch you." He pinched her nipples just enough.

Grace widened her stance, moving her feet

apart while bracing herself with a firm hold on Noah's upper arms. "Is that enough?"

He smiled gently. "A little more."

Grace hesitated, and Noah could see her thinking, trying to figure out how to obey. She wanted him to touch her, and that made him want to all the more.

Finally Grace reached for the hem of the skirt and hiked it higher, giving herself more freedom. She boldly met Noah's gaze, braced herself again, and said brazenly, "There."

Noah could see a few feminine curls and his knees nearly buckled. As he'd suspected, Grace wasn't wearing panties. And that fact pushed him over the edge.

He wedged one large hand between her thighs and stroked her. She was silky wet already, her soft flesh swollen and hot. Noah cursed even as he dragged her close and kissed her, taking her mouth hungrily while pushing his fingers into her, hard and deep.

Grace was so responsive, fingering her was more exciting than having sex with other women. She moaned and moved against him and clutched at him, and far, far too soon, Noah knew she was nearing a climax.

"I want to taste your nipples," Noah growled in harsh demand. He hooked one arm around Grace's waist to raise her.

Grace arched her back, forcing her breasts high, and Noah caught one swollen pink nipple in his mouth. He sucked strongly.

Grace cried out, writhing against his fingers, pumping her hips, grinding—and then she exploded, her hands tangled hard in his hair to keep him close.

Noah damn near came in his pants with her. "Yeah," he said against her breast, "hell yeah, Grace."

He still had two fingers pressed deep inside her, feeling the last squeezing spasms of her orgasm, when she went limp against his chest. The arm Noah held her with trembled.

His legs trembled.

His heart quaked. *Damn.*

As gently as possible, given his own heightened state, Noah lowered her feet back to the floor. In record time, he finished unbuttoning the uniform and tossed it aside. He cradled her head, loosening the band that kept her hair in the ponytail. He pulled it free and smoothed her hair.

Grace gazed at him through heavy, sated eyes, swaying a little, smiling in satisfaction.

Noah watched her, turbulent in his lust, peaceful in the comfort of being with her. He sensed that he'd known her forever, yet he'd never really known her at all. Emotions too foreign and deep to contemplate were forced aside. He couldn't deal with them this soon. Maybe not ever.

Determined to keep things physical, Noah lifted Grace into his arms, took two steps to the bed, and stretched out on top of the coverlet with her. When he started to move atop her, Grace lifted a hand to stall him.

"Noah, are you forgetting something?"

Grace reclining on a white comforter, wearing just that particular look, was as enticing as it got. He cupped her face as tenderness threatened to choke him. "What am I forgetting, babe?"

"My turn?" Her eyes were dark and smoky, filled with sensual suggestion. "You did promise, remember, before we got interrupted."

Lust surged, exploded. "Yeah," he croaked, "I remember."

"Good." Grace turned so that she was sprawled on top of him. She wiggled, causing her breasts to tease his chest, her belly to stroke his groin. "I've been thinking about this off and on all day, and I know just what I want to do."

"Tell me."

"Nope." Grace shook her head, and her smile was equally sweet and wicked. "I'd rather show you."

Grace felt charged, filled with power. She could easily understand why Noah enjoyed taking the lead. It was so exciting.

She pushed to her elbows and smiled down into his face. His silky black hair was disheveled, falling over his brow with rakish appeal. She smoothed it back, kissed his forehead, then the bridge of his straight nose, his long, lush lashes. "You are so incredibly gorgeous," she murmured, meaning it with all her heart.

Noah smiled. "Flattery will get you everything."

"It's true, you know." She stared into the pure blue of his eyes and felt herself turning to mush. Noah had eyes that expressed so much, and right now they were filled with a stormy glitter. "You're beautiful."

His mouth twisted with wry amusement. "Yeah. If you say so."

"Noah." Grace sat up next to him, uncaring of her own nudity with the prospect of his soon to come. Everything about Noah enthralled her—his innate strength of character, the incredible generosity in his heart, his protective nature.

But she also couldn't deny her appreciation of his physical assets. His body was a study of solid, perfectly sculpted muscles, silky dark hair, long bones, and masculine grace.

And his face . . . Grace sighed in wonder. Noah had the face of a dark angel, able to seduce with just a look.

Combined, his personality and his physique made him beautiful inside and out.

Noah gazed at Grace's bare breasts with avid attention while she trailed her fingers over his wide chest, absorbing the wondrous feel of him through his pullover. "You don't sound like you believe me."

Noah shrugged. "I look like my father, Grace, and I'm not altogether sure that's a good thing."

Her heart filled with pain. Noah had never been as vocal about his father as Ben had. He was more private, and he had a core of family loyalty that had likely been forged from desperation, from a burning desire to *have* a family. But Grace knew he was equally disappointed with Pierce Harper's lack of responsibility toward his sons.

Agatha shared that disappointment as well, though she'd never admit it.

Grace caught the hem of Noah's shirt and began working it up. "Pierce Harper was a very handsome man."

"I don't give a damn about that."

"Because of what he did to you?"

Noah raised his arms to assist her and gave a grunt of reply when she tossed the shirt to the side of the bed. "He didn't do anything, for me, to me, or about me."

"Noah . . ."

"I don't want to talk about this right now,

Grace." Deliberately, he trailed his fingertips up her thigh, higher and higher, until he stroked her pubic hair. "I'd rather fuck you instead."

Grace saw the stirring of desire in his eyes and the set expression on his face. Regardless of how Noah tried to hide it, she also saw his pain. His harsh, crude words were a cover, but she knew him too well to let them bother her.

She put her hands on his chest, spread her fingers wide, and explored the textures of iron-hard muscles, thick body hair, and warm skin. "Did I tell you," she whispered, "that I like it when you talk dirty?"

The pain left his eyes, replaced with burning need and a touch of amusement. "No. Do you, Gracie?"

She nodded slowly. "I like everything you say to me, but especially the sex stuff." She glanced up at his face and away. With her fingertips, she found his nipples. "I like everything you do to me, too."

Tension seemed to pulse off Noah in waves. "Then you'll definitely like this." He reached for her, his intent plain, and Grace caught his thick wrists.

"Ah, ah. It's my turn, Noah. You just mind your manners."

Noah laughed. "I'm a street rat, remember? I don't have manners, especially not in bed."

True enough, Grace thought. But then, he'd already shown her that bed was no place to be polite. Noah gave and took what he wanted, and made her burn with release in the bargain. She could find no fault in that.

"How about," Grace murmured, "if I promise to make it worth your while?"

Neither of them relented. Grace still held

Noah's wrists, and he still strained against her hold. "Yeah? And just how're you going to do that?"

"Well . . ." Her face heated; this was all very new to Grace, and she still felt timid on occasion. But more than anything in the whole world, she wanted to give Noah some of the same pleasure he'd given her. So she pushed the timidity aside, forced her gaze to his face, and lifted her chin. "I'm going to touch you all over."

"My cock?" Noah's blue eyes were direct, alight with challenge, with suggestion. Grace knew he was deliberately giving her the "dirty talk" she'd professed to enjoy.

"Especially . . . there."

His expression froze, his cheekbones colored with excitement and his nostrils flared with his in-drawn breath. He stared at her mouth as his eyes turned smoky.

"I'm going to kiss you, too," Grace added, emboldened by his reaction. "And . . . and *lick* you."

His whole body jerked and his jaw locked hard. "Grace . . ." He said her name as a warning.

"Even . . . even your cock."

Noah groaned long and low, ending with a strangled laugh. "Damn, you're good at this."

Noah's praise filled her with delight. Sliding over him and off the side of the bed, Grace held out her hand. "Come on, then. Stand up so I can get your pants off you."

"Lord have mercy." Noah pushed to his feet. He moved to stand between her and one of the tall posts at the foot of the bed. He smiled at her in anticipation.

Slowly, provocatively, Grace dropped to her knees. Being in front of Noah, naked and kneeling and wanting to please him, was a turn-on. His erection pressed against the front of his slacks, making her smile, too. Her heart beat hard, her pulse raced.

She felt Noah's fingers in her hair, gently massaging her scalp as she untied his shoes and instructed him to step out of them. She set the shoes aside and removed his socks. Noah braced his bare feet apart.

Grace looked up at him, saw the expectation in his expression. In her submissive position, she felt more like a sex slave than ever. It freed her from her inhibitions and made her wild.

She leaned closer and went to work on his belt buckle, anxious to see him naked, to touch him and taste him and hear him moan. Her knuckles brushed against his crotch again and again, and she became aware of the slight trembling in his hands as he continued to hold her head.

When she slid his belt free of his pant loops, his hands tightened in her hair. Grace paused, surveying Noah. He looked rigid and more than ready.

This was going to be so much fun.

Using one finger, Grace traced his long, thick erection through his trousers. "I've never done this before, but I know what I want to do."

"Yeah."

Grace hid a smile and wondered if Noah even knew what he was saying. His eyes were narrowed, his face flushed. His inky dark hair hung over his brow and his lips were parted.

With her own hands now shaking, Grace undid the button to his trousers. "If you don't like what I'm doing—"

"I'll like it."

Drawing out the anticipation, she slowly slid the

zipper down until his slacks opened. He looked uncomfortably contained in the tight boxers, his penis long and hard and straining against the soft cotton material. Taking him by surprise, Grace leaned forward and rubbed her cheek against him.

"Mmmm," she said with sensual realization, "you smell good." She hadn't realized that his scent would be so delicious, so hot.

"Damn." Noah pressed her head, holding her to him for a heart-stopping moment. "You little tease. You're killing me."

Grace laughed softly at his growled, barely audible comment. "Turnabout is fair play."

Noah edged his thumbs under her jaw and tipped her face up to him. "I'll get even," he promised gruffly, and Grace believed him. She shivered, already looking forward to his efforts.

Getting her mind back on the task at hand, Grace tugged his pants down his long, strong legs. She removed his boxers at the same time. "Step out."

Noah kicked the clothes away. Grace felt the stillness of him, the way he held his breath. She liked it that he was so excited, and she especially liked it that she was the cause.

Though they'd already made love and Noah had done incredible, awesome things to her, Grace hadn't yet had a chance to explore him. Now it was her turn, and no way would she waste it. She smoothed her hands up his hard, hairy thighs, all the way to the lighter, smoother skin of his hipbones. Noah shifted.

"Be patient with me, Noah, okay? I've never seen . . . *this*, up close."

"This?" he croaked, and even above his arousal,

she heard his amusement. Grace ignored it, too intent on her study of his male parts to be distracted
by his misplaced humor.

"You're hot." Tentatively, she cupped his hair-
roughened testicles. They were heavy, firm, drawn
tight. His skin there was very warm, and as she
leaned close to inhale his scent again, his penis
flexed, moved in reaction to her touch, her near-
ness. This part of Noah fascinated her. He looked
enormous, so long and strong.

"It's amazing that we fit."

His hands continued to gently clench and un-
clench in her hair.

While still cradling him in her palm, Grace
leaned forward and brushed a kiss over his right
hipbone. She liked that, so she did it again, this
time taking a small, delicate lick to taste his hot
flesh as well. He smelled good enough to eat,
musky and male.

"Grace . . ." he groaned.

She glanced up and saw that his head was
tipped back, his mouth slightly open. His strong,
tanned throat worked and he moaned again.

Keeping her touch light and careful, she
wrapped the fingers of her free hand around his
shaft. Noah jerked, then muttered, "Harder."

"What?"

He swallowed, drew a shuddering breath. "I like
it when you hold my balls so gently. That feels
great. But here"—he put his hand over hers, his
hold firm—"I want you to *squeeze.*"

And he helped her, tightening his grip and
breathing harder as he did so. "Oh, yeah, like
that."

"It doesn't hurt?" Grace stared at him in awe.
He'd begun moving her hand, helping her to

stroke him. Up, down, back up again until her fingers curved over the broad head of his penis, then pulled down to the base.

Noah released her and leaned back on the foot post, bracing himself. His eyes squeezed shut and his jaw tightened. "Ah, God, that feels good, Grace." His hands curled into fists. "I love having you touch me."

Grace stroked back down to the base of his shaft. He felt like warm velvet over solid steel, alive and powerful. A small drop of fluid appeared at the head of his penis. She stared, entranced.

Suddenly she couldn't wait. She leaned forward with a rush. "Will you love this, too?" she asked, and softly pressed her lips to him.

She started to draw back, but Noah caught her head and held her close, silently encouraging her. *"Yes."*

His excitement made her excited. Grace kissed him again, this time with her mouth open so she could taste him, too. She licked, felt a shudder go through him, and licked again.

Noah's head dropped forward and he watched her with burning eyes and fiery intensity.

Feeling wanton and sexy, her gaze locked with his, Grace held him still and licked up the entire length of his erection until her tongue slid up and over the head. She tasted the salty fluid at the same time Noah let out a raw growl of pleasure. His whole body shuddered.

"Grace?"

He sounded strained, almost in pain. Loving his reaction and her own sense of feminine power, Grace licked the head again and again, down to the base, back up. Her tongue swirled, teased. Then she'd start all over.

Noah shifted and groaned and he raised his arms, locking his hands behind his head. His broad shoulders pressed hard to the post, his legs stiffened, his abdomen pulled tight until every muscle was delineated.

His breath rushed in and out in broken pants and moans. Grace, sensing the time was right, closed her mouth over him and drew him in. He was large enough, and she was inexperienced enough, that it wasn't easy. She stretched her jaw wider, determined, hungry for him.

Suddenly Noah's long fingers molded around her head and he guided her, urging her to take him deeper, longer.

"Grace . . . *suck*," he rasped, and she did. Her own body was on fire. She curled her hands around his taut, narrow hips and held on as he began to rock into her, holding her steady, taking her mouth as he'd already taken her body.

"God," he moaned, and he stiffened, stilled. "Grace . . . that's it." He started to push her away. "I can't take it."

Grace held on, moving her tongue, drawing on him.

"Grace . . ." he warned on a growl so low and rough she could barely hear him.

She sank her nails into his firm backside, warning him that she wanted it all, she wanted to drive him over the edge.

And Noah let go. He came with a long broken moan, his hips jerking, his body burning hot and shivering, every muscle finely drawn. After long moments he slumped, his knees giving way so that the bedpost supported most of his weight. Slowly, he pulled back from Grace.

With shaking hands he smoothed her hair and then carefully, tenderly, tilted her face up to him.

Grace loved him so much, keeping the words inside was nearly impossible. She managed, but something must have shown in her face.

Noah stared down at her for a long time while he struggled to catch his breath. His eyes were the darkest midnight, filled with turbulent emotion. Finally he sank down to sit in front of Grace, then pulled her close, rocking her into his naked body, his face pressed to her throat.

"Amazing Grace," he whispered, and a second later she felt his smile.

Chapter Eleven

Noah woke with a dash of realization. Grace's bedroom was now dark, her sheets heated from their bodies. Grace was curled close to his side like a small cat and it felt right, even comfortable, to have her there. She had one leg over his lap, one arm over his chest, with her palm resting on his nipple.

Wide awake now, Noah turned his head to look at Grace in the shadows, and he heard her mumble something in her sleep. She stirred, snuggling tighter to his side, and her hand curled, inadvertently stroking him.

Damn. He silently commanded his cock to behave, but it was an impossible order around Grace. She grouched at him and he wanted her. She smiled at him and his blood heated.

She got to her knees in front of him and he caught on fire. He hadn't been this goddamned randy since his teenage years, when the only respite from life was wild, mind-numbing sex.

Well, Grace was here by her own volition, a decision she'd made without coercion. And better still, she enjoyed his excesses, and matched them with her own. He might as well take advantage of it.

But first he had a few questions for her.

Noah woke her by stroking her behind. Grace wriggled, moaned softly, shifted her leg over his crotch. Damn.

"Gracie?" He kissed her forehead, her upturned nose. Her fabulous hair trailed over them both in a wild tangle. "Wake up, Grace."

She moved again, then stilled with awareness. "Noah?" Her head lifted. "What's wrong?"

"Not a damn thing." He stroked her tush again, then gave it a squeeze. "Except that I want to know why you had that uniform on."

"What uniform?" she asked around a wide yawn. "What time is it?"

"The uniform you had on when I arrived, and I have no idea what time it is. What does it matter?"

Grace appeared to be pondering that, then he felt her shoulder shrug into his side. "It doesn't. I don't have to be at work till late afternoon tomorrow. I can sleep in." She shifted around until she was half atop his chest. She toyed with his chest hair, then asked in a husky, hopeful voice, "Did you want me again?"

Noah tried and failed to hide his smile. God, after she'd used her sweet mouth on him, he should have been dead to the world, down for the count with the way his body had exploded. Instead, he'd been insatiable.

Each time he loved Grace made him want her that much more. Where she was concerned, his body showed no moderation, and his stamina seemed inexhaustible.

"You like this slave business, don't you?"

She rubbed her breasts against his chest, nipped his chin, and purred, "Yes."

"Grace," he admonished, catching her bottom in his hands and holding her still before she swayed him from his purpose. "I want to talk."

"Oh." Her tone was filled with disappointment. "We could talk later."

"We'll talk now."

She sighed long and drawn out. "Okay. About what?"

Noah laughed. "You haven't been paying attention, Grace."

"Well," she teased, now nibbling on his bottom lip, "I've got this big, gorgeous, buck-naked hunk in my bed. If that's not enough to stop a woman's heart and scatter her wits, I don't know what is." And then, more seriously, "I never, ever thought anything like this would happen to me, Noah. I can hardly believe it. I want to relish every moment."

"Grace." Damn, she twisted his guts and tore at his heart. "I bet you've left a string of broken hearts behind."

She laughed. "Don't be ridiculous. Men never notice me."

"You, sweetheart, are just oblivious. I've sneaked plenty of looks at you over the years."

"Uh-huh." Disbelief dripped from her tone. "Sure you did."

"It's true," Noah insisted. Something about Grace had always drawn him. He'd told himself it was her quirky nature, her vibrating energy, and her staunch loyalty to her employer. He'd convinced himself it was respect and admiration.

He'd been so damn blind. "I was just subtle about it."

Grace tucked her head under his chin, rested her cheek on his sternum. In a small voice, she said, "Because you were in love with Kara."

"No." Noah traced her spine, loving the sleek feel of her skin, the voluptuous upward curve of her bottom. "Because I was engaged to her. I never loved her, not the way I should have loved a woman I was going to marry. I know that now."

"But you're worried about her."

Noah shrugged, admitting the truth of that. "I'm fond of Kara. She's a nice person, and in a lot of ways she's still like a child. I don't want to see her hurt. But I'm not in love with her and I never was."

Grace nodded in understanding and again leaned up to look at him. Noah could see the deep glitter of her eyes, the pale glow of her shoulders and breasts. "You're her friend, and you're afraid that whoever she's involved with will hurt her."

Noah stilled. "What are you talking about?"

She touched her nose to his. "I'm not an idiot, Noah. I know that Kara is involved with someone else. That's why you broke the engagement. I'm assuming it's someone at the restaurant, which is why she wants to hang out there."

Noah shook his head in wonder. "That quick mind of yours never rests, does it?" He was amazed at her observation, at her sensitivity to others.

Grace resettled herself, trying to get comfortable. She squirmed in a way that quickly made Noah hard. "It's obvious to anyone who knows you. It had to be something really personal, something insurmountable to cause you to call off the wedding. I'd say having a lover on the side would qualify."

Noah hadn't intended to discuss the situation

with anyone other than his brother, and that had only been to let off steam. He'd known exactly how Ben would react, cursing them all and offering Noah his support in whatever way he needed.

He hadn't discussed it with anyone else because he felt a lingering sense of protectiveness toward Kara. He didn't want to see her reputation ruined, didn't want to hear others condemn her.

But Grace wasn't accusing. The night was dark, the room quiet except for their hushed conversation. And Grace was a warm, gentle weight atop his heart.

Noah realized he wanted more than the blind support his brother so freely gave. He wanted understanding; he wanted vindication.

He wanted to talk out his thoughts with someone unbiased.

"I wasn't hurt when I found them."

Grace hugged herself closer to him. She was silent for a long time, then asked, "You found them . . . together?"

"Yeah."

"Must have been something of a shock."

He shrugged. "You'd think so, wouldn't you? I thought I had my life all figured out, thought I knew what I was doing. But damn . . ." Noah shook his head. "I walked in on them naked in the bed, literally *in the act*. And that's when I realized I didn't love her, because my biggest concern was how everyone else would take the breakup. For the longest time my grandmother planned on us marrying. She loves Kara."

"She loves you, too."

Noah laughed at that. "Yeah, so much so, she disowned me."

Grace stiffened, then pushed herself up and

spoke not two inches from his face. "Oh, Noah, don't think that way. You know Agatha reacts with her pride first and later regrets it."

"It's all right, Grace," he told her gently, feeling like a fool. How did Grace keep getting him to act so melodramatic? It was totally unlike him and left him feeling foolish. "I'm a grown man, not a little boy." *Not anymore.*

"But . . . Noah, I'm willing to bet that even now Agatha is trying to figure out how to get you back without losing face."

"You think so, do you?"

Grace nodded. "Everything is a strategy to Agatha. She thinks in terms of maintaining control. That's important to her."

Grace was very astute when it came to his grandmother. "All she has to do is ask me." Noah gave a wry smile. "Hell, I love the old witch."

In her gruff, strict manner, Agatha had taught Noah savvy business sense and the finer nuances to success. She'd shown him how to fit in with society, how to adjust.

For all that, he owed her.

What Agatha hadn't given him was pride and self-worth, because Noah had always had that, even when he'd had nothing else. Perhaps it was inherited, or maybe it had been formed from necessity. Noah didn't discount what Agatha had done for him, but he knew in his heart that somehow, some way, he'd have changed the circumstances of his youth with or without her assistance.

What he wanted most from Agatha—unconditional trust and love and loyalty—she hadn't given him.

Grace replied, as if she'd read his thoughts. "Agatha loves you, too, Noah, and she's proud of you. I think she'd like to take credit for all your successes, but she knows the truth, just as I do. You're the most capable man I've ever known. I would never doubt your ability to get ahead, with or without Agatha's influence."

Noah hugged Grace tight. He didn't have to guess at her motives, or her sincerity, because she spoke her mind and gave of herself with equal gusto. She was the type of woman who would open her heart completely to a man she loved.

She'd already opened herself to him.

That fact had become a burning awareness in Noah's conscience, sharper with each minute he spent near her. It disturbed him on many levels—especially since he found the idea so intriguing.

Noah changed the subject, saying, "I just realized, you haven't asked me who Kara is sleeping with."

"It's none of my business." Grace licked his throat, bit him gently. "But I'll admit, I'm glad she's not sleeping with you."

"Grace." Noah turned, pinning her beneath him. She was a soft cushion, inciting him, stirring him on so many levels. Without him asking, she opened her arms—and her thighs—to hold him close. "I want you to promise me something."

She didn't hesitate. "Anything."

Grim, hating himself but unable to keep the demand inside, Noah said, "Swear to me that for as long as we're involved, you won't let another man touch you."

It amazed Noah, but the idea of Grace lying down with someone else filled him with a killing rage. Seeing Kara naked and moaning with her lover hadn't really touched him, but if Grace did the same . . .

Her gentle smile was barely discernible in the quiet night. He expected her quick agreement, but she took him by surprise. "Noah, no other man wants me."

"Bullshit." How could she be so oblivious to her sex appeal? Her lack of confidence annoyed him. "Promise me, Grace."

She put her arms around his neck and pulled his mouth down to hers. "There's no need," she said, making him stiffen, and then she added, "But if that's what you want, then sure, I swear."

Noah kissed her hard, thrusting his tongue deep, biting her bottom lip. He was angry at himself, confused, but Grace gentled him just by stroking his hair, his shoulders. She made him feel both strong and weak with her complete giving.

By small degrees, Noah ended the kiss. He wanted Grace, wanted to lose himself in the warm, wet clasp of her body, in the sweet friction. But he was determined to get some of the talking done first.

"Why were you wearing that uniform, Grace?"

"Ben insists," she murmured, trying to catch his mouth again.

His suspicions confirmed, Noah jerked upright to sit in the bed. He glared at the small lump her shadowed form made in the bedclothes. "Goddamn it, Grace, I knew that dress looked familiar. Don't tell me this new job of yours is working for Ben."

The room was silent.

"Well?" he demanded.

The bed shook with Grace's philosophical shrug. "Do you want me to tell you or not?"

"Fuck. You are, aren't you?"

Slowly, Grace sat up. "Noah Harper, using that

word for sex, during sex, is *not* the same as cursing at me!"

Anger roiled inside him, spurred on by worry, by possessiveness. He could just imagine Grace bopping around Ben's bar in that getup, making every guy in attendance hot. It was intolerable.

He gripped her shoulders and bore her back down on the bed. He loomed over her, his nose touching her own, his breath on her mouth.

Punctuating his words with a small shake, Noah said, "I don't want you working there, Grace."

She huffed, and though he could barely see her, he knew she was glaring. "I never asked you."

An undeniable truth, and one he didn't like at all. "It's dangerous."

"I'm a *big* girl."

Her emphasis on *big* pushed Noah right over the edge. He growled and shook her again. "Damn it, Grace. You're gonna make one too many cracks on weight and I swear to God, I'm going to put you over my knee."

Her eyes widened, looking opalescent in the darkness. Breathless, she asked, "Really?" and damned if she didn't sound intrigued.

Noah burned, but he wasn't about to be sidetracked by sex. Not this time. "I can promise you won't like it."

In a huff, Grace flattened her hands hard against his chest and shoved. "Then forget it."

Noah refused to budge. "I wasn't asking your permission."

"And I wasn't asking for yours. We agreed to obedience in the bedroom, Noah, not in my entire life. Where I work is none of your business."

And that was what really pissed him off. He wanted everything that concerned Grace to be his business. He wanted to know that she was safe and happy and that she was . . . his.

Shit. Noah shoved himself away from her. Confusion churned inside him, making his head pound, his heart race. He'd just ended a long-term, complicated engagement, just ruined a close family relationship. His life, his future, was all up in the air.

Oh, he had no doubt he'd do fine; as Grace had pointed out, he knew how to take care of himself. He'd been a survivalist from birth.

But he had to get his life settled, had to put out the other fires before starting a new blaze. The last thing Noah wanted or needed was another entanglement in his life, and Grace was most definitely entangling him. She'd already turned him inside out.

Sex with Grace had seemed like such a great idea, a way to relieve his tension and stay unattached. In his usual fashion, he had made his decision to become involved with her. But he'd veered from his original plan in a big way, which was something he never did.

Now he wanted more than just the bone-melting sex, when he knew more was the worst thing. "I'm sorry."

Grace let out a long sigh. "I had no idea you'd react like this."

How could she have known? *He* hadn't known. He'd been engaged to Kara for years and had never been so controlling.

"Forget it." But then, because the worry was still there, despite everything he'd just told himself, Noah twisted to face her. "Grace, it really isn't the best place to work."

"Ben told me you wouldn't like it, but I promised him you wouldn't care."

He'd strangle Ben. "My brother can be astute on occasion, but this time his judgment was off. He should never have hired you."

Grace dropped back on the bed. "Here we go again."

"Don't be sarcastic, Grace. Ben runs a tight business, and I'm damn proud of him. But he caters to a lot of rough customers. It's not too bad during the week, but on the weekends, especially in the evening, it can get rowdy, even dangerous."

"He told me no one had ever been seriously hurt."

He supposed Ben didn't count his own stitches, bruises, and cuts as serious. Noah would have a long, serious talk with his little brother very soon. "It's only a matter of time. That's no place for a lady."

"He has other women working for him."

Grace's arguments were grating. Through his teeth, Noah said, "They're not you, Grace."

"And just what does that mean?"

She sounded so insulted, Noah shook his head. "You've never lived in that type of environment. You're not street smart. I've met Ben's other waitresses. Hell, I grew up with women like them. They know the score."

"And you're saying I don't?"

Hoping to sooth her growing temper, Noah stroked her thigh through the blankets. "I'm saying you're sweet and naïve."

"I am not."

"You just told me men don't notice you. If that's not naïve, then what is?"

"It's the truth, Noah. Men don't look at women who are . . ."

She hesitated, and he grinned evilly. "Remember my warning, babe. My palm is itching." He released her thigh and found her hip. He squeezed suggestively.

Grace scoffed at him. "You'd never hit me in anger, Noah, and we both know it."

She was right, damn it. Her faith in him was humbling.

Noah decided he'd just have to find another way to dissuade her. The answer came to him in a flash. "I wanted you to go to Florida with me."

"Florida?" Grace shoved up on her elbows. Moonlight fell softly over her breasts, making a pretty picture. "What's in Florida?"

Distracted, Noah said, "Rental property I bought. I already owned one condo complex there, but another has gone up for sale next door."

"You own a condo in Florida?"

Noah wondered if she had any real idea of his monetary worth. Agatha had shown him the value of owning land and property, and he'd quickly begun acquiring his own. But even Agatha hadn't been informed of all his purchases. For some time now, Noah had felt the need to guarantee himself financial security.

"My building has four posh condos in it, right on the beach. The one I'm thinking of buying has six units. They're smaller than what I own now, but the realtor says he has no problem keeping them rented. It'd be ideal to have them both, because then I could offer a wider range of rental fees."

Grace gaped at him. "Two buildings on the beach?"

Noah didn't tell her that he had property in a

few other vacation areas as well. "Do you like the ocean, Grace?"

"I don't know. I've never been to the beach."

"No?" He stared at the full, generous curves of her moon-washed breasts and pictured her in the bright sunshine, splashing along the shore, her smile as sweet and charming as ever. "You'd look great in a bikini, Grace."

She snorted, and though it was too dark to discern, Noah was sure she blushed. "Dream on."

Laughing, Noah decided he'd get her into a swimsuit sometime very soon. "I get down there about eight times a year, whenever I have to head that way on other business for Agatha. I like to keep up on things. I was hoping to fly down this weekend to check out the new property before I buy it." Hoping to tempt her into agreeing, he added, "I have one of the condos reserved from Friday to Monday, so I can find out firsthand how comfortable it is, and make sure everything is in working order."

Noah slipped his hand beneath the blankets and rested his palm on Grace's soft belly. The muscles tightened under his hand as she sucked in her breath. "You wanna keep me company?"

Grace fidgeted. "Our agreement was for sex and only sex. I don't want to . . ."

"Screw the agreement."

She looked uncertain.

Anger flared. Noah knew he was being perverse, because after all, *he* was the one who had stressed the terms of their involvement. But every time Grace hesitated, or pulled back, he wanted to draw her closer.

"Grace, there are bedrooms everywhere." He sounded reasonable, convincing. "Think of this as an adventure, as just another place to indulge our carnal games."

Still she held silent, and Noah added softly, by way of an incentive, "We could rent a boat and make love out on the ocean with the hot sun on our backs."

Just that easily, she nodded. "Okay, I'd love to." Noah grinned.

"But I might have to work."

She sounded disappointed at that possibility, and Noah decided to have a talk with Ben. He'd make sure his brother didn't schedule Grace on the busy, rowdier weekends. And Grace would never have to know he'd interfered. He instinctively knew she'd rebel against the idea of favoritism.

"Let me know as soon as you find out your schedule, okay?"

"Yes." She shifted slightly beneath his palm. Grace got hot so quickly, it sometimes astounded him.

Noah drifted his fingers lower, until he was just touching her pubic hair. Teasing, tempting. "Grace?"

"Mmm?"

He smiled at her breathless anticipation. "You're not going to wear that dress to work in, are you?"

"No, of course not." And then, forgetting his warning, she said, "Those uniforms were not made for heavy women. Hopefully Ben will be able to— *Noah!*"

In a flash, Noah had Grace up and over his thighs, her round behind available for a sound swat. She squealed and squirmed, making Noah hesitate. Then he thought, what the hell, and brought his palm down with just enough force to make her yelp.

"Noah!" She tried to sound outraged, but he could hear the laughter in her tone, could feel her jiggling as she snickered.

Noah smiled with lecherous intent. "I told you, babe, I don't like it when you keep putting yourself down."

"I wasn't!"

"You're not heavy. You look gorgeous, every single inch of you. All right?"

Grace struggled for balance in her awkward position. She flattened one hand on the floor and curled the fingers of her other hand into Noah's thigh. Twisting her face around to peer at him in the darkness, she said, "Be reasonable, Noah, anyone can see that I'm . . . *hey!*"

He swatted her again, a little harder this time. His palm tingled, and he had to hold Grace still when she tried to wiggle off his lap. He hampered her movements by flattening one hand on the small of her back and wrapping the other around the inside of her thigh. His fingertips touched her hot vulva. He stroked seductively—and Grace choked on a laugh.

"I'm ready to dole out more, babe. Be careful what you say."

"Okay, okay!" Grace sucked in air between her giggles. "This is a terribly ignominious position, Noah."

"I like it."

"You would."

Noah could feel her long silky hair hanging down to the floor, brushing against his hip, teasing him every time she moved.

He smoothed his hand over her back to the warm spot where he'd smacked her. He wished he'd had enough sense to turn the lights on so he could see her clearly. "I want to be positive sure that you understand me, Grace. Now say, *I have a great bottom.*"

At his demand, Grace started giggling again and couldn't stop. Noah squeezed one firm buttock. "Grace," he warned.

Still snickering, she said, "Okay, okay."

"Say it."

She drew in a breath. "I . . . I have a *sore* bottom."

Noah smacked her, then kept her still as she screeched with a mixture of stinging discomfort and hilarity. She almost got away from him, but he hauled her back up.

"Noah!"

"I have all night, Grace." He wedged his hand between her thighs and cupped her mound fully. "And you know, I think I'm enjoying this."

"I *know* you're enjoying it!" She peeked around at him again. "I can feel your erection on my belly."

Noah grinned. "Ah, but Grace"—his fingers pressed into her—"I've had that since I woke up and found you curled naked next to me."

"Oh."

She was already wet, hot. "Say it, Grace."

She went still and quiet, absorbing his touch. Without the humor, she asked, "You really do think I'm sexy?"

Noah turned her and cradled her in his arms. He kissed her softly on her lips, smoothed away her long hair. "Gracie, you're so fucking sexy, I can barely control myself around you."

Grace trembled. In the next heartbeat, she shoved him flat on the bed and moved over him, kissing him wildly, stroking him everywhere, using that incredible mouth of hers again to drive him insane. Noah forgot about everything but the intense pleasure she gave him.

Minutes later, when Grace straddled his hips and gently, insistently sank onto his cock, she dutifully whispered, "I have a great bottom," and Noah moaned his agreement.

When Noah awoke again, the sun shone bright through the pulled drapes, telling him it was late in the morning. He turned to his side and found the bed empty, only the soft impression of Grace left behind.

He reached over and smoothed his hand across her pillow. He was disappointed but not worried. It was the combined fragrances of coffee and bacon drifting into the room that had awakened him.

Grace was cooking him breakfast.

Filled with satisfaction, with peace, Noah stretched and smiled. Amazingly enough, his body was sore. He could only imagine how Grace felt this morning. She surely had a few . . . *intimate* aches and pains.

He remembered holding her legs high over his shoulders, making her vulnerable to his thrusts and driving into her so deep, he'd felt a part of her. He also remembered the gentle way she'd touched him, and the not-so-gentle way she'd come.

They'd been excessive through the long night.

Noah scratched his belly and looked at the nightstand, where several empty silver packets lay. He groaned, scrubbing a hand over his face, then finally laughed. Jesus, he'd brought half a dozen condoms with him last night—and they'd used every damn one. He'd always been a very sexual man, but he'd never been obsessed before. Around Grace, he couldn't get enough. Six times. He was equally appalled and amused.

Grace, it seemed, was a sexual dynamo. Who'd have ever thought?

Noah made a mental note to pick up a box of rubbers to leave at her apartment. He grinned, thinking of her reaction to that, knowing Grace would get a kick out of storing them in her bedside drawer. She had led such a sedate life, keeping all her pent-up lust quietly contained, that the smallest things made her feel naughty. And when Grace felt naughty, she was adorably accommodating.

Her bed was comfortable, Noah decided as he sat up and swung his legs to the floor. Even better, it smelled of Grace. The pillows, the sheets, all carried her unique, delectable scent. Not perfume, but the natural scent of woman.

Being surrounded by Grace's fragrance probably had as much to do with the sound, peaceful way he'd slept as it did with the overindulgence of tension-draining sex.

It was just as Noah found his boxers and pulled them on that he heard Grace arguing with someone. She sounded . . . upset, a little angry.

Protective, possessive instincts rose in a scalding wave. Without thinking about it, Noah stormed across the room, jerked the door open, and stalked into the living room. He promptly stalled.

Grace said, "Noah!" at the same time his grandmother gasped.

Noah was a little old to be blushing, but damn it, he was naked except for his underwear.

Agatha hadn't yet been seated, so Noah assumed she'd only just arrived. She was fashionably attired in a blue print suit with matching pumps, looking as pulled together, as business oriented, as ever. At the moment, she had one foot tapping impatiently.

Grace wore a long nightshirt, and her silky hair had been pulled back into a haphazard ponytail. She stood next to the sofa, where the ruined uniform lay in a rumpled heap next to a sewing kit. It appeared as though Grace had been reattaching buttons before Agatha's ill-timed arrival.

Grace fretted. Agatha scowled.

Noah decided there was nothing left to do but brazen it out, so he crossed his arms over his naked chest and summoned a firm tone. "Just what the hell is going on here?"

Chapter Twelve

Agatha Harper was not a fainthearted woman. It would take more than Grace's stammering discomfort or her grandson's surly tone to budge her from the spot. She mimicked Noah's aggressive pose and glared.

"I happen to be visiting Grace. Of course, I don't need to ask what *you're* doing here." She flicked her gaze over his sleep-rumpled hair, morning beard shadow, and naked chest, then shook her head in disapproval. It was quite obvious that Noah had just crawled out of Grace's bed. "My God, you've lost all pretense to polite decorum."

Once again, Grace rushed up and stationed herself protectively in front of Noah, making Agatha sigh. The girl was embarrassingly smitten and not even trying to hide it.

This was worse than she'd first assumed. Noah and Grace hadn't indulged in one indiscretion. They hadn't gotten carried away a single time, as she'd hoped.

No, they were quite clearly involved.

They also showed no signs of self-consciousness over the situation. Agatha wondered if either of them even tried to keep the affair private. Gossip would no doubt run rampant. The good Harper name was bound to take a beating.

If she didn't do something, and fast, Grace would end up irreparably hurt by it all, once Noah came to his senses and returned to Kara. When that happened, as it surely would, Agatha could hardly expect Grace to return to work and face Noah on a daily basis. And she definitely wanted Grace to return. With each passing hour, Agatha realized just how much she depended on Grace, and how much she missed her daily involvement.

Grace was a godsend, organized and precise and tactful. She didn't require constant supervision to handle things. She'd learned early on which appointments were important to Agatha and which invites should be politely turned down. The daily juggling of unexpected crisis, the numerous requests for her time or her input were now left up to Agatha, and she already didn't like it.

Since Grace had left, Agatha felt more abandoned than ever, and things were piling up around her. She'd lost her grandson and her right hand in the same week. Intolerable.

"Grace," Agatha said, never taking her gaze from Noah, "why don't you go get a shower and make yourself decent? Noah and I can entertain ourselves a moment."

Noah's hands settled on Grace's shoulders. "Grace is about the most decent woman I know."

Agatha narrowed her eyes at him. "This is difficult enough as it is. There's no reason to deliberately misconstrue my words."

Grace looked very undecided until Noah turned her around and started into the bedroom. To Agatha, he said, "I'll be right back."

It was the sight of Noah leading Grace away that gave Agatha a new idea. Perhaps she'd been looking at this all wrong. There was more than one possible way to get everything she wanted, for herself and for her grandson.

Agatha smiled in thought, her mind whirling with potential outcomes. As Noah gently tugged Grace into the bedroom, Agatha decided that it just might work. Everything was already in place.

All Noah needed was a nudge.

Noah shushed Grace when she started to protest the way he'd dragged her off. "I can handle my grandmother, Grace. You don't need to keep running interference."

Grace stalked behind him as he went to the chair by her bed and picked up his slacks. She watched him dress with grave misgivings. Despite what he said, she was afraid Agatha planned to inflict a few more well-meaning barbs. "Noah . . ."

"It'll be fine." He shrugged on his shirt. "Why'd you leave me this morning?"

Given the fact that his grandmother waited in the other room, Grace was amazed by Noah's change of subject. "I didn't. I was just cooking breakfast." She'd had plans to enjoy a peaceful morning meal with Noah—and then Agatha had shown up.

He sniffed the air and smiled. "Yeah, it smells great."

"The bacon is done. I was going to fix the eggs

and toast after you woke." She fretted again. "I suppose I could put more bacon on for Agatha . . ."

"No need. She won't be here that long." He sat on the side of the bed and reached for his socks. "Do you realize you're always trying to feed someone? First Kara, and now Agatha?"

Heat suffused her cheeks. Perhaps she had her mind on food too often.

Noah must have seen her look of guilt. He cocked a brow. "Is your bottom still sore?"

Grace blinked. "Um, no."

"Then maybe you need another swat."

She couldn't help but grin. She loved playing sex games with Noah, just as she loved his compliments. After last night, she had no doubt that he found every single inch of her desirable, regardless of her extra pounds. "No, sir. I've learned my lesson."

"Good." Now fully dressed, Noah stood and pulled her close. "Grace, you're not repairing that uniform so you can wear it, are you? It looks good on you—too good—but no way in hell is it appropriate for work."

Grace laughed. She could hardly credit that Noah was concerned about such a thing. "Of course I won't wear it." Her voice lowered, and she muttered, "But I didn't want Ben to see the buttons missing and think I'd popped them on my own."

Noah tilted her back in the circle of his arms so he could nuzzle her throat. "Want me to tell him how it happened?"

Grace swatted at him. "Don't you dare. Ben teases enough as it is."

From one moment to the next, Noah turned serious. "Grace, if you want a new uniform, just tell Ben. He doesn't give a damn what size you wear, and you know he'd never tease about something that might embarrass you."

"I know. Your brother is very sweet." But she still had no intention of sharing her size, or her weight, with anyone. Especially not Noah's brother.

Noah rolled his eyes. "I wouldn't go that far."

Grace saw no reason to belabor the point. "Actually, I tried on one of the other uniforms this morning, and it fits. So there's no reason to tell Ben anything."

Noah looked skeptical. "Maybe I should see it on you first. Now don't get riled, Grace, but I'm beginning to think you're clueless as to what's too seductive and what isn't."

Grace hid her smile. Noah was afraid other men might find her attractive. She knew better. After all, she was twenty-five, and men had never made a habit of pursuing her. She'd had male friends and known plenty of kind, likable men, but none of them had tried to rush her to bed.

Still, to her mind, it was a lovely compliment. She patted Noah's chest. "It's fits, Noah. Honest."

"Still . . ."

Grace shook her head at him. She loved him, but she wasn't about to let him start ruling her life. "If you leave your grandmother waiting much longer, she'll wonder what we're doing in here."

"Yeah, but a few lascivious thoughts might make her less rigid."

Laughing, Grace turned Noah and gave him a small shove. "Go. I'll be out in ten minutes."

"Take your time, Grace. I'll send my grandmother on her way so when you finish getting dressed, we can eat. I'll even cook the eggs."

Grace sighed as Noah went through the door and closed it softly behind him. She knew Agatha well enough to realize she wouldn't be budged a single inch until she was good and ready to move. And she was here for a reason, of that Grace was certain.

The moment she'd arrived, she'd informed Grace that she had a sound plan to get Noah and Kara reunited. Though the idea had felt like a fist around her heart, Grace hadn't tried to dissuade her. It wasn't until Agatha declared Noah to be bullheaded and selfish that Grace had disagreed— most vehemently.

Before Grace could get too wound up, Noah had walked in and the hostilities had really started. She hated the new tension that invaded the air whenever the two of them were in the same room together.

Grace decided it might be propitious to hurry through her shower. Left to their own tempers, Agatha and Noah would probably do more harm than good.

"So Agatha, what are you doing here?"

Agatha set her purse aside and smiled. "As I said, I came to visit Grace. I like her."

"Huh. S'that why you fired her? Because you like her so much."

"You're the one to blame for that, Noah."

"How'd you figure that?"

Agatha strolled over to a bookcase and surveyed Grace's eclectic collection of books. She pulled out one on baby names. Noah tried not to stare.

Baby names?

Lifting a brow as if to emphasize her point,

Agatha added, "You put me in a no-win situation. Grace is a friend as well as my personal secretary, but Kara is your fiancée."

"Ex-fiancée. I wish you'd try to remember that."

Agatha gave one condescending nod. "Be that as it may, Kara is still a close friend, and her parents are like family. I had to do something or risk alienating Grace and Kara both. With your actions, you forced me to fire Grace. It was the only solution."

Noah didn't want to accept that he might very well be to blame for Grace's current circumstances. And he was still distracted by that damn book, though he thought he hid it well. "I need a cup of coffee. You want to join me?"

"Thank you." Agatha strode forward. "I recall that Grace makes excellent coffee."

Noah ground his teeth together. As Agatha's secretary, Grace shouldn't have been assigned the duty of coffeemaking. Agatha had a housekeeper to take care of that chore.

He found two mugs in the cabinet over Grace's sink and set them out. Knowing Agatha favored both sugar and cream, he did some more rummaging around the pristine kitchen until everything was on the table.

The more he saw of Grace's apartment, the more he liked it. Her kitchen was small but brightly decorated with yellow-patterned wallpaper and sky blue rag rugs. Her canisters were shaped like smiling cows and her salt and pepper shakers were small pink pigs, one sporting a top hat, the other a Sunday bonnet.

Noah grinned as he helped himself to a slice of crispy bacon. He was ravenous after the long night of debauchery.

Rather than sit at the table with Agatha, Noah leaned against the sink. There was nothing he could tell his grandmother about the breakup, so he didn't address that issue at all, choosing to go straight to the point instead. "As you can see, Grandmother, you came at a bad time. Grace and I have plans."

"To do what?" she asked, her tone cool.

"Nothing that concerns you."

Agatha stiffened, then went through the routine of doctoring her coffee. Finally, she said, "I need to be at the restaurant soon. It seems we have a rebellion on our hands."

Noah gave Agatha a sharp look. Old instincts were hard to break, and he almost asked her to explain. As Grace had said, he had friends at the restaurant, people he cared about. Agatha's interference at this point would only make matters worse.

At the last second, Noah caught himself. It wasn't easy, but he managed a credible shrug of unconcern. "You mean *you* have a rebellion. I'm out of it, remember?"

"You can't tell me you don't care, Noah. I know you better than that."

He shook his head slowly. "No, I don't think you know me at all."

Agatha looked stricken for only a moment; then she rallied. She cloaked herself in belligerence. "I went out of my way to come here and I don't have much time. Surely you can see Grace whenever you like?"

She made it sound like a question, putting Noah on alert. He wondered what she was up to now.

"Not so." No way in hell was he going to leave

Grace alone with his grandmother until he knew what she wanted. "Grace got a new job and she has to work later, so her time today is limited."

Agatha froze. "Where is she working?"

Wondering what his grandmother's reaction would be, Noah sipped his coffee and looked at her over the rim. "She's waiting tables in the bar for Ben."

Agatha dropped her spoon to the tabletop with a clatter. She appeared genuinely horrified. "She's *what?*"

Gratified that his grandmother liked it even less than he did, Noah expounded on Grace's new employment. "She started yesterday, and from what I can tell, she loves it."

"But that's absurd!"

Noah shrugged, adding slyly, "Evidently, compared to her old job, working in a bar is a lot of fun."

Since her old job had been with Agatha, his grandmother looked ready to have a full-fledged fit. Noah hid his grin behind another sip of steaming coffee. He could see why Ben went out of his way to rile her. There was a certain pleasure to be found in making Agatha Harper lose her mask of cold hauteur.

Noah detailed Grace's duties. "She'll be waiting tables, serving food and alcohol. Not just during the day, but late at night, too."

Agatha sputtered, she was so indignant. "That place is . . ."

"Ben has it mostly under control," Noah interrupted before Agatha could go off on a tangent. "He's really turned it around. It was a complete dive when he first bought it, but now it's pretty respectable. Most of the time, anyway."

Noah couldn't let Agatha make slurs against Ben. But he appreciated, even welcomed, this proof that she cared for Grace. He should have already known it; after all, who could be close to Grace and not love her?

Those sentiments echoed in Noah's mind and he promptly choked. *He'd* been closer to Grace than anyone.

Agatha slanted Noah a curious look. "Regardless of Ben's admirable work ethic and all his well-meaning efforts, the hotel bar is still no place for a young woman like Grace."

Noah blinked twice at what clearly was a compliment for his little brother. Wait until he told Ben! He was likely to faint from shock.

Shaking himself, Noah said, "My sentiments exactly. Many of the men at the bar can be crude and pushy. Grace is too open, too caring, and far too naïve to deal with drunks. And every Friday and Saturday night, the bar has a few."

Agatha slapped her hand down onto the table. "Noah Harper, if you truly understand how naïve Grace is, then why in the world are you toying with her?"

Damn. She'd turned that one around on him. Noah took his time stealing another piece of bacon before answering. It gave him time to think, but unfortunately, he had no arguments to offer. "My relationship with Grace is my own business."

"A relationship implies there's more than what meets the eye." Agatha stared at him hard. "Are you telling me you actually care for Grace?"

"I'm telling you," Noah said through his teeth, "to butt out."

Agatha pushed to her feet, outraged at such rudeness.

Noah shoved away from the countertop, tired of her interference.

"Grace needs someone to look out for her. I'm taking on that responsibility."

"I'm not discussing this with you, Agatha." In the past, Noah had made a habit of trying to please his grandmother. That had obviously been a mistake. He'd already made up his mind that if they were to deal well together, it'd have to be on his terms for a change.

"I'd like to make you an offer."

Noah froze. His stomach tightened and his thoughts narrowed. "What kind of offer?"

"Despite your contrary determination to deny it, I know you love Harper's Bistro, and I know that I need you there. I'll accept that. I'll also accept that things are over between you and Kara."

Noah didn't so much as blink an eye.

Agatha drew a deep breath. "I'll gladly reinstate you into the family, and I'll hire Grace back."

Noah forced the words past his apprehension. "Yeah? So what's the catch?"

Agatha locked her gaze with his. "I want you to marry Grace."

Shock, followed by disappointment, slammed into Noah with blinding force. *"Goddammit."* He plunked his mug down on the counter so hard the handle broke off. He turned his back to Agatha, trying but failing to get a grip on his temper. "I fucking knew it."

"You watch your mouth, young man!"

His hands curled into fists. A red mist swam in front of his eyes, mostly because he'd been duped. He'd stupidly hoped she was sincere.

Noah's jaw ached and his words were hard and

clipped. "You just can't trust my decisions, can you?"

She waved that away. "Think about it. This will stop the gossip against Kara and it'll spare Grace's reputation. Sleeping around is one thing, but if you marry Grace, everyone will think it's romantic, that you were both swept away on love."

"And to hell with what I want?"

Agatha raised her voice in annoyance. "Well, given your intimate relationship, I assumed you wanted Grace."

He laughed at her audacity. "No."

She fell silent for a long moment. "What does that mean?"

Anger, not honesty, forged his reply. Noah braced his hands on the sink and concentrated on not shouting. "I said *no*. No I don't want your deal, and no I won't marry Grace. If I ever get engaged again, it'll be to a woman I choose, not one you line up for me."

"You won't even consider it?"

His voice rose with his irritation. Lately he'd done nothing but consider his relationship with Grace—and he still had no set answers. He shook his head, denying his grandmother, denying his own confusion. "Hell no."

"Then you should leave her alone!"

"That," Noah growled, "isn't your decision to make." No way would he walk away from Grace now. Hell, he doubted he could.

A very small voice intruded on his thoughts. "I agree."

Noah swung around. Grace stood in the kitchen doorway, her face pale, her eyes watchful. *Wounded.* She wore a long loose sundress of soft green that made her skin look creamy and emphasized her big dark eyes. Her feet were bare, her arms crossed protectively over her middle. Her long hair, still damp, had been neatly braided and hung over her shoulder to rest against her breast.

Noah took a step toward her. "Grace . . ."

She turned to his grandmother. "Agatha, I'd like you to leave now."

Agatha worried her thin hands together. "How long have you been eavesdropping, young lady?"

Grace gave a sad smile. "I heard the raised voices. I hurried to dress because I thought . . ." Her words fell into silence, then she shook her head. "Never mind."

But Noah knew what Grace had been about to say. She'd thought she might need to protect him again.

Instead, she was the one who needed protecting.

Noah wanted to curse, to punch the wall. He wanted to lift Grace up in his arms and hold her. But she didn't so much as glance at him, and the sudden emotional distance was unbearable.

"Please, Agatha." Grace kept her head high, her voice gentle. "I think you should go."

"Yes." Agatha glanced at Noah. She appeared as concerned, as apologetic as he felt. Neither of them had meant to hurt Grace. She'd been an innocent bystander in their verbal battle for control. "Yes, I need to be going. There are issues to be resolved at the restaurant."

She embraced Grace, even kissed her cheek. Grace held herself away, distant in a way Noah had seldom observed.

Agatha pretended nothing had happened.

"Please, if you find time, Grace, I'd love for you to visit."

At any other time, Noah might have been amazed at his grandmother's effrontery. She'd fired Grace and now invited her over for a friendly visit.

But at the moment he was too concerned with Grace's feelings to notice anything else. She escorted Agatha back through the living room. Noah stood in the kitchen doorway, watching in silence.

Agatha paused. "Grace, I didn't mean . . ."

"I know." Grace pulled the door open and waited.

With nothing more to say, Agatha left. Her step wasn't as spry as usual, and Noah spared a moment's worry for his cantankerous grandmother.

When Grace started back into the kitchen, Noah refused to move. He felt volatile with a mixture of guilt and determination.

Grace cleared her throat. "I'll start the eggs."

"I said I'd cook them."

She stared past his right shoulder. "Okay. I can do the toast."

Her agreeable tone rankled. Noah unfolded his arms and tried to loosen his knotted muscles. "This isn't going to work, Gracie."

"What won't work?" Now her normally direct gaze was on his throat. She obviously didn't want to look at him, but he wasn't going to stand for that.

Noah shook his head and pinched her chin. "You're pissed off at me, but you're trying to hide it."

Startled, she jerked her attention to his face.

"Of course I'm not mad. Why would you think that?"

"You won't look at me."

"I'm looking at you now."

"Sort of," he agreed. "But not like you usually look at me."

She edged past him into the kitchen. Her breasts brushed his chest, her belly brushed his hip. "I'm embarrassed, if you want the truth."

"I always want you to be truthful with me, Grace. You know that."

She went to the refrigerator and pulled out a carton of eggs and the butter. "All right." She looked expectantly at him. "Do you really want to cook, or do you want me to?"

Impatience nearly choked him. "I'll do the damn eggs." He strode to the stove and flipped on the burner switch to heat the pan. "Tell me what you're embarrassed about."

Her brow puckered with a small frown. "Your grandmother is trying to force you to do things with me that you don't want to do."

Noah put a pat of butter in the hot skillet and expertly cracked four eggs. "After last night, I'd think you'd realize there isn't much I don't want to do with you."

Grace dropped bread into the toaster, then watched it, as if making toast required her rapt attention. "Sexually, yes. That was our agreement."

Noah pointed the spatula at her. "I'll tell you what, Grace. I'm getting damned sick and tired of you throwing that stupid agreement into my face."

Like a small volcano erupting, Grace lost her temper. She whirled toward him, a butter knife clutched in her hand. "It was *your* agreement!" She poked the knife toward him for emphasis. "*You*"—

poke, poke—"came up with it and all *I* did"—she pointed the knife at herself—"was agree."

"Damn it, be careful before you stab yourself." Noah put down the spatula and wrestled the knife away from Grace. She started to turn away, but he caught her upper arm. "You know good and well what I'm saying here, Grace."

She yanked free of his hold, then went on tiptoe, her eyes blazing with dark fury. "You were very clear, thank you."

"Shit." He caught both her arms this time. "I'm not talking about my conversation with Agatha."

Grace scowled. "No? You're talking about our agreement, then?"

"Quit calling what we have an agreement." That damn word felt like a curse on his tongue.

"What would you call it?"

"Why do we have to call it anything?" he asked, for lack of a better answer. "Why not just enjoy ourselves?"

"I *am* enjoying myself." She sounded angry.

Noah rubbed her arms, trying to calm her. "Right. Sex and only sex."

Her chin lifted high. "That's what you said you wanted."

He laughed. Grace was rather cute in her pugnacious, antagonistic mood. "Lately, I've been a fool in more ways than one."

"Oh, no." She shook her head furiously. "You are not a fool. And in this case, you were right. Anything more than sex between us would be ridiculous."

It was Noah's turn to go quiet with anger. Here he was, struggling to figure out his relationship with Grace, and she flatly denied any relationship.

He curled his mouth without humor. "If we're

going to be accurate, I believe I said I wanted hot, wet, grinding sex and a woman who'd give it to me any way I asked."

Grace's eyes warmed, and some of her belligerence melted away, replaced by that awesome awareness that never failed to steal his breath. "Yeah, so?" Her glare lingered. "I remember."

Noah lowered his voice, rubbed her naked shoulders. "And still you said yes."

A pulse in her throat thrummed. "I've held to my end of the bargain."

Noah suddenly smelled the eggs and released her to take them from the pan. He put two in each plate and turned off the stove. "Breakfast will wait."

She took a step back. "What are you going to do?"

"Anything I want Grace, right?" Slowly, with precise movements, he pulled his shirt off over his head. "You're so fond of reminding me that we have an agreement. You want to stick to the letter of that agreement. Great. Who am I to complain?"

She eyed his naked chest and started breathing a little harder. "Noah, I . . ."

"Take off your dress, Grace."

She backed up against the refrigerator and stood there frozen. For the moment, he ignored her and went about clearing the table.

"Noah?"

He flattened a hand on the tabletop and tested the sturdiness. "I think this'll support us, don't you?"

She stared at the table, wide-eyed and apprehensive. "We . . . we were going to have breakfast." Noah could hear her breathing, fast and low.

Slanting her a look, he said, "I'd rather eat you than eggs anytime."

Her lips parted. She folded her hands over her belly, holding herself. "But . . ."

"You're not finishing your sentences, Grace." She looked confused, uncertain, and turned on. Already her nipples were puckered, pressing against the soft material of her dress. Her toes curled against the linoleum floor and her mouth quivered.

Noah wasn't sure what he wanted to prove, but determination to prove it rode him hard. "Hey, that's okay. I'd rather you get naked than talk anyway."

She looked around the kitchen—at the cooked eggs, the cleared table, then back at him. "You're angry."

"Nope." Noah opened the fastenings to his slacks and pulled down the zipper to ease the restriction against his erection. "I'm aroused. There's a fine difference there." He sat down and pulled off his shoes and socks.

Grace licked her lips while staring at his naked abdomen where the slacks parted. "We don't have any protection here."

"We'll work around that problem. Trust me, Grace, there are ways, things you haven't even imagined yet." She looked blank, nervous. Noah leaned back in his chair, stretched out his legs, and nodded at her. "Out of the dress, Grace."

Noah could tell she wanted to, but her modesty held her back. It was the morning, bright sunlight pouring in every window. They were in the kitchen.

He didn't repeat himself, just waited and watched her.

Very slowly, Grace caught the hem of the long dress and inched it up. Past her calves, her knees, her thighs.

Her face flushed, her breath came too fast.

Noah caught a glimpse of white panties, her belly, then her naked breasts drew his attention as she pulled the dress up and over her head. She held it in front of herself and looked at him.

"Drop it."

Biting her lips, Grace held the dress to the side and let it fall to the floor.

"Take off your panties." His voice was gruff, commanding. Noah felt wired, on the explosive edge. The night of excess might not have happened, he was so hard again. Always, Grace affected him this way. He wondered if ten years from now, he'd still go wild at the thought of having her.

He wondered if he'd even know her in ten years.

"I'm waiting, Grace."

She bent at the waist and started to push down her underwear. Noah said, "No, wait." His blood rushed through his veins, hot and thick. "Turn around first."

Her face flamed. "Noah . . ."

Again, he merely waited. Grace frowned, blushed prettily, and turned. For half a minute she didn't move, then in a rush she bent and shoved the underwear down so she could step out of it.

Noah groaned, seeing her delicate pink vulva, her soft white ass. She immediately straightened, and Noah reached out to catch her hand. "Come here, Grace."

Like a zombie, she allowed him to lead her. Noah pulled her between his thighs. He cupped her heavy breasts and stroked them, thumbed her erect nipples. "Lean down here," he said, and when she did so, he caught her left nipple in his mouth, sucking strongly.

Grace moaned and braced her hands on his shoulders.

Her breasts were so big and soft, he couldn't get enough of them. Grace hugged him to her, her heartbeat fluttering wildly.

"Up onto the table, Grace." He didn't wait for her to comply. He hefted her up onto the edge of the tabletop so that she sat facing him while he remained in the chair. "Open your legs wide. Here, brace yourself with your hands behind you and put your feet next to my shoulders, on the back of the chair."

He positioned her just as he wanted her, her thighs alongside his shoulders, leaving her open to him. His heart rapped hard as he gently eased her knees farther apart, which forced Grace to lean back on her elbows for better balance. He literally sat between her widespread thighs. She was a feast, laid out for him and his voracious appetite.

"I want you to watch me, Grace," he told her when he noticed she stared up at the ceiling. "Keep those big eyes of yours on my face. Or," he added as he brushed his fingers through her curls, "on my hands where I touch you."

Nodding, she whispered, "Okay."

Noah smiled. He used the fingertips of both hands to carefully part her outer lips. "Look at how pink you are, Grace." He felt her slight flinch and glanced at her face with concern. "Are you sore?"

She spoke on a nearly silent breath of sound. "No."

As Noah moved his fingers carefully over her,

pulling her farther open, examining her up close, her whole body shuddered.

"Then this doesn't hurt?" He worked his first and middle fingers deep into her.

She gasped and her head tipped back.

"Look, Grace."

Her throat moved as she swallowed, but she brought her attention back to his hands.

He continued to stroke, long and easy and deep. The sight of his dark, rough fingers pushing into her was erotic. "You look so tender, I don't want to hurt you."

"You're . . . you're not hurting me," Grace rasped.

Noah watched her clitoris swell, but he didn't touch her there, not yet. She was already wet, her whole body flushed, her thighs shivering. This close, she smelled like the soap and lotion she'd used after her bath.

She also smelled of womanly excitement.

Noah took her by surprise, saying, "Which feels better, Grace? My fingers—or my tongue?"

And he bent to lick her.

"Oh, God."

Her hips lifted off the table in response. Noah traced each slick, soft fold, licking, tasting, then he curled his tongue around her clitoris and tugged.

Grace gave a shuddering, husky moan and her hips twisted. Her arms gave out and she sprawled flat on the table while her feet pressed so hard against Noah's chair that she nearly turned him over.

Noah brought his hands up to her breasts to anchor himself and play with her nipples. The dual assault had her quickly beside herself, and Noah decided to bring her to an orgasm. Grace was so responsive, it never took long. Within minutes, she was crying out with her release.

She was still moving, her chest heaving, when Noah jerked to his feet and shoved his slacks down. He cursed the lack of a rubber but promised Grace, "I'll be careful," and he leaned forward to slide his cock along her mound, between her lips, without entering her.

She was so wet the glide was easy, maddeningly hot. Grace continued to lift and thrust against him, taking the small aftershocks of her climax. The direct contact against her still pulsing tissues had them both groaning.

Noah hooked his arms under her thighs, took her supple breasts in his hands and thrust against her, faster and faster, and then with a stifled roar, he came on her belly.

His legs shook and he slumped back into his chair. Grace lay there, stunned, staring at the ceiling. After she caught her breath, she muttered, "Wow."

Noah laughed, but the sound was weak and shaky.

Grace leaned up and looked down the length of her body to her belly. She wore an expression of wonder, surprise, as she saw what he'd done. With a touch of awe, she said, "Huh."

Smiling, feeling good from the inside out, Noah absently patted her soft thigh. "I think I could eat those eggs now, Grace. What about you?"

Grace plunked back on the table with a snicker.

Because it was the manly thing to do, Noah struggled to his feet and pulled several paper towels off the roll. He ran water in the sink. "Be still, Grace, and I'll clean you up."

She mumbled some incoherent reply. When he

turned back to her, Noah saw that her eyes were now closed and her legs dangled limply off the side of the table. He stroked the cool towels over her skin.

"If I served you at the restaurant," he murmured, "we'd all be billionaires."

Grace covered her face with her hands, but he could still hear her giggles.

Noah tossed the towels away, caught Grace under the arms, and hauled her up to face him. "One thing, Gracie."

She blinked big, still vague eyes open. "Yes?"

Her hair had come partly free from the braid and stuck out in wild disarray. Noah tucked several long, loose strands behind her ears. "You've never had sex, so you can't know. But what you and I have . . ." He struggled for the right words, trying to find a way to make her understand when he didn't really understand himself. "It's different."

A dose of caution crept into her expression. "How?"

Noah shook his head, mentally fumbling. "It's . . . better, more. Deeper."

Grace trailed one finger over his chest. "Definitely deep."

He wanted to groan again. "Forget what I said to my grandmother, okay? She has nothing to do with us."

Her smile was shy, sweetly accepting. Unconvinced. "All right."

Noah frowned at her. Any other woman he knew would have demanded an explanation, but not Grace. She adhered to that damn emotional distance he'd first asked for, and she'd so readily agreed to.

Now he wanted more, but how much more? Until he figured that out, he knew he couldn't push her. But at least the hurt was gone from her eyes, Noah thought as he handed her sundress back to her. He'd have to be satisfied with that much—for now.

Chapter Thirteen

Ben surveyed the crowd in the diner and wanted to laugh. Grace had been working for a week, and Noah had been there almost every night that Grace had. He watched over her like a guard dog and growled at any customer who gave her a second look.

He did a lot of growling.

With Noah's attention, Grace had bloomed into a self-confident beauty. Without realizing it, she exuded raw, earthy appeal, leading Ben to believe she and his brother were really burning up the sheets. Ben grinned. Not only did Grace look more sexually aware these days, but Noah was about as content as he could be.

Except for when other men came on to Grace. And they did, repeatedly. Most of Ben's regulars had already been on the receiving end of Noah's possessive stares, and they'd backed off to a tone of excessive politeness. But the others had no clue that Grace had been most thoroughly claimed. She smiled at men, and they melted. They also teased and flirted and made subtle suggestions that Grace either ignored or didn't catch.

Ben found it all hilarious. Rather than retreat to his rooms after a long workday, he found himself hanging out in the diner to watch the nightly drama unfolding.

It was on the downhill slide to midnight now, less than an hour till he closed. Yet the place had plenty of people hanging around. Most of those customers were directly linked to Grace somehow.

She brought in business.

So when Noah had requested that Ben not work Grace nights or weekends, he'd been all too happy to comply. Unfortunately, the schedule for the current week had already been set by the time Noah reached him, and Grace wouldn't hear of changing it. In the future, she'd work a few nights only during the week. Ben had no problem with that.

He'd also given Grace the coming weekend off so she and Noah could take a jaunt to Florida. Again, Grace had argued, seeing the free weekend as favoritism. Ben had convinced her by using her tenderhearted nature, and her feelings for Noah, against her.

Grace wanted to go, and Ben had convinced her that Noah needed her. Noah would have strung him up by his thumbs if he knew, but Ben considered it nothing less than the truth. His brother did need Grace, whether he realized it or not. Around her, he was a different man. Noah had always been attentive to Kara, but with Grace he was keenly aware of everything she did.

That told Ben all he needed to know.

Noah sauntered up to him. "I know why I'm

here," he said, gazing around at the mostly male clientele. "Why are you here?"

"Entertainment. If I went to my rooms, I'd just do paperwork or watch a movie. Here, I get to watch you watch Grace while everyone else watches her, too."

Noah made a sound of disgust but didn't refute that. He crossed his arms over his chest and leaned back against the bar.

Grace rushed past them to a table, seemed to remember something halfway there, and turned around to rush back. Her spectacular breasts led the way and did a lot of bouncing as she jogged by—which every guy in the place apparently noticed. Before Noah could get riled, Grace bounced past again.

"She does that a lot," Ben noted.

"Probably trying to catch her balance."

The two brothers looked at each other, then burst out laughing. Ben said, "She *is* top heavy."

"And that goddamned uniform you gave her shows it off."

Ben shrugged. "She has an asset that's hard to hide. I don't think it'd matter what she wore."

Noah groaned and ran a hand over his face. "Yeah, I know."

Three men came in. They wore ragged jeans, tight T-shirts, and work boots. And they sat at one of Grace's tables.

Noah was up and off his bar stool in a heartbeat. Ben silently wondered if he should be paying Noah a bouncer's salary, considering how much time he spent making certain Grace's work environment stayed pleasant. Noah didn't say anything to the men, but he did stop Grace, tip up her chin, and give her a lingering kiss right in the middle of the floor. Grace got so flustered, she nearly dropped her tray.

Noah released her, gave the men a long look, and positioned himself at an empty table—facing them.

Ben had to turn away so no one would see him laughing. If he ever got that smitten with a woman, he hoped someone would shoot him to put him out of his misery. Not that Noah seemed to be suffering. Just the opposite. But Ben knew he liked variety far too much to ever get so infatuated with a single woman. At twenty-nine, he had a lot of play left in him.

They'd long since quit serving anything besides drinks, and Ben looked around the diner, making sure everything was in order. Horace, who'd been with the diner since before Ben's time, would close up for him tonight. He was ready to call it quits and head to his rooms when another small crowd entered, catching his attention.

Ben turned—and knew there'd be trouble.

Grace was close at hand, standing at the bar to turn in a new drink order. Ben stepped up to her side. "Aren't those the guys who work at Agatha's restaurant?"

Grace turned, and a huge smile broke out on her face. "It's Andrew and Enrique and Benton."

Ben knew two of them from brief introductions. Andrew was the maître d', and Benton was the head chef.

The other man Ben knew by reputation. Enrique the bull. He shook his head.

It looked like he wouldn't be turning in after all.

* * *

Grace watched as the newcomers scanned the bar, located Noah seated at his corner table, and started toward him. She was very pleased that they'd sought him out.

Noah, however, didn't look the least bit happy about it.

They were still standing awkwardly next to Noah's table when Grace approached a minute later. Ignoring Noah's dark frown, she said, "Why don't you grab some chairs? There's plenty of room."

At the sound of her voice, Andrew turned—and did a double take. "Grace? What are you doing here?"

Feeling very pleased with herself, Grace gave a small curtsy. "I work here now."

Benton pulled out a chair, checked the seat as if he expected to find it dirty, then gracefully lowered himself. "That's right," he said. "Noah told us you got fired, too, after you hired that cretin to cook."

Grace flushed. "Hiring him wasn't my decision, it was Ms. Harper's, and that's not why I got fired."

Andrew pulled a chair around and straddled it. "Yeah? Why did you get canned?"

Grace cast a guilty glance at Noah, which she was afraid everyone noticed. Though Noah didn't seem to be doing much to keep their relationship private, she still felt hesitant to broadcast it.

Enrique walked from one side of her to the other. His ebony gaze moved over her in an insultingly intimate way. Before Grace could react, Noah was on his feet beside her.

"What do you want, Deltorro?"

Enrique shrugged and gestured toward the other two men. "I am part of the mutiny." He tipped his head and smiled at Grace. She saw that his inky dark hair was caught in a ponytail, and a fat diamond glinted in his ear.

Something about his black eyes disconcerted her. She wanted to ease her hand into Noah's, but she knew that would give too much away. It hadn't been that long since Noah had broken things off with Kara, and she knew speculation would be ripe.

Noah encompassed them all in a look. "I already told you, if you have a problem, take it to Agatha."

"That's pointless," Benton said on a righteous sniff. "She has no understanding of the finer nuances of running the restaurant."

"Not my problem," Noah stated.

Enrique looked disgusted. "Kara said you would be this way."

Noah's eyes turned ice blue and he smiled. "Kara was right."

"She hangs out in the dining room every night, Noah." Andrew shook his head. "I don't understand what the hell is going on."

Grace grabbed for another chair. "Here you go, Mr. Deltorro. Why don't you all get comfortable and I'll get you something to drink?"

Noah took the chair from Grace before she could position it under the table. "He's not staying, Grace."

She scowled at him. Under her breath, she said, "What is the matter with you? You're being entirely rude."

Noah smiled at her, then flicked the end of her nose. It always seemed to amuse him when she lost her temper. "I have my reasons, Grace."

And those reasons, she thought, were evidently

none of her business, because he didn't explain. Grace huffed. "Well, you're causing a scene."

Noah looked around and saw it was true. The ten remaining people in the diner were watching him with avid curiosity. "Isn't it about time to close up, anyway?"

Grace glanced at her watch. "Sorry. We have half an hour."

"Damn."

Andrew reached out to slug Noah on the arm. "C'mon, man. At least hear us out. Hell, if something doesn't happen soon, I'll have to quit. Michael already did quit and Dean's looking for a new job."

Benton nodded. "I as well."

Grace turned to Noah, horrified. At this rate, Agatha would lose Harper's Bistro in no time, and it had been in the family too long for that. "Noah?"

Groaning, Noah dropped back into his seat. "All right, I'll listen. But I don't know what you think I can do. I don't work there anymore." And with a stabbing look at Grace, he added, "I wish someone would remember that."

Hiding her relief, Grace took drink orders of beer and wine and scotch. Enrique shook his head, refusing a drink, while continuing to watch her with his penetrating, enigmatic gaze.

Ben waited for Grace at the bar. "What's going on?"

"I don't know." She handed in her order and turned to Ben. "Something's wrong at the restaurant and they want Noah's help."

He frowned in thought. "Agatha is sinking fast. I'm surprised. I really thought she'd hold it together longer than that."

"It's a different place now from when she started it all. The atmosphere reflects Noah and his values. He made those changes, those improvements, little by little, but Agatha isn't as subtle. She's probably trying to handle things as she always did, by bulldozing forward and making demands, and that won't work anymore."

Ben gave her a crooked grin. "All that, huh?"

Blushing, Grace shrugged. "I didn't mean to psychoanalyze. It's just that the two of them approach things very differently."

"It hasn't even been two weeks since Noah walked out."

"He oversaw everything. Without that constant supervision, things will fall apart." Reluctantly, Grace admitted, "I feel sorry for your grandmother."

Ben snorted at that. "She makes her own problems."

"Not on purpose. All her life she's been guided by pride. It's all she knows. Personally, I think it's up to you and Noah to show her another way."

Ben looked stunned by the accusation in her tone.

Grace collected the drinks and walked away while Ben was still sputtering. She didn't want to wait for him to find a rebuttal to her assessment. It'd be good for him to think about the situation for a while.

As she got near the table, Grace heard Noah say, "I think you should all write your grievances down and take them to Agatha. When she sees that there are more than a few small problems, she'll have to pay attention."

"I tried that." Andrew accepted his scotch and took a healthy drink. "Thanks, Grace."

Benton sipped at his wine. "It did us no good at all." He cast a glance at Noah. "She gave us the impression you might be returning to work soon."

Enrique lounged back in his seat, looking insolent and bored. The collar of his black silk shirt was opened so low, Grace could see a generous amount of curling black chest hair and three silver chains. "Your grandmother thinks that soon, *everything* will be as it was."

Noah ignored him, but Andrew said, "Knock it off, Deltorro."

Enrique shrugged. "Is it so?"

It was clear Enrique asked about more than the situation at the restaurant. Though Noah had said time and again that it was over with Kara, Grace held her breath.

Noah said only, "My grandmother is hopeful."

Grace turned to walk away—but not before she saw Enrique's hands curl into fists. She had a strong suspicion now about Kara's lover, and her heart ached for the other woman. True enough, her parents would not be happy. But then, how could Kara herself be happy?

Enrique was a womanizer of the first order. He wouldn't be an easy man to love.

Grace waved to Ben as she darted into the back room. She needed a break to think, and now was as good a time as any. The customers were thinning out by the minute and Noah was well occupied.

Grace dropped change into the pop machine and then plopped down at the round table. She propped her feet up on the chair across from her.

She'd just taken a long cold drink when Enrique pushed the door open and stepped in. He found Grace and slowly smiled.

"Enrique! This room is for employees only." A thought occurred to Grace, and she asked, "Were you looking for the boys' room?"

His bold gaze never left her as he shrugged and stepped farther inside. "So I said to the others. But I wanted to see you."

Grace dropped her feet back to the floor and straightened. "Why?"

"Necesito sentir tu piel contra la mia."

Grace scowled. Her high school Spanish was rusty, but she got the gist of it. *I need to feel your skin against mine.* She shook her fist at him. "I'll give you something to feel."

His dark brows rose and he looked delighted. "You speak Spanish?"

"Not well enough to converse, so perhaps you should . . ."

He moved closer, around the table, so that he stood at her side. Grace quickly stood. She didn't like having him loom over her.

He touched her cheek and murmured, *"Si tu fueras un postre, saborearia cada bocado, especialmente la crema azotada."*

Grace slapped his hand away. "How dare you! I am not a dessert and there's no whipped cream on me anywhere."

He looked sly, and his gaze dipped over her body. "Ah, but I think you are very creamy, *si?*"

Perhaps Noah was right, Grace thought with a hint of panic. She had no idea how to deal with a really pushy man. She was so embarrassed, she wanted to sink into the floor. And she was so outraged, she considered hitting Deltorro over the head with a chair.

He reached for Grace and she backed up, then tripped and sprawled into her chair. Grace was thinking she was lucky she hadn't hit the floor, until Enrique caged her in with his arms.

He leaned down very close to whisper, *"Tu tienes un cuerpo de un Diosa."*

Grace had had enough. She shoved against him hard. "You ass. Goddess's are not fat!"

Noah spoke from the doorway. "I warned you about saying things like that, Grace."

Grace's mouth fell open while Enrique moved back and away from her.

Noah's pose was casual, his words negligent. To someone who didn't know him well, he might not even look dangerous. But Grace did know him, and she saw right away that his crossed arms were tight with restraint and bulging muscles. His feet were braced as if he might lunge at any minute.

And his eyes blazed like hot blue flames.

"Noah," Grace squeaked as she scurried around the table and put herself between the two men. "Whatever you're thinking of doing, you can just stop thinking it."

He flicked a glance at her face and smiled. There was nothing amusing in that particular curl of his lips. "Not this time, baby."

Panic skittered down her spine. "Damn you, Noah. I will not have you causing a ruckus where I work."

Ben edged in around Noah. "Hey Grace. I own the place, and personally, I'm looking forward to watching Noah take him apart."

"Ben!"

He smiled and started to tug her out of the line of hostility.

Grace reacted before either brother could stop her. She threw herself against Noah and locked her arms around his neck. "This is not going to happen."

Noah tried to pry her loose, but short of hurting her, he couldn't. And she knew he wouldn't hurt her. "Turn loose, Grace."

"No." She pressed her face into his throat.

"I'll just hit him once or twice," Noah soothed, trying to convince her.

She tightened her arms around him. "No and no! You're not hitting anyone, so forget it."

Noah gave up with a growling sigh. With Grace hanging down his chest like a chunky necklace, he stalked toward Enrique. With each stomping step he took, Grace got jostled.

But she didn't let go.

Noah kept one hand on Grace's back, protecting her, even cuddling her. With the other he grabbed Enrique by the collar. Judging by the flex of chest muscles under her cheek, Grace knew he'd lifted Enrique right off the floor.

She heard the solid thump of a body hitting the wall.

"I'll say this just once, Deltorro." Noah's words were low, gritty, and so mean, even Grace flinched. "Touch her again, fucking *look* at her again, and I'll kill you."

Grace cringed. Good grief, that was rather blunt and to the point.

Their relationship was out of the bag now.

Surprisingly, Enrique didn't turn tail and run. "You did not fight for Kara," he spat.

"No, I didn't, did I?" There was another thump as Noah bounced the older man up against the wall again. "But don't think this time will be the same. You wanted Kara and now you have her. Be satisfied with that, because if you come near Grace again, I'll take you apart."

Grace could feel the rippling anger in Noah, the heat of rage pulsing off him, and she held on, uncertain what else to do.

Enrique, pulling the tiger's tail, growled, "And if I'm not satisfied?"

Grace wanted to groan. She pushed back from Noah, ready to give Enrique a piece of her mind.

A feminine gasp intruded on the room of pulsing testosterone.

"Enrique?"

Noah turned, which meant Grace and Enrique turned as well, being that he held one and the other held him. Ben pushed to his feet. A collective breath was held as Kara stepped through the kitchen and into the break room.

She stared at Enrique and big tears welled in her blue eyes, her bottom lip quivering.

Noah released Enrique with a shove and closed both arms about Grace. His hands rubbed her back distractedly. She felt him press a kiss to a temple, but all her attention was on Kara.

Her heart wrenched in sympathy at what Kara had just overheard.

Enrique looked at Kara as if she'd materialized from the air. *"Mi amor . . ."*

For a moment Kara looked ready to crumble to the floor. She was pale, her expression strained, tired, confused. And then she thrust up her chin. "You . . . you bastard!"

With her head high and her shoulders straight, she turned and strode back through the kitchen.

Ben looked at Enrique in disgust.

Noah just scowled at him.

But Grace pushed loose of Noah's hold. "You big jerk!" She didn't think about it, she just drew back and popped Enrique right in the nose.

He howled.

Noah stared at her and said in surprise, *"Grace,"* while Ben fell into the wall, laughing.

Shaking her bruised hand, Grace retorted, "You can damn well hit him, too, if you want. He deserves it."

Enrique held his bleeding nose and started out of the room, ignoring everyone as he shouted, "Kara!"

Ben cocked a brow. "Thank God she had enough sense to come in through the kitchen, otherwise this floor show might rival Enrique's performance at the restaurant."

Grace rounded on Ben, furious at his apparent insensitivity.

He held up both hands. "Don't hit me, slugger."

Grace thought about hitting him anyway, but her hand hurt too much.

Ben laughed. "Hell, I feel like I'm watching a soap opera, with all these twists and turns. Am I the only one not sleeping around on the sly?"

Noah gave him a shove and attempted to pull Grace close again. "Let me see your hand. Did you hurt yourself?"

Grace pulled back. "Noah, you should go check on her."

He shook his head. "Hell no."

"She's your friend."

"It's a private matter, Grace, between her and Deltorro."

Grace scowled at him. "But he hurt her."

Noah took her hand again, examining her

knuckles. "Kara's a big girl and she chose him. As long as he has enough sense to stay away from you, they can work it out on their own."

Grace slapped his hands away and stalked out. Noah started after her. "Damn it, Grace."

Her hips swayed righteously, but she didn't slow down.

Ben grinned and followed them both. "I'll admit I'm curious how this will play out."

Grace heard them both stomping after her. They found Enrique in the kitchen, boxing Kara into a corner. He held a dish towel to his nose while rambling in mixed Spanish and English.

Kara kept half-heartedly attempting to push him away. "Forget it, Enrique." She sniffed delicately. "I should have known better than to ever trust *the bull.*"

"I did not choose the nickname!"

"No," Kara said, sounding defeated, "but you chose to live up to it."

Enrique shook his head. His normally melodic voice was nasal, given the way he pinched his nose with the towel. "You are the one ashamed of our love. *You* are the one who said I should continue to flirt, so no one would suspect."

Kara's stricken expression darkened with guilt. "I never told you to flirt with her!" She pointed over his shoulder at Grace.

Grace, feeling sheepish, rushed to explain. "He was just trying to rile Noah because he's mad that Noah didn't fight for you."

"*Sí, sí!*"

Kara looked skeptical, but then, so did Noah and Ben.

"I'm supposed to believe that after what I just

heard? I'm not that big a fool, Enrique." More tears welled in her eyes. "You said you weren't satisfied with me."

"No, no," Enrique muttered. *"Tu eres el aire que respiro."*

Grace could tell Kara didn't understand and leaned in to translate. " 'You are the air that I breathe.' "

Kara smacked at him, and he let her. "Why is it," she demanded, "you only speak Spanish when you're trying to seduce me?"

He waved a hand, gesturing to his head. "Thinking English is impossible when I want you. And I always want you."

Her expression softened, her chest expanded. "Now?"

"Sí." Enrique cupped Kara's cheek with his free hand; it was shaking. *"Necestio probarle."*

Kara, frowning suspiciously, looked at Grace. Grace smiled and said, " 'I need to taste you.' "

Ben nudged Noah. "I never thought I'd hear Grace talking dirty to another woman. It's sort of a turn-on, huh?"

Glaring, Noah smacked Ben in the side of the head.

Enrique edged closer to Kara. He didn't kiss her—after all, his nose was bloody—but he did cuddle her. Close to her ear, he said, *"Yo estube solamente medio vivo hasta el momento en que te conosi."*

Grace spoke sotto voce. " 'I was only half alive until I met you.' " Her own heart fluttered. *How romantic.*

Predictably, Kara melted. "Oh, Enrique."

"Yo te amo." His expression of love was plain to one and all, so Grace didn't translate *I love you.*

Enrique pulled Kara into his chest and began mumbling soft Spanish apologies mixed with more words of deep affection.

Contented, Grace went to the sink, got a clean dish towel, and reached over Enrique's shoulder to exchange with him.

He spared her a glance. His black eyes were solemn. *"Gracias."*

She turned to Noah with a huge smile and her own sheen of tears. "Isn't love grand?"

Ben looked at the ceiling and whistled.

Smiling, Noah hauled her close. "I thought your right hook was grand." As he led her out of the kitchen, he added, "I can't believe you wouldn't let me hit him, but you sure as hell didn't hold back."

Grace blushed, especially when she heard Ben laughing again behind her. "I lost my temper." She shook her hand, looking for a tad of sympathy. "And it hurt, so you can believe I won't do it again."

Noah lifted her hand and kissed her fingers. "If Ben is ready to call it a night, I'll take you home and . . . make you feel all better."

Ben gestured magnanimously. "Yeah, go on, Grace. It's time to close up anyway."

"Are you sure?" Normally Grace would have stayed till the very last minute. But it had been an eventful night, and they were leaving for Florida in the morning. She was so excited, she could hardly contain herself.

Ben bent and kissed her forehead. "I'm positive. But don't forget to pick up your tips."

While Grace collected money from the empty tables, Noah said his final good-byes to Andrew and Benton. A few minutes later, Enrique came out. He was no longer holding his nose, but it was swollen and red.

Andrew gave Enrique an incredulous look. "Is the john through an obstacle course?"

Enrique ignored him.

There was no sign of Kara. Grace assumed they were still keeping their involvement secret. She shook her head, and now her sympathy was for Enrique as well.

The three men were still standing there when Noah called, "Grace, you ready?"

She looked up in surprise. "Uh, yes."

"Come on, then. We can all walk out together."

Unsure of Noah's purpose, Grace approached. Noah slipped his arm around her waist and gave her an affectionate squeeze. His actions announced to one and all that they were together.

Andrew's eyebrows rose, Benton grinned, and Enrique looked away.

Noah said, "Grace and I are heading down to Florida for the weekend, but when I get back, I'll see what I can do about the situation at the restaurant."

"Thank God," Andrew muttered, but he was still distracted by Noah's possessive hold on Grace.

"I'm not making any promises," Noah warned, "but Grace is trying to make me feel guilty about the whole thing and I hate to disappoint her, so I'll see what I can do."

Grace went very still as she considered Noah and what he'd said. He made it sound as though her wishes were important to him. Grace liked that, probably more than was sensible. But at the same time, she didn't want Noah to do anything for her that he wouldn't do for himself.

A lot had changed in one night.

Grace wasn't at all sure what it meant, but it still made her heart swell, and it still made her foolishly hopeful. Because the more time she spent with Noah, the more she wanted to spend her whole life with him.

But Noah had been honest up front—he wanted her for sex, and only sex.

She wouldn't make him regret their bargain.

Chapter Fourteen

"Kara is a fool."

Noah hadn't meant to speak aloud, but as he watched Grace unpack a long floral sarong, realizations bombarded him. Damn, but he'd fallen in love with Grace. Or maybe he'd always loved her.

When he'd seen Deltorro eyeing her, his blood had boiled. When Andrew and Benton had eyed her in speculation, he'd been compelled to protect her, to make their relationship public. Unlike Kara, he wanted the world to know that Grace was his.

From the time he'd been a child, alone, always on the outside, Noah had thought about what he'd need to be happy, whole. He'd made plans and worked toward his goals. He'd seen others with large families and had put that at the top of his list. Family meant you belonged, that you were someone rather than a nobody sitting in a dark alley, wishing for unattainable things. He'd wanted a home to return to each night, money so he would never wear hand-me-downs or stolen clothes again.

Noah shook his head. He had more than one

property now, but nowhere had really felt like home. Not until Grace. She brought sunshine into every room, and Noah had no doubt she'd somehow make a cardboard box feel cozy. He could probably sit in that same dark alley with Grace and be content.

He also had expensive clothes tailor made to fit his tall frame. Shopping had been one of the first things Agatha had taught him. She claimed the right clothes were important to make the best impression. Noah smiled.

He'd rather be naked with Grace any day than wear fine clothes.

Grace's impact on him was disturbing, and had at first scared Noah spitless. But he was getting used to it, accepting it. Noah snorted. Hell, he'd more than accepted it, he loved it. Long before Grace had crawled into his bed, she'd been in his heart. He just hadn't dared to recognize his feelings, because recognizing them meant all his other plans had been awry. It would mean he'd put too much importance on the wrong things, that he'd been planning to marry the wrong woman.

He wouldn't make the same mistakes Kara made by trying to hide his feelings. He wouldn't let Grace think he was ashamed of her.

Grace glanced up, for once oblivious to his mood in her excitement about the small trip. "Kara's understandably afraid, but you know, I think Enrique is really in love with her. It hurts him that they have to sneak around."

There was no accusation in Grace's tone, nothing to indicate how she felt about their present situation. Noah had thoroughly enjoyed their little game of sex slave and master, but with every passing minute he wanted more.

He wanted everything.

"Grace, would you be involved with a man you were ashamed of?"

Her gaze flew to his. She held the colorful sarong to her chest. "No, of course not." She looked confused for a moment, then went back to unpacking.

Noah propped himself against the dresser and watched her. "Grace?"

"Hmm?"

"You have a baby book on your shelf at home."

Her head lifted, their eyes met and held. Hot color flooded her face, and Grace winced. "It's an old one."

"Yeah?" Noah couldn't look away from her. "How old?"

She fidgeted. "Um . . . I got it when I was twenty."

"Why?"

Shrugging, she said, "A lot of the other women I knew then were seriously involved, engaged, getting married. It made me think about those . . . things."

Noah pushed away from the dresser and went to her. Being near Grace and not touching her was almost impossible. Especially when discussing things like babies. He could so easily picture Grace as a doting mother. The image of a tiny baby tugging hungrily at her nipple squeezed Noah's heart and made his lungs constrict.

He needed to know exactly how Grace felt about him. "Do you think about all that still?"

Grace actually winced; Noah had no idea what to make of that. Was she uncomfortable with his questioning? Was he crossing the line for her?

She replied carefully, her expression masked.

"Right now, today, I'm just happy with how things are." She reached up to touch his jaw in a feather-light caress. "Very happy."

Noah was at a loss. With Kara, everyone had assumed they'd marry, and it was discussed around them quite often. He'd never been forced into a formal proposal.

With Grace, it wouldn't be that easy. Not only was she far more complex than Kara, but she was also a stronger woman. She wouldn't marry a man for any reason other than love.

Did Grace love him?

Noah watched her, wondering if her evasiveness was her subtle way of letting him know she didn't want to get married. He knew Grace cared about him. He could still recall in vivid detail the way she'd rushed to his defense when Agatha had disowned him. The memory of that would live with him forever.

But did Grace care enough to tie herself to him for life? What could he offer her other than mind-blowing sex?

Just as Noah's past didn't matter to her, he knew his present situation of wealth and influence wouldn't matter either. What did Grace see in him? What did she need from him?

Noah tried a different tack. "My grandmother seems to think we should give marriage some thought."

Grace stiffened, then walked away from him. She opened the balcony doors and wandered out. She'd done that several times since their arrival, continually drawn by the ocean and the balmy breezes. This time felt different.

The sound of the ocean was a droning roar in Noah's ears. The air was humid and thick and fresh. Palm trees swayed in a gentle breeze. Noah followed her out.

Grace had her face tipped up to the sun, and as he stepped up behind her, she said, "It's beautiful, isn't it?"

Noah braced his hands on the railing at either side of her waist, caging her in. He pressed his chest to her back and kissed her ear. Softly, he whispered, "You're beautiful, Grace."

He could feel her smile. And her avoidance. "Will we really make love out on the water?"

He kissed her neck, her shoulder. "We can make love anywhere you want to."

She put her head against his shoulder. "Where do you want to?"

Noah considered her question before answering. "When I was a young man, I'd screw anywhere. In the alley, at the theater, in the front and back-seat of a car. Once, I took this girl in the rear of the subway with passengers sitting up front."

"Noah!"

He nuzzled her nape. "Back then, sex got so mundane, so boring, I needed the extra kick of maybe getting caught."

Grace elbowed him hard. "So you're saying sex in the ocean is no big deal to you?"

Noah grinned and hugged her, restraining her arms so she couldn't prod him with that pointy elbow again. "I'm saying sex anywhere with you is great. No matter how many times we make love, Grace, I just want you more."

Grace went very still, not even breathing. Then, in the tone of voice he now knew signaled her arousal, she murmured, *"Noah."*

He reached around her and pressed his hand to her belly. Grace was always soft, warm, and giving.

If all they had was sex, he'd use that to win her over. He'd get her as addicted as he felt.

"Right here, Grace?" A breeze lifted her hair, blew it back against his jaw. Noah stroked her as he felt his balls tightening, his blood heating. "You wanna watch the ocean while I fill you up? It's deep this way, Grace, but you'll need my fingers"— he touched her suggestively—"right here, so you can come."

Her bottom pressed and wiggled back into his groin. She wore only a thin sundress, and the feeling was incredible. Breathlessly, she said, "Okay, sure."

Noah almost laughed. Grace was always so willing, so eager, she amazed him. "Think you can be real quiet while you come? The people on the beach might wonder what you're doing if you start making all those sexy little noises I love so much."

"I'll be quiet," she promised, and wiggled again, trying to urge him to hurry.

Noah lifted the back of her skirt. He stroked her thighs, her bottom, slid her panties down her legs until they dropped to her ankles. All the while, he kissed her throat, her ear, the nape of her neck, her shoulders.

When Grace was ready, he opened his slacks and freed his cock. For the first time, Noah resented putting on a condom, but he knew he'd never risk Grace's feelings that way. If and when she wanted more from him, then they'd discuss it further.

But as he slowly sank into her, he couldn't stop himself from saying, "You'd be an incredible mother, Grace."

Grace groaned and clenched around him. Noah

wasn't sure she'd even heard his words. If she had, she didn't comment.

"Push back, Grace. That's it. Now brace your feet apart so you can take my thrusts."

Within minutes Grace was ready to climax. Noah reached between her legs and touched her just right, then had to use his other hand to muffle her shout of release. In the next instant, he closed his mouth over her shoulder to hide his own raw groans of completion.

They both slumped forward on the railing.

After a moment, Grace giggled. "Noah," she whispered, sounding scandalized. "We have to move."

"No. Can't." His legs were awkwardly braced, and if he moved, he'd fall on his face. Thinking of babies and forever-after while Grace milked him dry had zapped him of strength.

"People are looking," she insisted.

Noah cocked one eye open. Sure enough, people below were glancing their way curiously. He smiled. "Nosy bastards." He was still inside her, as closely connected as two people could be, and he hated to pull out. "They're just jealous that I'm the one here with you."

"Yeah, right." Grace chuckled again, but Noah also heard the hint of embarrassment.

He slipped out of her, patted her rear, and said, "Marry me, Grace."

He nearly groaned as he heard the echo of his own words—and Grace's stunned silence. Damn, he really had to quit blurting things out like that. Sex had never before made him melodramatic, but sex with Grace did insane things to him.

Grace suddenly whipped around to face him and almost tripped because her panties were twisted around her ankles. Her eyes were huge when Noah caught her.

"Hold on, sweetheart." He bent and held the underwear as Grace stepped free. Without a word, she hurried around him and back through the doors to the bedroom.

"Are we playing tag here, Grace?" He followed her back inside, but halted by the door. Grace was pacing.

Noah hated to admit it, but he felt very uncertain. Grace didn't look overcome with joy at his proposal. No, she looked dumbfounded and ill at ease. His stomach roiled.

"Grace?"

Her hands were clenched together when she turned to face him. "Mathew Dean and Jessica Marie."

"What?"

"Those are the names I decided on, from the baby book. I wanted two children, a boy and a girl. Matt and Jessie."

Noah watched her. "Good names. I like them."

"I know it'd be tricky to have one boy and one girl. But remember, this was just the ideal. If it was two boys, or two girls, I'd still be thrilled. I just wouldn't want to stop at one." She looked up, her expression earnest. "Children should have siblings. They should never be alone."

"I agree." A battalion of kids would be fine by him, as long as Grace was the mother.

"I pictured them as average, healthy, happy kids. They'd run around and be noisy and play, and I'd love every single minute with them."

Noah would love every minute with them, too. "As I said, you'd make a great mom."

"I hope so." She turned away, and tension radiated off her. Her head dropped, her voice lowered. "Noah, I can't marry you."

Her words hit him like a punch in the gut. "You don't think I'd make a good father. I never had one, so I've never seen how it should be."

"No!" She whirled to face him, now taut with anger. "That's not it at all. I think you'd make a wonderful father. You'd love your children and guide them and . . ."

"Then you think I'd make a lousy husband?"

Grace rubbed her forehead. "You'd make a wonderful husband, too." And with some acerbity, "How could you think otherwise?"

"What am I supposed to think, Grace?"

She stormed up to him. "It isn't about you, Noah. It's about me. All my life I've been boring. I've been ignored and overlooked."

"I find that so hard to believe, Grace."

She shook her head, making her hair whip around. "But it's true. Before they passed away, my parents were disappointed with me. I was heavy and shy, the opposite of them. Other kids weren't exactly mean, but they didn't go out of their way to befriend me either. And guys always ignored me."

"I haven't ignored you."

"No. But you're the first man who's ever wanted me. And now other men seem to be noticing me, too. It's all so new and so fun. Better than fun."

Noah barely got the words out. "You want to fool around with other men, is that it?" Like hell. He'd find a way to get that idea out of her head real fast.

"No!" She looked genuinely stunned that he'd come to such a conclusion, and Noah managed to relax. "It's flattering, but that's all. I'm not interested in other men."

"That's good, Grace, because I'm not about to share."

She scowled. "I wasn't asking you to. I like what *we* have, Noah. I like your attention and I love having sex with you." She bit her lip, blinked hard. "It's . . . it's enough for me. Please try to understand."

Oh, he understood well enough. Grace wanted nothing more from him than sex. Noah almost laughed at the irony of it.

Grace gave him exactly what he'd asked of her, when almost from the first he'd known it wouldn't be enough. Grace was sunshine and happiness and loyalty, the type of woman who made a man better, more complete. She was sexiness personified, real and caring and good deep down to her soul.

She was everything to him, and he'd blown it.

Noah wanted to rage, to shake her. But Grace stepped up to him and hugged him tight. "You're very important to me, Noah. I've always cared about you, you have to believe that. But this is all so new, so . . . unexpected." She looked up at him and smiled. "Let me enjoy it, please?"

He'd die for her, so how could he refuse her now? Noah touched her warm cheek, smoothed her long, thick hair. "Anything you want, Gracie."

Her eyes darkened with deliberate suggestion. In an effort to relieve the tension between them, she teased, "That's the spirit."

Noah managed a smile over his aching sense of loss. *Amazing Grace.* How long would she be content with him? The thought of her with another man put him into a rage. He couldn't, wouldn't, let that happen. He'd keep Gracie so sexually satisfied, so limp and sated, she wouldn't have the strength to look at other men. "Tell me what you want, honey."

"I want what you promised. Sex on the beach, on the ocean. I want to explore Florida and see your condo. I want to enjoy *you*, all of you. I want to pack as much pleasure into this weekend as we can."

And then what? Noah wanted to ask. Instead, he said, "You got it."

The panicked shadows left Grace's dark gaze and the strain eased from her face. "Where do we start?"

He squeezed her waist and kissed the tip of her nose. "I'll rent a boat." He stepped toward the desk and the phone book. "You can get into your bikini."

Grace blushed. "I already told you that's not going to happen. But I did splurge and get this nice tank suit that matches the sarong."

Noah looked her over as she pulled the suit from her case and held it up in front of her body. He nodded. "That'll be fine." Then he added, "I'll have it off you in no time anyway."

Grace drew in a shuddering breath. "I'm counting on it."

With some trepidation and a lot of antagonism, Ben rapped on the front door of his grandmother's mansion. He'd been to her house a handful of times and was awed by the size and elegance of it each time. In comparison, his rooms at the hotel were no more than a hovel.

He still preferred them.

Surprisingly, Agatha's housekeeper, Nan, wasn't

the one to open the door. Agatha saw to the chore herself.

Ben was deliberately ten minutes late and he waited for Agatha to mention it, but she didn't. Instead, she said, "Thank you for coming, Ben."

Ben tried to relax, but it was impossible. He stepped inside. "Yeah, well, you didn't give me much choice."

Slanting him a look, Agatha said, "Well, well. I had no idea I had such control over you. That kind of information will come in handy." She turned and headed toward the library, leaving Ben to follow.

He scowled at her narrow, straight back. Her sarcasm was misplaced, but then, he'd asked for it by dishing out his own. Ben was fair, so he said nothing.

As usual, Agatha wore an expensive silk suit, this one a stormy gray, with low-heeled pumps that made her steps echo throughout the large entryway. Her silver hair was in a severe, elegant twist and she wore a simple silver pin in her lapel with matching studs in her ears.

For a fleeting moment, Ben wondered if Agatha Harper had ever been a soft woman, if she'd ever been a loving mother. Perhaps Pierce, his father, had merely been a product of his rigid upbringing. Ben shook his head and shut the library door behind him. He'd be damned before he started making excuses for the man who'd gotten his mother pregnant, then turned his back on her.

"Okay, Aggie, let's hear it. What dire circumstance do you envision me dealing with?"

Agatha flicked her gaze at him while tidying a stack of papers on a dark, massive desk that Ben wouldn't keep if it were given to him. "This is serious, young man, so you'd be better served to stop baiting me."

She was probably correct, at least partly. Ben sighed. "Yeah, all right. So what's up?"

"It's about your brother."

Ben raised both brows. "Hold on here. Are you acknowledging that Noah *is* my brother?" His shock was only half feigned. "But Aggie, you do realize that would have to mean Pierce was my father."

"And I your grandmother, yes." Wearily, she seated herself behind the desk and nodded toward a chair. "Please, take a seat."

A little numb at the turnaround, Ben scooted the padded leather chair a little closer. It was unaccountably heavy. The damn thing likely cost as much as his hotel. He dropped into the posh padding with a sigh. "I gotta admit, I'm waiting with bated breath."

Agatha folded her old, wrinkled hands on the desktop and eyed Ben. "Noah is ruining his life."

A guffaw of hilarity escaped Ben. "Yeah right. He's happier than he's ever been."

Agatha frowned. "On the surface, maybe. He's a proud man and wouldn't want others to know how he really feels."

"He'd tell me." Ben stared at her, taking pleasure in pointing out the truth. "He tells me everything."

Agatha seemed startled by that news, but not unhappy about it. "Tell me, Ben, how can he possibly be happy? He's built up so much at the restaurant, and now he's walked away from it all. He's in love with Kara, yet he's pulled out of the engagement. He's destroying his reputation, his business associations, and his love life."

Ben shook his head with a disparaging show of pity. "Christ, you really don't know him at all, do you? I figured since Noah was your chosen one, the heir apparent, you'd paid closer attention. I sort of assumed you were an astute woman, given all your wealth. Hell, Aggie, you might as well have been wearing blinders, you've missed so much."

That was one too many insults for Agatha to calmly ignore. She shot to her feet, then had to grab the edge of the desk to steady herself. Ben slowly stood, watching her with concern. She looked . . . wobbly. He'd never seen her that way before.

Guilt over his appalling behavior crowded in. Agatha was an elderly woman, in her late seventies, and he'd taken pleasure in his insolence.

Ben shook off the guilt. He owed her nothing. Yet his concern remained.

Agatha took several moments to gather herself. She stared at the desk while doing so. When she finally looked up at Ben, she was once again in control. "I do know my grandson. He's a mover and a shaker, a man who likes to see things through. I've let the restaurant go because I know it'll be impossible for Noah to watch it fall apart."

Ben narrowed his eyes. "You love that restaurant."

"So does Noah."

He shook his head impatiently. "No, I mean I thought you loved it too much to let it crumble."

Agatha stepped out from behind the desk to pace. "I don't think that will happen. Noah will return before it does. But . . ." She looked up and held Ben's gaze. "It's worth the risk."

Because she loved Noah. Oh, Ben doubted she'd ever admit it, she was such a crusty old witch, but it was there in her faded blue eyes, in the strain on her aristocratic face. Ben turned away from her to run a hand through his hair. Everything was suddenly more complicated.

"So what the hell do you want from me?"

"Your help in setting things right."

"Yeah?" He faced her again. "And how do you figure to do that?"

In an uncommon show of nervousness, Agatha bit her bottom lip. Just as quickly, her chin lifted in imperious demand. "How do you feel about Kara?"

Ben shrugged. He considered Kara spoiled and self-indulgent and weak—typical of her upbringing. But he didn't say any of that to Agatha. "She's all right."

"She's perfect for Noah."

"Not even close."

Agatha didn't appear to hear him. "I want to prod Noah back to his senses. To do that, I need you to temporarily replace him."

Shock rolled through Ben. "Replace him . . . where?"

"Everywhere that counts. You can step in as my manager, for the restaurant and my other business ventures. Given your success at the hotel and diner, it's obvious that you're capable of handling the task. At least for a short time."

Ben didn't dare blink. He had no idea when he'd see anything this bizarre again. Agatha giving him a compliment? Or had it been? She'd stipulated that "for a short time." He was still pondering that when she threw the rest at him.

"And I want you to pursue Kara."

His mouth fell open. Only Aggie could be that outrageous.

"That ought to shake Noah up," Agatha went

on. "If he thinks he's losing Kara, he'll realize his mistakes and come back where he belongs."

A slow burning in his gut made Ben shake. He rounded the desk toward Agatha, and given the way she backed up, he knew he didn't look exactly receptive to her idea.

"You old bitch." The words were spat out from between his teeth, but Ben couldn't remember ever being so angry. "You would connive and plot against your own grandson. Noah gave you everything he had, and all along you've just been using him."

Agatha reached behind her until she found her chair. She dropped into it, then braced her hands on the arms. "That's not true."

"Bullshit." He leaned over her. "You act like you took care of him . . . well, that's backwards, Aggie. Noah's been propping you up since the day he arrived. But were you ever grateful? Hell no, you ground him under every chance you got."

She clutched a hand to her chest. "That's a lie! I did my best for Noah."

Ben snorted. "Like you did your best for Pierce? Yeah, we all know how that turned out, don't we? The man was a waste of humanity as far as I'm concerned."

Agatha pushed upright, heaving in her anger. Her chair skidded out behind her on the hardwood floor. "How dare you!" Her voice rose to a shout. "He was my son and I loved him!"

"Like you love Noah?"

Her thin nostrils flared and her eyes filled with tears. "What would you have me do, damn you? Just give up on Noah, watch him ruin his life?"

"Gee, I don't know, Agatha. Maybe you could

try being honest? Maybe you could tell Noah how much you appreciate him? Give him the respect and admiration he deserves?"

For a long, frozen moment, neither of them moved. Agatha hugged herself and stared beyond Ben. "Pierce was a great man, a wealthy man. As his son, you could have had so much."

Ben narrowed his eyes. Was that a threat, an enticement? He had no idea. "You just don't get it, do you? Pierce had nothing I wanted, including himself, including you. Hell, I count myself fortunate that he stayed out of my life. And believe me, he wasn't missed. My mother and I managed just fine."

"You could have had more. New cars, luxury vacations, influence, and—"

"Everything Pierce had?"

Her mouth trembled. "Yes."

Gently, feeling a twinge of pity, Ben said, "And look how he turned out."

Agatha turned away. Her shoulders were hunched, making Ben feel like a monster. But damn it, she had to stop tampering with Noah's life.

Ben knew it was time to go. But first he said, "Noah is a better man than Pierce ever was."

Seconds ticked by, and Agatha finally said, "I know."

Ben stared at her back. "Come again?"

She straightened, turned. "I said I know. The same can be said for you."

Suspicion bloomed. "Still trying to finagle, Aggie? Use any old trick, including false flattery, to get what you want?"

"No." She shook her head. "It's true, Ben. You're a fine young man."

His anger on the rise again, Ben told her, "I'm not that easy. You made it clear what you thought of me years ago."

"Yes." Her smile was slanted, real. "And you've made it quite clear what you think of me."

Damn her, did she want his sympathy now? Panic crawled over Ben, joining the uncertainty, the hesitation.

The neediness. *No.*

Ben drew one breath, then another. He had to get out before he said something stupid. "One question before I go, Agatha."

She agreed with a weary nod of her head. "All right."

Ben folded his arms over his chest. "What the hell do you have against Gracie?"

Surprise flickered over her face. "Why, nothing. She's a lovely person."

"Yeah, I think so. One of the finest people I know. Then why are you so hell-bent on breaking her and Noah up?"

Agatha shook her head. "No, you've misunderstood. I tried to encourage Noah to marry her."

Ben closed his eyes, then slowly reopened them. "Oh God, this is just great." Incredulity rang in his every word. "You *encouraged* him?"

"Yes. I offered to accept him and Grace both back if they married."

For the first time, Ben began to wonder if Agatha truly did mean well and was merely shortsighted in her methods. She'd learned to bulldoze her way through life and didn't know any other way. He laughed and propped one hip on her enormous, ostentatious desk. It was sturdy, he'd give her that.

"So, in other words, you tried to bribe him?"

"I didn't see it that way."

" 'Course you did, Aggie." He pointed at her and winked. "You're not that dull-edged yet. You knew exactly what you were doing. In fact, I'll bet you thought such a ploy might push him back at Kara, didn't you?"

She flushed in astonishment, which was all the answer Ben needed.

"Aggie, Aggie," he said in mock reproach. "You really don't know Noah at all, do you?"

She bristled, then shocked the hell out of Ben when she snapped, "Oh, stuff it, will you?"

Stuff it?

"Yes, I tried to get him back with Kara," Agatha admitted. "I thought she'd be his perfect match, though I am forced to rethink that."

"Doubts, Agatha?"

"Yes. Doubts and remorse. My plans backfired. Grace overheard Noah refusing my suggestion, and my God, I've never seen a girl look so devastated." Her gaze narrowed on Ben, piercing and direct. "I feel wretched enough about it without your smart-ass mouth."

Ben blinked several times, then burst out laughing. Agatha shoved him, nearly knocking him over the desk. Ben righted himself with an effort. "Damn, Aggie, you've got a regular gutter mouth on you."

"Like you'd even notice, with the foul way you speak?"

Ben grinned. "I must have inherited it from you."

Agatha looked ready to combust, but slowly her scowl lifted into a smile. She even chuckled. "Oh, shut up, you . . . miscreant."

"Yes, ma'am."

Agatha gasped, then grabbed her chest, alarming Ben until he realized she was pretending shock at his courtesy. She blinked her eyes at him and said, "You were actually polite!"

"Har har."

In the next instant, Agatha turned businesslike. "I've thought about Grace a lot since that awful incident, Ben. I hurt her and I hate myself for it. It didn't take me that long to realize Grace might just be everything Noah wants. She's strong like him, capable like him, good and honest like him. They'd make a fine pair." Her hands twisted together. "But I messed that up."

"Yeah, well, shed the hair shirt, Aggie, because unlike you, I do pay attention, and I can tell you, Noah is still hooked."

"On Grace?"

"Oh, yeah." Ben pretended to cast a fishing line. "Hooked, reeled in, and gutted."

"But . . . what about Kara?"

Considering what he'd just learned, Ben decided Noah could maybe use a little help after all. And Agatha made a hell of an ally when she chose the right side.

Ben would help her choose wisely.

He nodded toward her desk chair, which rivaled the desk in pretentiousness; it was large enough to hold two grown men. "Park your old bones in a chair, Aggie. You're already looking a tad pale, but I've got something important to tell you, and it may be a bit of a shock."

Chapter Fifteen

Grace waited for her pounding heart to slow, for the sweat to dry on her heated skin. Tears threatened, but they were tears of happiness, of satisfaction—and melancholy.

Noah dropped onto his back beside her. "Good God, you get better every time, Grace."

A smile was about as much as Grace could manage at the moment. She felt sensitive everywhere, her skin still tingling, her nipples throbbing.

Noah laid one hot, heavy hand over her belly. There was a new stillness about him, a strange mood that had taken hold of him almost from the moment they'd arrived in Florida two days past. He'd been alert, thoughtful, edgy. He'd been relentless in his sexual demands, pushing her hard, making her scream.

And he'd asked her to marry him.

Grace drew in a shuddering breath and squeezed her eyes shut, affected once again just by the memory. The urge to say yes had been so strong she'd nearly choked on it. But Noah's grandmother had manipulated him enough. Grace wouldn't let his sense of responsibility toward her force him to allow yet another manipulation. She couldn't bear that.

Just as she couldn't bear to lose him.

She felt pulled in half, wanting to say yes, bound by her honor and her love to say no. Their time in Florida had been wonderful—and yet tinged with a new strain that hadn't existed before his proposal. This was their last day at the beach. Grace didn't want it to end.

Overwhelmed by those thoughts, she turned into Noah's side and hugged him.

His arms automatically came around her, as secure and comforting as ever. "Hey."

Grace pressed her nose to his damp chest hair and inhaled his wonderfully masculine scent, now intensified by their vigorous lovemaking.

Normally after sex, Noah took inordinate pleasure in tending to her, bathing her and making her comfortable. Out on the rented boat, floating on swelling waves, he'd tidied her in the bright sunshine. All the while he'd complimented her body and kissed her everywhere.

On the shore at night, he'd held her hand and waded with her into the surf. Moonlight had carved his harsh features as he'd cupped his hand between her thighs, exciting her even as he'd soothed her flesh.

He made love to her everywhere in the condo, from the shower to the balcony to the bed. Even when Noah was merciless in giving her pleasure, he was tender and careful. Grace felt cherished by him.

This time Grace wanted Noah to feel cherished. "Lie still."

She lifted one leg over his lap and crawled

across him. Her breasts, still flushed and too warm, brushed his chest.

Noah groaned, then said, "I'll give you a dollar to do that again."

Grace laughed despite her confusing jumble of emotions. "You're a sex maniac, Noah Harper." She patted his hairy thigh. "And no, that's not a complaint."

Noah was still grinning when Grace returned with a damp washcloth. In leisurely fascination, she removed the spent condom, then took her time drifting the cool cloth over Noah's body, his thighs, his hard abdomen. His penis and testicles. She dragged out the chore, enjoying herself. Before she was through, Noah's legs were shifting on the bed and his hands had curled into fists. He was erect once again.

Their gazes met and caught, Noah's bright with hunger, Grace's dark and mellow.

"I want you to ride me, Gracie."

Stunned, she asked, "Now?" Noah had always had a voracious appetite, but a half hour hadn't passed since they'd both yelled out their releases.

"Yeah." He growled and reached for her. "Right now before I die."

Grace snagged another condom off the nightstand, amazed but more than willing, and Noah's cell phone rang.

They both stared at the phone across the room on the dresser. Noah cursed and lifted Grace to the side. "I'm sorry, Gracie. The only one who has this number is Ben, and he wouldn't call unless something was wrong."

Naked, Noah padded to the phone and flipped it open. "Yeah?"

Grace came to her knees on the bed. Her heartbeat accelerated with dread. When his expression darkened, she said, "Noah?"

He held up a hand while he listened. Sexual excitement was quickly replaced with worry. His head dropped forward and he paced. "You've seen her?"

Her who? Grace wondered. *Kara, Agatha? What had happened?*

Noah glanced at Grace with a silent apology. "Yeah, we'll be out of here in less than an hour. I'll take the first flight I can get." He hesitated, then asked, "Ben, will you stay with her?" He nodded. "Good. Thanks."

Noah canceled the call and opened the dresser at the same time. "Agatha's in the hospital. She and Ben were arguing when suddenly she went pale and dropped. Ben barely managed to catch her. She's in ICU now."

"Ohmigod!" Grace leapt off the bed and scrambled for clothes.

"Take it easy, Grace," Noah told her as he stepped into his slacks. "According to Ben she's doing fine now and is kicking up a fuss at all the attention. To quote Ben, 'She's pitching a bitch about looking old and frail.'"

"She would." Grace jerked a shirt over her head, got her arms caught, and felt Noah straightening the garment out for her.

When she got her head free, she said, "Noah?"

"Yeah?" He pulled on his own shirt and then opened their luggage on the mussed bed.

"What was Ben doing with her?"

Noah glanced up. "Damn. I have no idea. I didn't even think to ask."

Shaking her head to clear it, Grace began loading clothes. "Never mind. It doesn't matter right now, and I'm sure Ben can fill you in as soon as we get there."

"Yeah." But Noah stood still in the middle of the floor, a frown on his brow.

"Noah," Grace said gently, seeing the stark concern in his eyes. He loved his grandmother very much, despite their recent differences. "Why don't you call the airlines while I finish packing? I can have us ready to go in ten minutes flat."

"Yeah, I'll do that."

Within an hour and a half, they were on a plane headed back to Gillespe. Grace held Noah's hand, but he was silent, his thoughts private. She could see he was hurting, and that made her hurt, too.

They went to the hospital straight from the airport—and walked into a small mob.

Kara stood between two female friends, her cheeks stained with tears. Ben was off to the side, adequately ignoring the slanted admiring looks continually cast his way. Noah squeezed Grace's hand and walked toward them all.

"How is she?"

Kara looked up, saw Noah, and burst into fresh tears. She threw herself against him, leaving Noah little choice but to catch her. Grace was forced to move to the side, making Noah feel very alone.

Fear clawed at him, and he sought out Ben with his gaze.

"She's fine, Noah." Ben gave Kara a disgusted look, then rolled his eyes. "They're running some tests right now. She evidently had heart failure, and she's still a little weak, but she's awake and talking—or rather complaining—and the doctor says with medicine she'll be all right."

Noah almost went limp. He set Kara away from him and reached for Grace. Grace came into his arms without hesitation. She held him and said, "Thank God."

Kara's friends came to stand beside her. Noah recognized them both but couldn't remember their names. They glared at Noah and Grace.

Ben rudely stepped in front of them. "We should talk."

Noah nodded and allowed Grace to move to his side. She clasped his hand in comfort.

Ben drew a deep breath. "Agatha had asked me to visit her. I hadn't said anything to you because I knew it might piss you off. Or worry you. But it was dumb. She had some half-baked idea of making you jealous over me, so you'd rush back where you belong. We were arguing and I noticed she looked more piqued than usual, but I thought it was just because she was fretting over things. You know, she's old and all."

Grace squeezed his hand, and Noah said, "What happened?"

Ben looked over his shoulder at Kara and the other two women, then took Noah's arm and led him and Grace a short distance away. When they stopped, Ben propped his hands on his hips and stared down at his feet. "I told her the truth. At least part of it." He looked up and shook his head. "I'm sorry, Noah. It's just that at first she made me so damn mad, and then I realized she really had no clue. She sincerely wanted to make things right for you, but she didn't understand that they'd never be right with Kara."

"You told her about Deltorro?"

"No, not that. But I did tell her how much you care for Grace, and that it was Kara who fucked things up, not you. I think she'd pretty much figured out there was a third party involved, but then she got short of breath and looked real sickly and just . . . she nearly collapsed."

Noah squeezed Ben's shoulder. "When can I get in to see her?"

"I don't know. The doctors are with her now."

"This isn't your fault, Ben."

He rubbed his forehead. "I goaded her."

"Knowing Agatha, she probably enjoyed it." Noah allowed a small smile. "And believe me, she'd have expected no less from you. You two remind me of each other, did I ever tell you that?"

Ben choked. "The hell you say!"

Grace pulled free of Noah. "I'll go get us all three some coffee. I know I can use it."

Noah gave Grace an absent smile. She looked tired, strained, but still strong. The only flight he could get on such short notice had two connections. Grace hadn't relaxed once. He knew she loved Agatha, too. "Thanks, babe."

But as Grace went to ask if Kara or the others wanted coffee, one of the women confronted her. Noah heard her whisper, "You should be ashamed of yourself, coming here now."

Grace pulled up short. "Excuse me?"

And the woman said, "Haven't you done enough damage? You ruined Noah's engagement and his relationship with Mrs. Harper. It's probably the stress that's done this to her."

Horrified, Kara stepped forward, but she wasn't fast enough. Noah beat her to it. He pulled Grace into his side and said to Kara, "Get them both out of here. Now."

Kara fretted. "Noah . . ."

He caught her arm and pulled her closer. "I put

up with a lot from you, Kara, but I won't tolerate insults to Grace. Get rid of them or I'll tell them the truth."

Big tears filled her eyes.

Noah felt no sympathy. "And pull yourself together if you want to see Agatha. I won't have you upsetting her more with your bawling."

Kara nodded, but her friends gasped. The same woman who'd verbally attacked Grace now turned her cannon on Noah. "You don't have a single ounce of shame, do you? I can't believe you brought *her* here." And she aimed a malicious sneer at Grace.

Grace just shook her head and rested a hand on Noah's chest. "It's okay, Noah. Really."

Ben muttered, "Stupid bitch," loud enough for the women to hear.

Noah narrowed his eyes. "I've had enough, Kara."

Kara grabbed both women and hauled them away. There was a brief argument at the sliding doors before her two friends were convinced to leave.

Kara returned to them with a lagging step. "Noah, I—"

"This isn't the best time or place, Kara. So I'm only going to say it once. I won't have people bad-mouthing Grace. Set the record straight or I will."

"What do you expect me to do?"

"I expect you to tell the truth and to act like an adult. How long do you think Deltorro will put up with this game you're playing? Do you even care what he thinks or feels, or do you only think about yourself?"

She bit her lips. "My parents . . ."

"Only have the control you give them. What

matters the most? The man you love, or your parents' acceptance?"

Dejected, mouth trembling, Kara nodded. "All right."

Grace patted her back, making Noah marvel. "It'll be all right, Kara, you'll see. Once your parents understand how much you and Enrique love each other, they'll be supportive. They only want you to be happy."

Kara wiped her eyes and drew a shuddering breath. "I hope you're right."

Nothing more was said as a doctor approached them. "Mr. Harper?"

"Yes?"

"Your grandmother is asking for you and a Grace Jenkins."

Grace stepped forward. "How is she?"

"Ornery." The doctor smiled. "And surprisingly fit for her age. I have her on a diuretic by IV and I'd like to keep her a few days to monitor her. However, she's not keen on that idea."

"She'll stay." Noah would tie her down if he had to, the blasted stubborn woman.

The doctor smiled again. "I'll get her started on some medicine that will strengthen her heart. Also, a low salt diet, so don't let her convince you to sneak food in. She'll need to be watched—"

Noah, Grace, and Ben all said at once, "She will be."

They looked at each other.

The doctor nodded in satisfaction. "We're moving her out of ICU. As soon as that's done, she'd like to see you."

Noah glanced at Grace and Ben. Grace said, "We'll be right here."

The doctor said, "Are you Ben Badwin?" At Ben's nod, he said, "She requested to see all three of you. And Kara?"

Kara hurried forward. "She wants to see me?" She sniffed and dabbed at her eyes.

"That's right. She said something about killing two birds with one stone, then she ordered me out here to fetch you all. When I told her she'd have to wait until we got her settled, she wasn't happy." The doctor appeared bemused as he added, "She threatened to have my job."

"She's going to be difficult," Noah predicted when the doctor had walked away.

"Damn right." Ben nodded. "And I intend to let her."

"I suppose we shouldn't upset her," Grace agreed.

Kara dried her eyes and smiled. "I'm so relieved that she's okay."

Fifteen minutes later, Noah led the way into Agatha's room. She was half propped up in bed. Her gray hair, normally styled in an elegant twist, was half pulled free, which made her look somewhat demented. Her face was more pale than Noah had ever seen it. She looked both determined and drawn. It scared him.

Agatha turned her head on the pillow toward him. "Damn it, Noah, what took you so long?"

Surprised at her vehemence, Noah sauntered up to prop his hip on her bedside. "I've been in the hall just waiting for you to be moved to a room. How do you feel?"

"Better than I look. Hospitals have no respect for dignity."

"You look fine, Agatha."

"You're a lousy liar, Noah." And before he could reply, she snapped, "You three, quit hiding. Come here where I can see you."

Ben went to the other side of her bed; Grace came to stand next to Noah. Kara stationed herself at the foot of the bed.

"Now," Agatha said, doing her best to look stern, "you all have some explaining to do. And Ben, don't you dare roll your eyes at me!"

Ben said, "No, ma'am."

"Now, as you can all see, I'm not up to my usual strength. The damn doctor pointed out that my ankles are swollen and I've gained some weight. I told him he was rude, but that didn't stop him. He insists I'll need time to rest and relax." Her eyes were shrewd as she stared up at Noah. "Under the circumstances, you'll certainly come back to work." Her eyes narrowed and she added, "I need you."

Noah sighed. Agatha was right—under the circumstances, he had little choice. Despite her bossiness and tyrannical inclinations, he did love her, and now wasn't the time to try to prove anything. Except for his love for Grace. He had to get that cleared up. He'd come back, but he was bringing Grace with him. If Agatha had a problem with that, they still had some things to work out.

Because he wasn't letting Grace go.

Having made that decision made every other problem seem simple. Noah grinned at Agatha and said, "Yeah, I'll be back."

Grinning in pleasure, Grace patted Noah's arm.

Agatha surprised them both when she groused, "As for you, Grace, you'll return as well."

Grace blinked. "But . . ."

"No buts!" Agatha glanced from Noah to Grace. "I'll give you plenty of time off to continue this courtship with my grandson. But for the time being, I need you, so you *will* be there for me."

With the shoe on the other foot, Grace scowled. Knowing how she felt, Noah squeezed her hand, and Grace finally muttered, "All right."

Ben was chuckling at their predicaments when Agatha turned to him. He gulped.

"And you," she said, and she now sounded as demonic as she looked. "You're my damn grandson."

Wearing a facade of disregard, Ben cocked a brow. "Which makes you my damn grandmother?"

"Exactly." Looking satisfied, Agatha suddenly smiled. "I like all this cursing. It's sort of fun."

Ben sputtered, and Agatha added, "Oh, hell, you're too old to get tongue-tied, Ben, so knock it off."

Ben stared up at the heavens and pretended to pray.

Strange how things had changed so suddenly, Noah thought. It wasn't under the best circumstances, and it certainly wasn't anything he'd planned on. But his whole family was with him, his brother, the woman he loved, a dear friend, and his crusty old grandmother.

Life was good.

Noah looked at Ben and saw he was slightly red around the ears. And he could feel Grace shaking with humor beside him. His grandmother was all vinegar at the moment, very full of herself. She probably thought she had them all where she wanted them.

She was right.

"Now," Agatha said, looking down the length of

the bed to Kara. "You'll have to officially cancel the wedding."

Kara didn't hesitate, but her voice was small, uncertain. "Of course."

Agatha continued. "Good. I'm glad you're not going to argue with me, because Noah and Grace can't very well set a date until that's taken care of."

Grace jerked hard, but Noah held on to her. He looked at his grandmother and said, "What makes you think Grace and I are going to get married?"

As if she'd been saying it all her life, Agatha growled, "I love you, Noah, I really do, but you can be horribly dense at times."

Noah was speechless.

Grace said, "He is not dense!"

"No? Has he told you yet that he loves you?"

It was Grace's turn to fall silent.

Agatha snorted. "That's what I thought. It's a failing he no doubt got from me."

Ben muttered, "Yeah, one of many," and without looking, Agatha swatted him upside his head.

Ben pulled back and laughed.

"Well?" Agatha demanded. "God knows I've been remiss in saying it, but Noah, I do love you. The years have been better because of you. Don't make the same mistakes I made. Tell Grace."

As usual, Grace started to object, more than ready to defend Noah. But Noah beat her to the punch. "Yeah, I love her."

Grace blinked at him. Her mouth fell open and she clutched his shirt. "You do?"

Agatha snorted again. "Grace, you're not an idiot. Too tenderhearted maybe, but not dumb. Of course Noah loves you. It's as plain as the nose on my face."

"Now that is obvious," Ben quipped, then ducked before Agatha could get him. To Noah's surprise, Agatha appeared to enjoy Ben's needling, and judging by the grin on Ben's face, he was having a ball.

Noah opened his hand on the small of Grace's back. "Your turn, Gracie, and no, Agatha, don't say a word. I won't have her coerced."

"Coerce Grace? Ha. She's like an old-fashioned white knight where you're concerned, Noah. I doubt anyone could coerce her."

Grace turned pink. Her gaze darted around the room from Agatha to Ben to Kara and back to Noah. Their gazes caught and held. Noah could feel her uncertainty, her embarrassment at being the center of attention.

And he could feel her love even before she spoke.

She touched his jaw, and a tremulous smile bloomed on her pretty mouth. "I've always loved you, Noah."

Very slowly, Noah felt himself relax. His heart expanded, his soul filled with joy. "Always, huh?"

"Noah." She threw herself against him and held on tight.

Agatha tried to discreetly dab at her eyes. She saw Ben smiling at her and grumbled, "The stupid medicine is making me maudlin."

Ben said, "Uh huh."

Kara dabbed at her eyes, too, then she leaned forward to touch Noah's shoulder. "Can I be the first to congratulate you both?"

Noah hooked an arm around her and dragged her up to his other side. He kissed her cheek and said, "Thanks, Kara, for helping me to come to my senses." Grace gave a watery, tear-filled laugh.

Kara smiled. "You're most welcome. I'm so glad it's worked out for you, Noah."

Agatha gave an impatient sound. "If all of you are done with your effusive shows of affection, I have more to say."

Ben folded his arms. "Oh, this ought to be good."

Agatha ignored Ben. "Kara, I love you like a daughter, you know that. But it's past time you got some backbone. Here's what I think you should do."

As Agatha spoke, Kara looked horrified. But she listened.

Noah thought his grandmother was, for once, exactly right.

Epilogue

"Say please," Grace murmured, and then kissed Noah's abdomen again.

Noah tangled his hands in her hair and growled, *"Please."*

Grinning to herself, loving the power of it, Grace cupped his testicles gently and prompted, "Pretty please."

"Grace," Noah moaned, "paybacks are hell."

"Is that a threat?" She licked him at the base of his shaft, right above where her fingers curled around him.

"A promise," Noah assured her, and then directed her so that her mouth was at the head of his erection. "Grace . . ."

She opened her lips wide and drew him in, tasting the heat of him, the salty secretion, his urgency. Noah's body went rigid and he arched hard. Grace slicked her tongue over him, around the head, down—and Noah jerked her away.

"I've created a monster," he muttered thickly and quickly positioned her over his lap. "I need to come, Grace. Bad. I'm shaking like a virgin, but you've got some catching up to do."

That wasn't true. Grace was so turned on, she felt ready to explode.

Noah held her gaze as his cock prodded her slick opening. "No barriers, Grace."

"No." Though they'd only been married a month, they'd decided to try for children right away. Agatha was thrilled with their plan. She wanted great-grandchildren before she was too dotty to enjoy them.

"I'm going to fill you up," Noah promised and slowly began to penetrate.

Grace gasped at the burning, enticing sensation. "I love you, Noah."

He stilled at her words, his every muscle flexing, straining. He cursed low, laughed roughly as he lost control. *"Witch."*

In the next instant Noah gripped her hips hard and thrust fast, deep, over and over again.

Grace watched the pleasure darken his beautiful features, watched his blue eyes turn vague and smoky, heard his rough sound of release.

She closed her eyes, dropped onto his chest, and joined him. Sometimes she thought the pleasure was so intense she couldn't bear it.

Noah's heart was still thumping beneath her cheek when he said, "I'll always love you, Grace."

Despite her repletion, she smiled with confidence. "I know." After a few more minutes of recuperation, she pushed herself to her elbows.

Noah gave her a sleepy look and smoothed her hair. "For most of my life, I've been trying to plan things, to ensure that no one and nothing would ever take me by surprise again. Agatha took me in and I liked it. I didn't want to end up homeless again, or alone."

Grace gently kissed his mouth. "So you planned things. Like your life with Kara."

"Yeah. But I never planned on you. I had things all mapped out, exactly how my life would run, what I needed, what I wanted." He shook his head. "All I really need and want is you."

"You have me."

Noah cupped her bottom and leaned up to give her a long, leisurely kiss. "At first," he said against her mouth, "I just wanted to get you into my bed and keep you there."

"That was easy enough, huh? It was where I wanted to be."

Noah laughed. "Yeah, well, you didn't just stay there. From that first night, you were in my head, crowding my thoughts all day. And you were in my dreams, and in my heart." His voice went husky when he added, "You are so goddamned sexy."

Grace grinned. "I'm glad you think so."

"Every man thinks so." His expression darkened. "You've got guys salivating over you at the diner every damn night. But it's not just how you look, Grace. Like me, they see beyond your great bod."

"To what?"

"To who you really are. You're a . . . comfortable woman. Genuine and sincere and so damn sweet, I just want to eat you up." He scowled. "And I know every guy chatting you up is thinking the same thing."

Grace tried to hide her pleasure. It wasn't that she wanted Noah to be jealous, just that jealousy from him was still so incredible. "It's very manly of you to put up with it."

Noah snorted at that. "If anyone touches you . . ."

"Shhh." Grace rested back against him, content. "You're the only man who will ever touch me."

Noah squeezed her. "Damn right."

Grace loved working at the diner, and she was glad Noah wasn't still peeved about it.

Once they had married, working for Agatha seemed awkward. Grace still helped her out with a few necessary things, but both Noah and Agatha had claimed that, as Agatha's granddaughter-in-law, she could not work for her. So she worked at the diner.

Noah hadn't liked that much better, but he'd learned real quick that Grace made her own decisions. She might give him the lead in the bedroom, but it was only in the bedroom. And even there, she was learning to dish out her own form of sensual torture.

Noah loved it. Because he loved her.

"Do you think Kara and Enrique are enjoying life in Florida?"

Noah had opened another restaurant in Florida not long after buying the condo. He'd named it Grace and trained Kara to be the manager of both his rental property and the restaurant, which was located nearby. Enrique, at home in the relaxed, sunny lifestyle, performed at the restaurant nightly.

Agatha had carped and complained about Noah branching off on his own, then went about bragging to everyone about all her grandson's accomplishments. To Grace's amusement, Noah now seemed chagrined by Agatha's praise.

Agatha also exaggerated that half the customers from their restaurant had relocated south just to see Enrique. But since it gave Kara and Enrique a fresh start away from her parents, Agatha had supported the move.

At Harper's Bistro, Noah had replaced Enrique with a lovely young woman who sang mellow folk songs. The customers, after a brief segment of adjustment, claimed to love her. Harper's Bistro might have lost some of their female patrons, but hordes of young men crowded in each night.

"If Enrique is half as smart as I'm hoping he is," Noah said, "he's making sure Kara loves it there and is spending his free time keeping her happy. Her parents left it entirely too open for her to return home."

"I know." Grace absently touched Noah's nipple beneath his thick chest hair. "Overall, they reacted well. Once they got over the shock."

"Especially with Agatha there, acting like an expert on parenting, lecturing them to accept Kara and her decisions or lose her." Noah spoke with a touch of irony. They were all having problems adjusting to the new, more sensitive Agatha. Ben said it turned his stomach, but Grace could tell he was pleased.

"She's trying, and so are Kara's parents."

"It didn't help that Enrique showed up in leather pants and an open shirt." Noah chuckled with the memory. "The dumb ass could have at least gotten a haircut before telling Jorge he was going to marry Kara."

Grace again propped up to look at him. "Kara likes Enrique's ponytail, and probably his leather pants, too. I think Enrique wanted her to accept him completely, to prove she wasn't ashamed of him." Grace studied Noah in thought, and added, "You know, you'd look really hot in leather pants, Noah."

"Not in this lifetime, Grace, so get that gleam out of your gorgeous brown eyes."

Grace laughed. "Okay." She bent and kissed his chest. "But only because you look as good out of pants as in them."

Noah curved his big hands over her and held her snug against his groin. "Since I'm presently out of my pants, you know what I think I'm going to do to you, Grace?"

At the suggestive heat in his words, a wave of awareness washed over Grace. She shivered. "Okay."

"Grace." Noah smiled tenderly. "You're always so quick to agree, and I haven't even told you what I'm going to do yet."

"I'm yours, Noah. You can do anything you want."

Noah groaned, and in the next heartbeat, Grace found herself pinned beneath him—a position she much enjoyed. "Damn, I do love you, Grace."

She smiled. "That's why I'm yours." Grace drifted her hand down Noah's body to his hip, then slipped her fingers over one muscled buttock. "Now, Noah, tell me exactly what you have in mind."

If you liked this Lori Foster novel, you'll love
her other books available from Zebra . . .

When it comes to love, he plays to win.

There's only so much frustration a guy can handle before he gets a little nutty. For Jude Jamison, his frustration has a name—May Price. She's everything the former Hollywood bad boy actor came to Stillbrook, Ohio, hoping to find: open, honest, lovable, and full of those luscious curves you don't find on stick-figure starlets—curves May doesn't seem to appreciate in herself. Every time Jude tries to get close to the skittish business woman, to take her in his arms, she thinks he's joking. Joking? Joking does not involve lots of cold-shower therapy.

Time for new tactics. If May can't respond to his sly compliments and sexy innuendos, he'll just have to spell it out for her. Jude Jamison is going to lay down the law for May Price. And after that, she'll have no delusions about just how much he wants her. . . .

Jude pushed forward until he stood directly in front of her, close, so close he could smell the combined scents of lemon shampoo and powdery lotion. "Hello, May."

Her lips trembled, then firmed. She turned her face up to his. "Jude." Her smile wobbled. "Hello. How are you? I didn't realize you'd be here. You're usually waiting when I open the doors. But today you weren't. What with the rain, I assumed—"

Only with him did she chatter. His presence made her nervous. He found that cute. And encouraging.

Resisting the urge to push a shushing finger to her lush lips, Jude said, "Storms don't keep me inside." He stared at her mouth. "I think they're sexy."

"You do?"

"Yeah. All that crackling energy. The heat. The moisture."

Her mouth opened, but nothing came out.

"You ever made love in the rain, May?"

She shook her head, then squeaked, "No."

Desire pulsed beneath his skin. "Would you like to?"

Their eyes met, and she stepped backward, almost knocking a tray from a passing waiter. On the guise of assisting her, Jude caught her arm and drew her forward again.

Even through her suit coat and blouse, her arm was plump and soft and warm. Gently, his fingers caressed her.

Rather than send her running, he retreated a bit. "You know I never miss a showing. I've been looking forward to this all week."

"You have?"

Because she held her arm out to the side like a broken wing, he released her. But at the same time, a pulse tripped wildly in her throat. She had so much repressed sensuality, he burned just thinking of the moment when she'd let loose.

May needed him—in more ways than just the sexual.

If it weren't for him, he doubted she could stay in business. The arts rarely, if ever, gained priority from the denizens of Stillbrook. The town consisted mostly of farmers and blue-collar workers, more concerned with their schools, their local sports, and the neighborhood bar.

Because he usually secluded himself behind the heavy gates of his property, much of the crowd showed up just to see him. Jude knew it, and he suspected May did too.

"Your showings are one of the few highlights of the town."

"Thank you." She bit her lip. "It's just that you were late—"

Trying to resist you. "A minor inconvenience slowed me down, that's all."

"I see." She blinked big brown eyes at him, and visibly gathered herself. "Was there something particular you wanted to look at tonight?"

You. Naked. "I'm not sure." The house he'd built had more walls than he could count. "I'm still working on the downstairs. I need some things for the home theater and the guest room. Something . . . friendly. Bright. Large."

Unable to resist, he smoothed back a tendril of her hair, tucking it behind her ear. Silky and soft, warm and sweet. Would she be that sweet all over?

At his touch, May's dark eyes widened. Deep with intelligence and gentle caring, her eyes fascinated him.

She said, "I have some ideas."

One eyebrow lifted. "Do you?" Unable to help himself, he glanced at her hands clasped in front of her stomach. Then at the gaping lapels of her suit coat and the silky blouse beneath, buttoned up over her breasts.

"You should come by the house." His voice dropped. "We could discuss your . . . ideas."

Her soft gasp drew his attention back to her eyes. Bright color tinged her soft skin, leaving her blotchy. Never, not with anyone else, did May blush. With him, she often looked like a boiled lobster.

A lobster with untidy hair and mouth-watering breasts.

"I . . . I don't know." Her hands fluttered and she looked around the room, but found no salvation. "I'd have to check my schedule . . ."

"You know where I live, right?"

She choked on disbelief. But then, even though he'd built on the outskirts of town, everyone in Stillbrook knew where he lived. Hell, he was practically a tourist attraction. Having a well-known personality move into their area was big news a year ago. Because of the rag mags teeming with accusations, speculation, and outright lies, his location remained big news. Even here, in a town barely on the map, the past followed him.

Feeling cynical and annoyed, Jude ran a hand through his hair. "Of course you do."

She turned businesslike, straightening her rounded shoulders while her brows came down in a slight frown. "You have forty acres, Jude. Your house is . . . well, magnificent. A mansion. No one around here has ever seen stone fencing like that. The trees alone are so beautiful that . . ." The frown smoothed away, her expression eased. "Well, besides all that, you're a celebrity. I bet everyone has driven past your place a time or two."

When May went into protective mode, she lost her timidity. More than once, she'd acted protective toward him. A novelty, that; but also kind of sweet. "Have you?"

Her lower lip caught in her teeth, and she gave a guilty nod. "I wish I could say I drive by there anyway, but you'd know I was lying." She stared at him, weighed her words, then shrugged. "I stopped by last week, just . . . looking at things, and your security camera aimed right at me. I had the odd feeling that . . ."

"What?"

Her chin came up. "That you were watching me."

The grin appeared unbidden. He didn't deny or confirm her accusation. "You should have come up the drive. I'd love to show you around."

Her eyes widened. "But you have NO TRESPASSING signs everywhere. You keep your gates locked. The security cameras are always on . . ."

He touched her again, this time just running his

thumb along her jawline. "None of that applies to you."

Retrenching again, he gestured at the display of artwork. "Like I said, I could use some help picking things out."

Though she continued to blush, a dimple appeared in her cheek. "You have incredible taste and you know it. You're more sophisticated than I'll ever be."

Because he'd been in movies?

Or because he'd survived one of the most celebrated murder trials of the decade?

Anything that can go wrong . . .

Nothing is going to go wrong. Ashley Miles has worked too hard for her independence to let some Bentley-driving hunk named Quinton Murphy interfere with her plans—or her freedom. Yes, the chemistry is phenomenal. Kind of scary, actually. But that's it. NO emotional commitments.

. . . will.

But he's SO wonderful—a woman could fall in love . . . How did that happen? That wasn't part of the plan! But can she trust him? Really trust him? The man is just so mysterious. There's only one solution: put it all on the line and see what Quinton does when she tells him how she feels. And hope everything that can go wrong . . . won't . . .

With building impatience and anticipation, Quinton Murphy leaned against the cinderblock wall and checked his watch for the tenth time. How pathetic for a grown man to go to such lengths to talk with a woman.

A woman who had refused him—*after* kissing him senseless.

He didn't leave. He *wouldn't* leave. Not until she showed up and he had a chance to set things right with her.

Loosening his tie and pulling at the collar of his dress shirt, he cursed the unseasonable warmth of the October night and the stifling stillness of the parking garage. He checked his watch yet again; and then, finally, her yellow Civic pulled through the entrance.

Headlights flashed around the gray, yawning space, now mostly empty except for his Porsche Carerra and the vehicles of the night shift workers. Her brakes sounded a little squeaky, and she parked with a jerk of the gears that shook the aged automobile.

Always in a hurry—that described Ashley Miles. At least, from what little he'd seen of her. He had to wonder if she ever relaxed or took a day off to laze around.

As soon as her engine died and her headlights went dark, the driver's door swung open and she stepped out. Quinton soaked in the sight of her, letting his gaze meander along the length of her long legs, her trim midriff, the understated curves of her small breasts, before settling on her face.

Once again, he mulled over her startling effect on him—and wondered at it. At thirty-three, he was hardly a monk. He'd had infatuations, relationships of convenience, and once he'd even been in love.

But something about Ashley, some indefinable nuance in her nature got to him in a most unusual way.

Pieces of her were perfect: her dark eyes, her long silky hair, and her mouth . . . God, he loved her mouth.

She smiled easily, had a sharp tongue, and said no far too often.

But she kissed with an enthusiasm and hunger that made her impossible to dismiss, almost as if she'd never kissed before and the sensation of it overwhelmed her. He wanted more. He wanted everything. Until he had her, he wouldn't be able to get her out of his thoughts.

Put all together, Ashley made a mostly average appearance. But when she spoke, all that sassy attitude came crashing out, and it made her seem appealing yet unattainable, brash yet vulnerable.

She said things he didn't expect, behaved in ways unfamiliar to him. She smiled, and he wanted to strip her naked.

Her car door slammed hard, and she looked around the garage behind her, talking to herself in low mumbled words that reeked of irritation and disgust.

Unaware of his presence, she said, "For God's sake, Ashley, get a pair, why don't ya?"

Never taking his gaze off her, Quinton pushed away from the wall. Patience he told himself. He'd have her, and soon.

"A pair of what, Ashley?"

She screeched. The high-pitched yell of panic bounced around the cavernous garage in deafening force, causing Quinton to wince. "For God's sake, it's me."

Eyes wide, she whipped around, zeroed in on him, and went from startled to furious in a heartbeat. The change was something to see.

And she looked as desirable pissed as she did impatient.

After stomping across the concrete floor, she thrust her chin up close to his face. Since this was the second time he'd startled her in the garage, he felt a little guilty. Holding up his hands in concession, he said, "My apologies."

She didn't soften a bit. "You're making a habit of this, Murphy, and I don't like it."

Quinton gave in to a half smile, gently touched her hair, and lied through his teeth. "Not on purpose. I just finished some late business. Since I knew you were due in soon, I decided to wait to say hi before heading home." The last time he'd seen her, he'd been with a client. A sexy, blond female client; and though he knew Ashley wouldn't admit it, she'd misinterpreted the situation.

Now he needed to make her understand his interest for her and her alone.

For a single suspended moment, she stared at him, mostly at his mouth, her expression soft and giving . . . then with a frustrated growl, she strode away from him.

Damned contrary woman. She wouldn't make this easy for him. But she did make it interesting.

Quinton propped his hands on his hips and watched her long-legged retreat, undecided whether he should say anything more.

But after only three steps, she halted. Her straight, stiffened back still to him, she snapped by way of explanation, "I usually don't scare so easy."

An olive branch? He gladly accepted it. "I gathered as much." He hadn't known Ashley long, but already he accepted that she wasn't a timid woman, definitely not a woman who jumped at shadows. In fact, he'd have described her as ballsy beyond belief. "So what's going on? Why are you so jumpy?"

"It's nothing."

She shut him out and he didn't like it.

Dear Readers!

I'm so pleased that Kensington chose to reissue *Too Much Temptation*. Ever since the first release back in March 2002, I've heard you tell me, again and again, that this is your favorite of my books. A few of you say it's because of Noah, while others say it's because of Grace. I think it's mostly the two of them together.

Some characters are just that way. They come to me fully fleshed and very real in my mind. They *click*, and they win me over. Then they win you over.

As soon as I started writing them, Noah and Grace did and said as they pleased, and my only job was to get it down on paper. I could barely keep up! If only all my books were that easy to write.

Many of you, after reading the sequel *Never Too Much*, have asked me for more so you can catch up with the characters and "see" them again. As a Christmas present to you, I did that in the October '07 anthology *I'm Your Santa*. The short story presents a new romance with Noah and Ben's stepsister, while at the same time giving a brief look at the different couples, at how some things have changed and others stayed the same. I hope you enjoyed that chance to revisit all the characters.

Thank you for picking up *Too Much Temptation*. I do hope you enjoyed it! I also hope you'll try some of my other books. You can find out more about my entire booklist on my website at www.lorifoster.com. Write to me with any questions or comments at lori foster1@fuse.net.

Happy reading!

Lori Foster